D0792987

"Time travel, ancient legends, and seductive romance are seamlessly interwoven into one captivating package."

    –*Publishers Weekly* on Midnight's Master

"Dark, sexy, magical. When I want to indulge in a sizzling fantasy adventure, I read Donna Grant."

    –Allison Brennan, *New York Times* bestseller

5 Stars! Top Pick! "An absolute must read! From beginning to end, it's an incredible ride."

    –*Night Owl Reviews*

"It's good vs. evil Druid in the next installment of Grant's Dark Warrior series. The stakes get higher as discerning one's true loyalties become harder. Grant's compelling characters and continued presence of previous protagonists are key reasons why these books are so gripping. Another exciting and thrilling chapter!"

    –*RT Book Reviews* on Midnight's Lover

"Donna Grant has given the paranormal genre a burst of fresh air..."

    –*San Francisco Book Review*

Contemporary Paranormal

DRAGON KINGS

(Spin off series from *DARK KINGS SERIES*)

Dragon Revealed (novella)

REAPER SERIES

Dark Alpha's Claim

Dark Alpha's Embrace

Dark Alpha's Demand

Dark Alpha's Lover

Tall Dark Deadly Alpha Bundle

Dark Alpha's Night

Dark Alpha's Awakening

Dark Alpha's Redemption

Dark Alpha's Temptation

Dark Alpha's Caress

DARK KINGS

Moon Struck

Moon Bound

ROGUES OF SCOTLAND

The Craving

The Hunger

The Tempted

The Seduced

Rogues of Scotland Box Set

THE SHIELDS

A Dark Guardian

A Kind of Magic

A Dark Seduction

A Forbidden Temptation

A Warrior's Heart

Mystic Trinity (connected)

DRUIDS GLEN

Highland Mist

Highland Nights

Highland Dawn

Highland Fires

Highland Magic

Mystic Trinity (connected)

SISTERS OF MAGIC

Shadow Magic

Echoes of Magic

Dangerous Magic

Sisters of Magic Boxed Set

THE ROYAL CHRONICLES NOVELLA SERIES

Prince of Desire

Prince of Seduction

Prince of Love

Prince of Passion

Royal Chronicles Box Set

Mystic Trinity (connected)

MILITARY ROMANCE / ROMANTIC SUSPENSE

SONS OF TEXAS

The Hero

The Protector

The Legend

The Defender

The Guardian

Check out Donna Grant's Online Store, www.donnagrant.com/shop, for autographed books, character themed goodies, and more!

This is a work of fiction. All of the characters, organizations, and events portrayed in this novel are either products of the author's imagination or are used fictitiously.

THE GUARDIAN
© 2020 by DL Grant, LLC

Excerpt from *The Hero* copyright © 2016 by Donna Grant
Cover Design © 2020 by Charity Hendry

ISBN 13: 9781942017608
Available in ebook, print and audio editions

www.DonnaGrant.com
www.MotherofDragonsBooks.com

THE GUARDIAN

SONS OF TEXAS, BOOK 5

DONNA GRANT

St. Petersburg, Russia
Yesterday

"They know."

The whispered words from behind him caused Luka to stiffen. He'd been careful. So very careful. Trusting only his best friend, Vladimir, because he knew what kind of monsters he was trying to avoid.

Luka tried to calm his racing heart as he scanned the faces of those rushing past him on the street. He'd given his life to the Federal Security Service—the FSB, formerly the Soviet KGB. He'd been an excellent spy, and he'd taught many of the younger generation. So many times, his superiors had come to him with one problem or another, and he always managed to find a solution.

"You're on your own."

Luka didn't turn around. It wouldn't do any good. Vladimir would have already blended into the crowd. That was his specialty. If Vladimir didn't want to be found, it was damn near impossible to locate him.

Then again, it wasn't just anyone after the two of them.

Luka thought about his flat. There was nothing there for anyone to find. Nor in his office at FSB headquarters. He wasn't that stupid. When they came for him—and they would—he was prepared for the torture they would inflict while demanding he tell them everything he knew. Luka had been down this road before when captured by an enemy. He'd just never expected his own country to turn against him.

He brought the cup of coffee to his lips and blew on the steaming liquid. His hat was pulled low, covering his salt and pepper hair and brows. With the rim near his face, he glanced at his watch. Two minutes until he was supposed to walk across the street and board the train that would take him west out of the city to Estonia.

If Vladimir could be trusted—and he could— then anyone was a potential threat. Luka knew firsthand not to discount anyone. To see everyone as a potential enemy. But he wasn't just any spy. He was one of the best. He'd survived two years of torture. He wasn't going to let some nameless group keep him from getting out of Russia and sharing the truth with the world.

He took a drink, but he didn't taste the coffee. His mind was trying to find threats in the crowd. He picked out two women standing fifty meters to his left. Ahead of him, a man dressed in business attire hadn't quite hidden the earpiece he wore well enough. To his right, three other men stood out like sore thumbs. It was all so obvious. Too obvious. Yet nobody made a move.

That's when it hit him. They *wanted* him to think he'd beaten them. He'd let his guard down, and that's when they'd strike.

Luka's mind raced to find a way out. Every direction he turned, there they were, waiting. He couldn't go home. He couldn't go to work. He couldn't flee his beloved homeland. That left only one thing for him to do.

He drew out his phone and sent a two-word text. Then he started walking to the train. He threw away his coffee and put his hands into the pockets of his coat. The fingers of his right hand wrapped around the pistol, while his left found the grip of the small dagger.

No one stopped him. He entered the train station and made his way to the platform. The hairs on the back of his neck stood on end. He was being followed, and he had a suspicion that more enemies surrounded him. Still, he didn't slow. He reached the car and took the steps up and inside.

He walked through car after car until he found one that was nearly filled to capacity. He went to the very back and took a spot opposite a mother with a toddler in the seat facing him. Luka nodded in greeting. He glanced to his side to see three men in their early twenties wearing jeans and hoodies. One listened to music or something through earbuds. Another was reading. The third played on his phone. They looked unassuming, which meant they were most likely people he needed to be wary of.

He sat back and looked out the window. His

thoughts skidded to Vladimir again, and he wondered if his old friend had gotten away. Despite the normalcy around him, Luka was on high alert. He knew better than most how a good operative could get a job done—even in a crowd.

The moment the train began to roll, his senses became even more heightened. If this were his mission, he'd wait several minutes before he made his move. It would give the prey a sense of security and let them think they had gotten away.

Just a few minutes into the ride, the mother across from him made a sound and spoke softly to the child. The harried woman gave him an apologetic look as she shifted the cumbersome toddler, who was now whining. She shushed the boy, rocking him. As she moved, she knocked over her coat and bag. He smiled and continued studying the other passengers while the mother shifted the child and tried to gather her items.

"Excuse me," the mother said, just loud enough to get his attention.

Luka's gaze slid to her, and his brows rose in question.

"Would you mind getting the bag for me, please? I don't want to wake him," she said, looking at the child who now lay limply across her chest.

Without question, he bent to retrieve the bag and coat. No sooner had he leaned over than he felt something sharp near his ribs. He froze, unable to believe what had just happened. He tried to sit up, but he couldn't move. Blood flowed, thick and hot, from the wound in his side. As he struggled for breath, he managed to turn his head to look at the mother. She was gone. The only thing left was a life-like doll he had mistaken for a real child.

His last thought as his eyes closed was that there was no escaping the monsters.

2

Amsterdam, The Netherlands
Today

There were monsters in the world. Maks knew that all too well. He surveyed the bustling city at night, the tourists moving from one hotspot to another. The red-light district teemed with people until the narrow alleys were nearly bursting. People watched the scantily clad women in the windows—some curious, some judging, and others not bothering to hide their hunger.

Some feared the night because they knew there were horrors there. Most believed that's when the monsters came out to play. And they did.

But the real beasts, the brutes so evil, so morally corrupt that there was no saving their souls, well... they preferred the daytime.

This was the second night in a row that Maks had taken to the streets. He'd been restless since he got the encrypted text the day before. He wasn't even sure why it had been sent to him. After decoding it and figuring out that it had come from Luka, Maks had been even more confused.

He'd met Luka only twice. The older man seemed nice enough—for a spy. Any words exchanged between them had been for business and nothing more. So why had Luka sent that cryptic text? And how did he even get Maks' number? Maks initially thought it might have been done on accident. Then he'd heard that Luka had been murdered on a train.

Maks leaned his shoulder against the corner of a building and looked down at his mobile. The screen only had two words: "Watch yourself."

He put the phone away and blew out a breath. No matter how he looked at it, there was only one thing Luka could be talking about—the Saints. Unease slithered through Maks. The secret organization was global, with the heads of states of all countries involved in some form or fashion. There wasn't a country that the Saints *didn't* have control of somehow.

The alliance was so well-formed and implemented that most had no idea they even existed. Maks had discovered the organization when he was in Delta Force. He'd gotten an up-close-and-personal introduction that had left a sour taste in his mouth. He hadn't told a single person what had transpired that day.

A few months later, the Central Intelligence Agency came calling, offering him a job. He had known exactly why they were there. He'd wanted to refuse them, but he was also driven to learn everything he could about the Saints. He couldn't do that if he wasn't involved. He joined the agency and did everything they asked. Every mission was completed, every target eliminated. They questioned him often about seemingly inconsequential things, but he wasn't stupid. The root of their queries was always about the Saints.

It took years of Maks keeping his head down, not asking questions, and doing minimal digging. For every mission and each person he met, he made notes. Little by little, he'd pieced together parts of the bigger puzzle. But it wasn't until the agency asked him to go undercover in the FSB that he found a treasure trove of information.

With his ties to Russia through his family, he'd known that he would eventually be sent there. His grandfather had emigrated from Russia to San Francisco at the age of seventeen. San Francisco was a destination for many Russians, and it was there that he'd met his bride, another Russian immigrant.

Maks had grown up speaking both English and Russian fluently, and it played a large part in the CIA's interest. He used it to his advantage because he knew the more he was sent on missions, the more information he could obtain.

It wasn't an easy process, and it took far longer than he liked. But with an organization like the Saints, he had to work carefully. He couldn't trust anyone, because he didn't know who was working for them. That was until he discovered that one of his friends from his days with Delta Force was going head-to-head with the Saints. Wyatt Loughman, along with Wyatt's two brothers, had gone searching for their father, Orrin. The elder Loughman had gone missing after finding a bioweapon that the Saints wanted to release on the world in an effort to control the population.

Maks just happened to be working undercover for Major General Yuri Markovic at the time. It made it easy to help Orrin escape and assist Wyatt with taking out some of the Saints. Yuri had been secretive enough that Maks hadn't known for sure if he worked for the Saints or not. In the end, Yuri teamed up with the Loughmans in Texas for a battle on their ranch, and Maks joined them.

As much as he wanted to stay with the Loughmans, Maks knew that it would be better for them if he was gone. He could disappear, go off the grid for a few days, but if he didn't resurface, the agency would stop at nothing to track him down. While the Saints had the Loughmans in their sights, they had gone up against the Texan family and lost. The organization would come at the family again—it was only a matter of when.

Maks wanted to be sure that he knew about those plans so he could help his friends. After all, he trusted no one else in the fight against the Saints. To that end, he had made sure to ditch the two trackers his friends had put on him in an effort to know his whereabouts. It wasn't because they didn't trust him. It was so they could find him easily if he got into trouble.

The thing was, he would never ask them for help. They had their hands full as it was. Not to mention, the three brothers had found their wives in their fight against the Saints. And while the women had all helped in one way or another to take down the Saints, Maks knew the brothers would do anything and everything to make sure nothing happened to their women. And *he* would do whatever he could to help, as well. Because if anyone knew what it was like to lose someone you loved, he did.

Maks blinked and shut off his memories before they took him down a road he wasn't prepared to travel. His thoughts turned back to the text he'd gotten from Luka. The CIA may have planted him in the FSB, but he knew that it was really the Saints who controlled his movements. What he didn't understand was their motivation.

There wasn't a government or security agency on the planet that wasn't controlled by the Saints. So why take him and put him in Russia? He'd been told it was to uncover Russian secrets, but that was a lie. He'd thought that he would be working as a spy in the FSB—and in a way, he was. Except he wasn't spying on Russian enemies. He was spying on Russians.

And it was easy to determine that those he was told to focus on were either those who weren't with the Saints or Saint members who had made someone doubt their allegiance. Luka had never come under Maks' scrutiny.

A fat raindrop landed on Maks' cheek. He wiped it away and glanced at the sky. Rain was a part of life in Amsterdam, especially in the winter. And it did nothing to deter the tourists. He put away the mobile and did a quick sweep of the area. His gaze moved over a man who was staring at him. Maks acted as if he hadn't seen him. Shifting subtly, Maks used the window of a shop nearby to scan the area more closely. He found two other men that drew his interest.

Living the life of a double agent whose agenda was his own left a man ultra-vigilant. He was always careful, but he'd let himself delve into his thoughts in an open area where others had been watching without him knowing.

Maks pushed away from the store and started toward a narrow alley. There were so many people staring at the half-naked women that he had to squeeze through them just to get past. The city was laid out in a grid, so while one man followed him, the other two men took to the side streets to cut him off.

Maks kept his steps even, giving no sign that he knew he was being followed. As he came out of the alley, out of the corner of his eye, he saw one of the men rush into the street. Maks kept walking through more red-light sections, restaurants, *coffee houses* that sold marijuana and not coffee, and tourist shops. He ditched both his phones in case that's how he was being tracked.

When he came to the intersection, he quickly turned left into yet another busy alley, this one slightly wider. The crowd swallowed him, giving him time to provide the coded knock. The door opened, and he gave the woman clad only in a skimpy bra, panties, and heels a wad of money as he entered.

No words were exchanged between them as he quickly disappeared behind a curtain and headed down a hallway. He ran to the stairs and took them three at a time up to the third floor. Maks took a moment to peer out the darkened window to the ground below, where the three men had gathered, each looking around for a sign of him.

That had been a close call. He didn't know if it was the Saints, the FSB, or the CIA who had sent the men, and it didn't matter. Someone wanted to talk to him, and instead of calling him in for a chat, they had sent men to force him to go wherever they wanted. That meant that someone knew about the coded message he'd received on his secret phone.

Maks spun on his heel and stalked out of the room, heading to the roof where he jumped to the next building. Five buildings later, he made his way to the ground via the fire escape. There was no going home for him now. But he'd been preparing for this moment since before he joined the CIA.

3

Vienna, Austria

"Dammit," Eden said as someone jostled her, making her spill coffee on her coat.

She stopped and wiped it off, but it didn't do any good. Her new white winter coat would have to go to the cleaners. She adjusted her purse on her shoulder and continued on her way to the office building, along with the hundreds of others headed to work that morning.

Stifling a yawn, she hurried through the revolving doors to get out of the cold, then lengthened her strides to the elevators. She drank some of the hot coffee that was loaded with cream and sugar, hoping it helped to wake her up. It was her fault that she felt so sleepy. If only she hadn't binge-watched *The Witcher* into the wee hours of the morning. But how could anyone start watching that and not finish it? Especially when Henry Cavill was the main character.

There was a smile on her face when the elevator doors opened, and she stepped inside, moving so others could crowd on, as well. She bit back a yelp when an overweight man stepped on her toes. Eden looked down at her coffee and wished there was some extra caffeine in it. Or liquor. At this point, she just wanted to be awake during the meeting.

The elevator stopped on every floor, others getting off a little at a time until only she and three others were left. The four of them all got off on the top floor. She smiled in greeting to the guards as she and the other occupants each carded their way through security. Then she went to her desk, put her purse in the bottom drawer, and locked it. After grabbing a pen and paper, along with her coffee, she straightened and headed to the conference room, only to have Kyle step in her way so she nearly collided with him.

Eden pinched her lips closed instead of letting loose the string of curses she wanted to say. She didn't particularly like Kyle. He'd never been rude or mean to her, but he was the worst gossip in the office, and that was even worse. He loved to talk about anyone and everyone, and she could only imagine what he said about her.

"Sorry," he said, though his smile was anything but apologetic.

She glanced away, trying to regain her composure. "You scared the hell out of me."

Like her, Kyle was one of a handful of Americans that SynTech had brought over from the States because of their skills as information brokers. But there was a reason Kyle had chosen this profession—he didn't work well with others. Which was why he used to work out of his home office. But he had particular skills in cyber-ops.

"I know," he said, his creepy smile never faltering.

Eden cleared her throat. "Did you need something?"

"You look pretty this morning."

"Thank you." She tried not to sound ungrateful, but he'd told her that every morning for the past two years. He'd also attempted to ask her out on numerous occasions, and she had declined as politely and nicely as she could. He just hadn't gotten the hint. Eden tried to walk around him. "We're going to be late for the meeting."

"There's no meeting."

She turned to face him. "What? Why?"

"Check your email."

With her temper flaring, Eden shook her head. "Why didn't you tell me that?"

"That's why I stopped you." With that, he turned and walked back to his desk.

Eden glanced out the wall of windows to the beautiful city beyond. She'd worked on her own for three years, and there were times—like now—that she missed that. She didn't have to get dressed, worry about making meetings, or getting along with coworkers. It had just been her, her computer, and the jobs that came in.

But as she stared out at Vienna, she remembered why she had taken this job. It wasn't just the pay, although that was certainly nice. It was the opportunity to live in Europe, so she could do all the traveling she'd always dreamed of doing. And over the past two years, she had racked up a lot of miles on the train and had seen a ton of beautiful places. There were so many more on her list, but she was getting really tired of working for someone. It paid well, and for a while, the pros outweighed the cons. However, that wasn't the case anymore.

Eden looked around the office with its many cubicles and corner offices. She didn't have an office, but she didn't have a cubicle either. Her workspace was somewhere in between. There had been a time when she'd thought that was a good thing. Now, she wasn't so sure.

She sank into her chair and logged into her computer. The moment her email popped up, she saw the message flagged as important. Eden quickly read it. Then she reread it. She sat back, a frown in place as she looked around the office once more. Nothing seemed out of the ordinary. They were often given names and tasked with finding any and all information on them. It wasn't illegal because the information was out on the internet as part of public record. It was just that most people didn't want to spend the time or know-how to garner such data.

That's where information brokers came in. They were trained on how and where to look for things. Long hours were spent online, poring through websites, scanning documents, and scouring pictures. To Eden, it was like a puzzle. She had the starting piece—i.e., the name of a person, business, or organization—and it was her job to find all the bits that went along with that, no matter how tiny or inconsequential she believed them to be. They all made up a bigger picture.

She had done a lot of data mining over the last

two years. A couple of times, she had even been asked to stop what she was working on and turn to the new, emergency project. Not once had a Monday morning meeting ever been canceled for a job, though.

As she stared at the office again, she began to feel a surge of panic. When she homed in on individuals, that feeling intensified as she watched them frantically searching the internet or going through a list, clearly not finding what they looked for. Was everyone looking for the same individual?

Her gaze moved back to the email, and she reread the name. She rose slowly and walked down the middle of the cubicles toward the toilets while glances at her coworkers' monitors. The same name and face in her email was on everyone's computer. While it wasn't unheard of for an IB company to give all the employees the same thing to search for, it was rarely done. There were too many jobs coming in, and only so many hours in a day. Teams of data miners might be pulled together for a big job, but not an entire office.

By the time Eden reached the bathroom, she was more confused than ever. She walked to the sinks and washed her hands before drying them thoroughly. Then she returned to her desk. On the way, she looked at the corner where the CEO of SynTech had her office. Janice Ahlers stood in a white and black blouse and a black pencil skirt, her arms crossed as two men spoke to her.

The men had their backs to Eden, unfortunately, so she couldn't see their faces. The moment Janice's gaze slid to her, Eden looked away and kept walking to her desk. When she sat, she immediately pulled her chair forward and opened her browser. There, she typed in the name: Maks Volkov.

Because of social media, there was generally tons of information on the internet to find. Even on the first search of just a name. Not so with this one. Eden glanced around the office once more, finally understanding everyone's frustration.

She took a deep breath and settled in to do what she did best—find information. She printed out the picture in the email and taped it to the side of her computer as she looked through numerous photos, searching for him. After thirty minutes, she had yet to find even one picture of Maks Volkov. Very few people could stay off social media. A few old-school individuals didn't believe in putting every little thing of their lives out into the world, but it was rare.

Those people made her work harder. Eden actually liked those jobs. With so many posting pictures of their food, or taking dozens of selfies, not to mention snapping shots of themselves with everyone else when they went out and then putting those on social media, it wasn't hard to dig up information.

But Eden loved challenges, and she had a feeling that Maks Volkov was going to be one of them.

She didn't lift her head again until lunch. And it was only the fact that her stomach was growling, and she had a headache from not drinking any water, that she even stopped for a break. Eden took time for a quick lunch and to stretch her legs. She made sure to have water with her when she returned to her desk. Then, she was back at it.

Unfortunately, when the day ended, she still didn't have more than a few instances of the name. The dates of birth were all over the place, so she couldn't be sure if any of them belonged to her Maks.

On the way back to her flat, she kept thinking about how she had yet to find anything on her quarry. And then something began to niggle in the back of her mind. Worry settled around her like a suffocating cloak she couldn't get off.

Inside her flat, she locked her door and put down her purse before taking off her coat and scarf. She began unzipping her dress on the way to her room. The image of Maks filled her mind as she quickly changed into comfy sweatpants, a sweatshirt, and thick socks. She then stood in front of her open fridge, trying to find something to eat, but her mind was still on Maks.

Alone in her house now, she allowed herself to think the thing she hadn't wanted to mull over before. Was Maks a spy of some sort? That was the only explanation she could come up with for him having no digital footprint of any kind. No credit cards, no photos, no credit report, no mobile phone listing. Nothing.

It was like Maks Volkov didn't exist.

But even spies couldn't stay off the grid completely. There was something out there somewhere, and she was going to find it. Not because she wanted to expose Maks. It wasn't her job to know why someone wanted information on him. She was going to do it because it was what she did. It was why she had been hired. And she loved a good challenge. It had been a while since work had followed her home.

She poured a glass of wine and ordered takeout for delivery. Then she went to her sofa. Eden picked up one of the books on the shelf that hadn't been read yet and tried to fall into the story. She wasn't able. It was by one of her favorite authors, so it wasn't that. She just couldn't concentrate because her brain was still locked on Maks.

Eden set the book down and sighed. She alternated between reading and watching TV most nights. She read fast enough that she could finish a book in a night. Tonight wasn't going to be spent reading a book, however. She reached for the remote and scrolled through the saved series and movies on her to-watch list, but nothing looked interesting at the moment.

A knock on the door, signaling the arrival of her food, saved her from making a decision. After handing a tip to the delivery guy and getting the food, Eden locked the door and found herself at her desk. Since she'd spent all day on the computer, she rarely turned hers on anymore. But she couldn't stop thinking about Maks or seeing his face in her mind.

"A very handsome man," she said as she waited for her computer to boot up.

She had stared at the printout of his face all day. She knew the way his blond hair was cut short on the sides and left longer on top. She knew the small scar above his left eye that cut through his brow slightly. She could even pick out the exact shade of bright blue for his eyes.

"They're contacts," she said to herself.

They had to be. No one had eyes that unnaturally bright, as if they could see straight into her soul. His stunning eyes, along with his hard jawline and full lips made him, in a word, gorgeous.

Eden propped her feet up on the edge of her desk as she leaned back in her chair to eat. In between bites, she continued her search. She needed to know more about Maks Volkov, because the more she thought about him, the more she needed answers. It was a dangerous road she walked.

An IB didn't allow themselves to feel anything for those they looked into. They couldn't. Otherwise, it could jeopardize their work. Eden had never found someone like this before. Everyone else had just been a face or a name. She didn't know or care why someone wanted information. She got paid to find it, and that's exactly what she did.

But Maks...there was something about him that she couldn't shake. She wished she knew what it was. And until she figured that out, she would have to be careful.

4

As Maks walked through Amsterdam, his strides were long and purposeful as he quickly covered ground. It didn't matter if it was the CIA, the FSB, or the Saints after him. His cover had been blown. This moment had been inevitable. He'd hoped to have more time to gather intel on the Saints, but he hadn't finished going through everything he'd accumulated over the years. There might be enough. And if there wasn't...well, then he would do whatever he had to do to get what he needed to bring the Saints crashing down.

They had governed the world for long enough. They had no right to decide who would run countries, or who lived and died. It was time they were exposed. It wasn't going to be easy, though, and Maks knew that going against them would likely mean his life. He was prepared to give it. Especially if it meant that the world could be free. That people could actually elect officials as they were supposed to. That they could speak out against the powerful and not incur some accidental death that was anything but accidental.

Maks made his way to Amsterdam Centraal. Once inside the train station, he headed toward the east wing and the luggage lockers. He halted in front of his number and glanced to either side of him. The attendant that was always on duty glanced his way but otherwise seemed uninterested. Maks opened the locker and reached for the black backpack inside.

He slung it over his shoulder and walked to the train. As he passed one of the many shops, he swiped a baseball cap as he passed and put it on. He didn't slow until he reached his platform. As he heard the train approaching, he glanced around him. No one appeared to be following him, but he wasn't going to take that for fact.

Just as the train was slowing at the platform, he jumped in front of it and rushed across the tracks to the opposite side where another train had just stopped, and passengers unloaded. Maks fell into step with the crowd. As he walked up the stairs, he glanced back to the other platform and saw two men looking his way and rushing back up the steps.

When Maks reached the main floor on his side, he kept with the crowd and used the opportunity to get out of the station. The area in the front of Amsterdam Centraal was a tourist mecca, even at night. It offered boat rides, trams, and dozens of people on bikes, ringing their bells to alert unsuspecting passersby that they were in the bike lane. The city had few cars, but that didn't deter Maks. He wound his way through the maze of streets and waterways, checking each vehicle along the canal until he found one that was unlocked. He slung his pack into the passenger seat and got inside. In minutes, he had it hotwired and pulled onto the narrow lane.

He needed to get somewhere out of the city, a place he could take a few minutes and think. But getting out of Amsterdam was easier said than done with so many thoroughfares blocked off. He'd memorized the street map long ago, though, so he knew which intersections to avoid and where to go to get out the quickest.

Once he was on the highway headed east toward Germany, he relaxed a little. He didn't stop until around two in the morning, parking at a rest area. Maks turned off the ignition and grabbed his pack. He looked through the different passports he had with various names, all of which he had acquired on his own without the CIA's, FSB's, or the Saints' knowledge. Years spent cultivating relationships with shady individuals had given him access to various things he knew he'd eventually need.

He flipped through the passports but set them aside since he didn't know where he needed to go. Blowing out a breath, he dug out a water bottle and drank the contents. Since he didn't know who was after him, it limited his destination choices. Nothing had seemed out of the ordinary the day before. Everything had begun with that text.

Maks thought about the message. The phone was encrypted, which only meant that it was difficult for someone who didn't know how to break through those protocols to get in. It wouldn't stop someone who really wanted information. Honestly, there was only one set of people Maks could trust right now, but getting in touch with the Loughmans would be dangerous. But he didn't have any other choice.

He blew out a breath and started the car again to pull back out onto the road. He didn't stop until the sun had come up. The small village he'd entered was perfect. He parked the car and wiped it of any prints, then he grabbed his pack and walked away. Maks found a store and bought a water bottle, some protein bars, and a disposable mobile phone, all while making sure his face couldn't be seen on any of the security cameras.

After he left the shop, he found an abandoned building and kicked in the door to get inside. He checked the area to make sure no one was around, then he placed a call to Texas while tearing open one of the protein bars and taking a huge bite. He chewed as the phone rang once, twice. On the third ring, the line connected.

"Hello?" said a female.

Maks smiled as he recognized Callie's voice. "I wondered if the number would still work."

"As long as you're out there, it'll always work." Then, sounding muffled, she called, "Maks is on the line."

Maks cleared his throat. "I'm in a bit of a bind. Hoping you can help."

"Always. Switching you to speaker now," Callie told him. "Everyone but Cullen and Mia are here. Tell us what's going on."

Maks looked down at the debris at his feet. He kicked a broken piece of glass. "I don't know, exactly. Everything seemed to be fine. I was in Amsterdam when I got a peculiar text on my encrypted phone that I didn't think anyone knew about."

"Number?" Callie asked.

Maks quickly gave her to digits.

"You got rid of it, didn't you?" Owen, the middle Loughman brother, asked.

"As soon as I shook the men following me." Maks ran his free hand down his face. "I know I've always been watched, but no one's ever sent anyone after me before."

Wyatt grunted. The oldest brother then said, "You think it has something to do with the text?"

"I can't imagine what else it could be."

Natalie, Owen's wife, asked, "What was the text?"

"I was just about to ask that," Callie said.

Maks tightened his coat around him for warmth. "*Watch yourself.* That was all it said."

"Do you know what it means?" Wyatt asked.

"Not a clue. More concerning is who it's from, and how they got my number. I was able to trace it. His name was Luka Fedorov. An agent for the FSB."

There was a beat of silence, then Owen said, "*Was?*"

"He was killed on a train out of St. Petersburg just minutes after he sent the message," Maks explained.

The sound of fingers tapping on a keyboard came through the phone. "Give me a sec," Callie said.

She was the best hacker he knew, which was why he'd called. If there had been a way for him to gain the information without involving the

Loughmans, he would have. They wouldn't understand it because, in their eyes, they were part of his mission to take down the Saints. And they were.

But they had survived attempts on their lives and still managed to come out ahead. If Maks could keep them out of the line of fire, then he would. They had earned at least that.

"Tell us about Luka," Owen urged.

Maks briefly closed his eyes. "I knew him from the FSB. He was a high-ranking official who earned his position after years as a spy. He trained most of the assets currently out in the field. He'd even been captured and tortured by the Chinese for a few years back in the day. He's a fucking hero."

"You liked him," Natalie said.

There was no denying it. "I did. Even though I didn't exactly trust him and only met him a couple of times. He seemed genuine. His love for his people and country were evident."

"Who do you think killed him?" Owen asked.

Knowing that would make things easier for Maks. "It could be the CIA. But they usually try to flip people like him to their side, not kill them."

"Unless they thought he was about to spill some secrets," Wyatt interjected.

"Maybe. But if there was something against the US, it would've been mentioned, and I heard nothing. That's not to say there wasn't something. Then there's his agency."

Natalie asked, "Do you think the FSB would do that?"

"They've done more for less," Wyatt said.

Maks twisted his lips. "Wyatt's right. They

have. Every agency has. So, it could be them, especially if he was about to leak something about the head of the FSB or Russia."

"Then there's our favorite group," Callie said, her voice heavy with sarcasm.

Maks rubbed his eyes with his thumb and forefinger. "Yeah. It could be any of those three."

"FSB, huh?" Wyatt asked. "How deep are you?"

"Deep."

Owen sighed loudly. "And there's nothing else going on that would put a target on you?"

"Other than me continuing to gather information about the Saints? No," Maks told them.

Callie let out a whoop. "Okay, I got past the firewalls at the FSB. I won't be able to stay long before they figure out their system has been breached. I looked up Luka Fedorov, and his record is stellar. He's someone the US would want as an agent."

"And someone his country wouldn't want to let go of," Natalie added.

"Wait," Callie said before pausing. "Oh, shit."

Maks frowned, wishing he could see whatever it was she was looking at. "What is it?"

"His record is being wiped as I'm reading it," Callie said.

"Do they know you're there?" Wyatt asked.

Maks listened as Callie furiously typed on the keyboard.

Finally, she answered, "I don't think they did."

"Did you get the file copied?" Owen asked.

A chair squeaked, then Callie said, "Unfortunately, no. There was too much information. What I did get was his address, email, and a phone number. I'm digging through that now."

Silence stretched as Maks finished off the protein bar and downed some water. He didn't know when he'd get to eat again. If there was time, he'd get a few minutes of sleep, but that would have to wait until he found a better location.

Minutes felt like years before Callie's voice reached him again. "Maks, how well did you know Luka?"

"Not well. I met him a couple of years ago. I wasn't part of his department. We attended a few of the same meetings. It was more just a nod in passing, though, nothing more. I think the most we spoke was in an elevator once where he said he had seen my record and was impressed by it. He wanted to know who had trained me because I was so good. I knew from those who worked for him that he was hard but fair."

Wyatt then said, "He had your file. Or at least a copy of it. It's on his desk in his home."

Maks wasn't surprised that Callie had managed to get into the surveillance cameras of Luka's home. "I knew he'd read it. He told me as much."

"When was that?" Natalie asked.

Maks shrugged. "About a year ago."

"Then why would he have it now?" Owen questioned.

Maks shook his head. "Maybe he wanted to recruit me to his division?"

"Or perhaps he wanted to know if you were someone he could trust," Callie said.

Maks leaned against the wall and considered

that. "Maybe. There is any number of reasons he could have my file."

"Could he have known you were really CIA?" Natalie asked.

Owen made a sound in the back of his throat. "It's possible."

"Give me another few minutes," Callie said.

Wyatt quickly seconded his wife. "You can't see, Maks, but she's getting a lot of information. We're copying it now in case the FSB tries to wipe this, as well."

"Understood," Maks said.

He might have learned patience as a spy, but that didn't mean he liked it. His mind began to drift, thinking over the last few hours, when the sound of a chair being rolled brought him back to the present.

"Uh, guys," Natalie said. "Look at this."

Maks wanted to demand that they tell him what it was, but he held his tongue.

"I hate to be the bearer of bad news, my friend, but your face is plastered everywhere in Europe," Wyatt said.

That certainly got Maks' attention. "Why? What does it say?"

"Just that you're wanted for questioning, and to detain you if seen," Own answered.

Callie halted that line of talk when she said, "I think Luka had a second phone. I can't find any texts or calls going to either of your mobiles. I'm taking the encrypted line you gave me and reversing the search. Yep, there it is." A few keystrokes later, she said, "This was a burner, so there's no record."

Maks had hoped there would be something for him to go on, but it wasn't looking as if that would happen. "Thanks for trying."

"I didn't say I was finished," Callie told him, still typing.

Owen said, "Both Callie and Natalie are working. Hell, Callie even has Wyatt at a computer, going through what she copied from Luka's home computer."

"Please tell me there's something," Maks said. But he knew there wouldn't be. Luka was too smart to get caught like that.

"Damn," Wyatt said. "I honestly thought I'd come up empty, but I'm on my third email, and I've figured out who killed him."

Maks braced himself. "Who?"

"The Saints. In an email, he mentions a private, world organization that is taking over. We'll have to do more digging to figure out what he found, but I think it's a safe bet to say that the Saints are responsible."

Maks swallowed, his thoughts racing. "Since Luka texted me, they must think I'm part of whatever he was doing."

"Uh...I think that's a good assumption," Natalie said. "Callie showed me a couple of tricks, and I just used one to figure out who plastered your face everywhere."

Owen said, "It's the Saints."

"But they're hiding behind a company," Callie said. "Right?"

"Yep," Natalie agreed. "It's called SynTech, and it's based in Vienna."

Maks wasn't that far from Vienna.

Wyatt interrupted his thoughts by saying, "Don't do it. You can't go into a company like that and erase everything about you."

"He's right," Natalie said. "They're information brokers. That's all they do."

Callie made a sound of frustration. "Which means that they're not just looking for your name, they're looking for your face everywhere. I hope you covered your tracks well because IBs dig deep to uncover everything about whoever or whatever they're looking into."

Maks pushed away from the wall. "I can't just sit here doing nothing. I'm here, undercover in the FSB, specifically to gather intel on the Saints."

"We can get you back to the States," Owen said.

"We all know there isn't anywhere I can go where the Saints won't find me. I won't put all of you in jeopardy like that. Thanks for the offer, but I'm staying here."

Callie said, "We'll keep digging. If we find anything else, I'll let you know."

"Until then, be safe," Wyatt told him.

Maks disconnected the call and strode from the building.

5

The next morning, Eden was at her desk before anyone else. She hadn't been able to sleep. In fact, she'd spent most of the night continuing her search for Maks. Which proved much more difficult than she wanted to admit.

When Kyle walked into the office, Eden followed him with her eyes. He got situated for the day and typed in his password before pulling up the page he'd been working on. As his specialized algorithms began to work with the facial recognition software they all had access to, he rose and went to get coffee.

Eden knew she couldn't get to his computer in time to discover anything before he returned. Not to mention, his desk was out of the way, just as hers was. The last three big clients they had competed with each other for had him winning two, and her one. She didn't care about that, though. What mattered was that she found Maks first. She couldn't explain *why*, only that she knew she had to.

She looked to where Kyle was and glanced at

his computer again. Something in a red box kept flashing on the screen. She couldn't read it from her location and the fact that he had a film over his screen that prevented others from seeing what he did.

With nothing to lose, Eden got up and walked toward his desk. Her hands were shaking, her heart racing. She knew that she could get caught by Kyle at any moment, and she didn't know what she would say to him. The more she tried to come up with a plan, the more her brain refused to work.

Her mouth was dry, her ears ringing. How did anyone do things like this for a living? She feared that her heart might burst from the stress and kill her right then. But, somehow, she reached Kyle's desk without incident. Once there, she didn't know what to do. She looked around, hoping something would jump out at her. But there was nothing.

She turned her head, her gaze locking with Kyle's. She tried to smile, but she wasn't sure her lips actually lifted in a grin. Kyle started toward her, anger blazing in his eyes. Eden moved a lock of hair behind her ears and glanced at the screen. She memorized the location then faced Kyle when he reached her.

"What are you doing here?" he demanded.

She laughed. "I work here."

His lips didn't even twitch.

Eden cleared her throat and licked her lips. "I wanted to apologize for yesterday. I was rude to you, and I'm sorry."

He continued staring at her, his face showing nothing.

"All right then," she said with another forced smile. "Later."

On the way back to her desk, she felt her knees shaking. She didn't breathe normally until she was once more seated in her chair. When she looked up, Kyle was still staring at her. She ignored him and hurriedly typed *Amsterdam Centraal* into her search. She put in filters for the last week and then added in the facial recognition software.

While that ran in the background, Eden looked at every Maks Volkov in Europe between the ages of twenty-eight and thirty-eight with blond hair and blue eyes. That narrowed down her search to four hundred thousand seven hundred and forty-eight. She'd done the same search last night on her home computer and had come up with the same number.

She hadn't had his photo to scan in to match, however. Eden did that now, and it didn't take long for the computer to give her an answer: *No Match*.

Wanting to be sure she hadn't missed anything, she ran the search twice more. Each time, it came back with the same answer. The next time, she expanded the search worldwide. It gave her over two million hits.

It took longer for the detailed search to run, and she was confident that she would find something this time. No sooner had that thought gone through her mind than her computer dinged that she'd gotten a hit. But it wasn't on the name. It was on her search of the Amsterdam Centraal train station.

Eden switched screens and found a snippet from a CCTV camera that showed someone who looked like Maks, at least in profile. She glanced at Kyle, but he wasn't at his desk. When she searched the floor, she found him in Janice's office, no doubt giving her the news. That didn't deter Eden, however.

She hadn't actually thought she would get a hit on Maks so soon using facial recognition and the cameras from the train station. Based on what she saw, he'd definitely been there the night before. She quickly got the footage from the other cameras in the station and added in the facial recognition software. To her surprise, she caught sight of a man who could be Maks twice more, but he was always careful about his face being turned away from the cameras.

That was something someone who had been trained did. Something done consciously. Normal people didn't notice or care if a camera picked up their face. But a select few did. Criminals.

And spies.

Which one was Maks?

Eden continued looking through the CCTV footage to see if she could find anything else. Just as she was about to shut it down, thinking it was a dead end, her gaze snagged on a man leaping in front of a train. She feared that she might have found someone committing suicide, and she had to know if they were okay. She lost sight of him as the train stopped, so she switched cameras to find another angle.

She found him again. He wore the same type of jacket that the other man in the footage had, but he now carried a backpack and had on a baseball cap. He landed from jumping in front of the train, easily clearing the tracks. Then he took off running to the other side before climbing up to that platform. No sooner had he straightened than the train opened its doors, and people flooded out, swallowing him.

But she had her gaze locked on him. Switching from camera to camera, she followed the unknown man up the stairs to the main floor of the train station. When he turned a corner, she got another profile shot of him. This time, she was positive that it was Maks Volkov.

Instead of taking the information to Janice, Eden encrypted all of it then pulled out a pen drive from her purse and put all the footage on it. Kyle might be able to uncover what she had eventually, but she wasn't going to worry about that right now. Eden wasn't even sure why she was suddenly rooting for Maks. She didn't know him, but something kept telling her not to give the information she had gained to SynTech or the client wanting to find Maks.

"He better not be some serial killer," she mumbled to herself.

With her taste in men, it would be just her luck. She shook her head, refusing to go down that road again.

Eden decided to try and find out who it was that wanted the scoop on Maks. That wasn't something shared in an environment like this. Though she had worked on her own long enough that she had gotten used to knowing who her clients were. SynTech's policy was that it didn't matter who the client was. They were paying for a service, and every IB had a duty to deliver.

This time, Eden wasn't okay with that. Yet no amount of digging gave her anything. She wasn't used to coming up empty. There was always *some* information—good, bad, or ugly—out there on anyone and everything. For Maks and this unknown client to both have nothing out there? Yeah, something wasn't right.

Eden closed her eyes and stretched her neck to give herself a little break. The ding on her computer had her back at it again. She'd done a worldwide search for Maks' name. Not a single result matched the picture they had been given.

Maks had been caught on camera in Amsterdam, so he wasn't some made-up individual as a test for them. But if his name didn't match any records around the world, then that could only mean one thing: Max Volkov wasn't his name.

By the time lunchtime came, Eden could barely contain her frustration. She decided to get out of the office and grab a bite as well as meditate a bit to try and get herself back in balance. As she rose to leave, she saw that Kyle was still in Janice's office. The two men from the previous day were also there. She didn't give them a second thought as she left the building.

Once outside, she drew in a deep breath. The temperatures were still chilly, but the sun was shining, and the sky was a beautiful, clear blue. Eden found herself relaxing as she walked the streets. There was something about Vienna that drew people. After all, it was the best city to live in the world. Not only was there culture, history, and amazing architecture, but the people were also friendly, and the vibe of the city was a beat that pulled in tourists as well as those who moved there permanently.

Eden chose her favorite café and grabbed a seat

near the window. Locals sat outside, but she preferred not to shiver as she ate. After she ordered, she found herself watching passersby. People watching was something she loved. As her gaze moved from face to face, she did a double-take, her breath locking in her lungs as she thought she saw Maks.

But as she searched again, he wasn't there. She inwardly gave herself a shake. Her brain was too focused on Maks if she was seeing him in the crowd. Thankfully, her food arrived, and she could stop thinking about him. At least that's what she told herself. As she bit into her sandwich, her mind went back to what little she had learned about Maks. It wasn't much. The only one who seemed to have found anything was Kyle, and she wasn't sure if Kyle had found the CCTV footage of Maks jumping in front of the train and going up the opposite platform.

"Stop," she told herself.

Eden put in her earbuds and turned on some music as she ate. By the time she was finished with the meal, she felt a little better. Then, she got comfortable and switched to a quick five-minute meditation. She closed her eyes and let the words of the guided session clear her mind and balance her once more.

When it was finished, she felt immensely better. There was a smile on her face, and she had some direction for what she needed to do next. Eden paid for her food and gathered her things to leave. She kept one earbud in to continue listening to music. She still had about fifteen minutes before she had to be back at her desk, and she wasn't going to go back any sooner than she had to.

She walked slowly, soaking in the sun's rays. Her mind drifted to the items she needed to pick up at the market since she hadn't cooked all week. The weekend was fast approaching, and she was seriously considering making a short trip to Prague. She loved the city, and with so much to do there, it kept calling her back.

Eden was about to walk into the office when a man standing and staring at her while others walked past caught her attention. She searched for him as the crowd moved by, but by the time the area was clear, he was gone. Once more, she would've sworn it was Maks.

"I'm losing my mind," she said.

She hesitated about going into the office. The fact that she had slept very little last night and her unconventional connection to this new assignment made her take a step back. She had vacation days. Perhaps she should take a couple and extend her trip to Prague. Eden pulled out her phone and called Janice before she changed her mind. The secretary answered the call.

"Hi," Eden said. "Please tell Janice that I won't be coming back into work this afternoon, and I'll be taking Friday off, too. I'm not feeling well."

She dropped her phone into her bag and looked back at where she had thought she saw Maks. That was twice in less than an hour. Eden thought about walking across the street and seeing if she could find him, but she knew it was a ridiculous thought. Maks wasn't there. He might be a spy, but he couldn't know who was looking for him, or where the office was located.

Could he?

Eden shook her head. She needed to sleep. That's all this was. She'd go home, take a nap, and then book her trip to leave either later tonight or first thing tomorrow morning. Without a second thought, she walked away from SynTech and toward her flat.

The moment she was in her home, she let out a sigh of relief. Without preamble, she locked her door and went to her bedroom to undress and get back into bed. In seconds, she was asleep.

6

Getting to Vienna had been easy. Maybe too easy. Maks looked at everything and everyone as an enemy now. He needed to get into SynTech, but the office had security everywhere. Not only were there badges that let the workers through a gated area, there were also metal detectors that everyone had to walk through.

It would take some time for Maks to find a way into the building. Time he didn't have. So, he set up to watch. He recorded the comings and goings of everyone in the building. It was the woman who caught his attention that morning. First because she was one of the first to arrive. Second, because she was breathtaking.

Her shoulder-length dark blond strands caught the morning sun and held him transfixed. She walked with a confidence he'd not seen in many. As if she didn't let the weight of the world affect her. Her camel-colored coat was buttoned and belted and hung past her knees, preventing him from seeing what she wore beneath. She had a cream and black plaid scarf around her neck, black gloves on her hands, a large black purse slung over her shoulder, and black stilettos on her feet. The fact that she was more dressed than half the people who had gone into the office was something he took notice of. She glanced his way, giving him time to see her oval face, full lips turned up in a greeting, and a cheery disposition.

Besides, someone with a face like hers would catch anyone's gaze.

A couple of hours later, after most everyone had gone into the office, he went into a neighboring building and made his way to the roof. With the scope in his backpack, he scanned the windows of those within the building, moving from one floor to the next. Then he moved to the adjacent building and repeated the surveillance process a second time.

Maks was on the top floor when he froze as he spotted the woman. She sat at a desk with windows to her back. It wasn't an office, nor was it a cubicle, it was something in between. She wore a black skirt and a goldish-colored top. When he saw his picture taped to the side of her monitor, his lips flattened. For several minutes, he watched her scanning the footage from the train station in Amsterdam. He didn't wait around to find out if she'd found anything. Instead, he spun around and went back downstairs.

He kept out of sight, waiting to see if she would come out for lunch. When she did, he followed her. The temperatures had warmed up enough that she had left her coat open and her gloves and scarf in her purse. She kept tilting her face to the sky with her eyes closed as if she couldn't get enough of the sun.

The moment she entered the café for lunch, Maks remained close to watch her. Maybe too close because he feared she might have seen him. Something spooked her, because she scanned faces as if she were looking for someone. She also spoke to herself, seemingly unaware and uncaring if anyone noticed. Once she had her earbuds in, it was like the outside world didn't exist for her. Then she did the strangest thing, she sat in the café with her eyes closed. He couldn't figure out what she was doing.

On her way back to the office, she took her time as if she weren't ready to leave the sun. He'd been so engrossed in watching her that he'd forgotten that he was supposed to be hiding. Then her gaze locked with his. He wore sunglasses and a ball cap, but it didn't matter. He knew that she saw him.

Maks waited until there were enough people between them before he ducked out of sight and moved to another location to observe her. He waited to see if she would tell someone that he was there. But she didn't. She kept looking for him, though.

It wasn't until she used her mobile that he worried she was calling someone about him. Not that he was worried. He'd been trained by some of the best operatives in the world. If he wanted to disappear, he could do it. Maks remained where he was, and a moment later, the woman walked away from the building instead of going inside.

She didn't seem to be in a hurry or upset. It was more like she was happy. He kept a safe distance as he trailed her back to a set of flats. When she was inside, he went to the door and tried it but found it locked. He looked at the buzzer buttons on the side to see six. Looking around to see if anyone noticed him, he ran across the street and ducked into an alley to use his scope to locate which floor the woman was on.

He found her on the third floor, south side. Scanning the flat, he saw no movement within. It wasn't until he spotted her in bed that he got an idea. Maks made his way back to her building. Before he could pick the lock, someone opened the door from the inside, which allowed him entry. He bypassed the elevator and used the stairs to get to her floor. Then he stood in front of her door.

Maks easily picked the door lock and two deadbolts before he let himself in. He waited, looking around for an alarm system, but didn't see or hear one. Quietly, he walked through the flat. It was an open floor plan. From the door, he could see the living room, kitchen, and eating space. A small area to his right held a desk with a computer. The only other door he saw was the bedroom.

He walked toward it and peered inside. The room, like the rest of the house, was immaculate. Nothing was out of place. Even the clothes the woman had worn earlier were carefully placed on the bench before the bed. The closet door was shut, but he spotted the bathroom from his position.

Unable to resist, he walked into her room and looked at her. She was on her side, the covers tucked close against her as she slept. Her dark blond locks fanned out behind her as one foot rested outside of the covers. Her lips were parted slightly, her breathing deep and even. He couldn't help but smile. She'd come home to sleep, not to report on him.

Maks turned around and walked back into the main area. As he looked around, his gaze landed on her purse. He went to it and dug out her wallet to find her ID. Eden Fontaine, originally from Idaho. His gaze locked on her photo, big hazel eyes fringed with thick lashes stared back at him with a smile that made him feel welcome. He was curious as to what had brought her to Vienna and SynTech. Maks put her wallet back and then went to her desk. He hit the spacebar on her keyboard, and the computer woke. A screen asking for a password waited for him.

In the space, he typed THE SAINTS and left the same way he'd come in.

Once out on the street, he called Callie once more. "I need you to find out everything you can on Eden Fontaine of Idaho, who now lives in Vienna and works for SynTech."

7

E den came awake slowly. She stretched her arms over her head and turned onto her back. When she lifted her lids, she saw her room was dark. She had thought to only take a short nap. Had she known she was that tired, she would've set an alarm so she didn't sleep all night. Not that it mattered, she was taking tomorrow off.

She threw back the covers and rose from the bed. After pulling on a pair of sweats and an oversized shirt with her slippers, she checked her phone for the time. It was not yet seven, so she'd slept a solid six hours. She had to admit, she felt better. With her phone in hand, she walked into the kitchen and turned on the lights. Her stomach was growling. That's when she remembered that she had meant to go to the market for food.

"Looks like more takeout," she said with a chuckle and pulled open the drawer that held all the menus.

It didn't take her long to pick a place and call in an order for delivery. Then she grabbed a glass and filled it with water, drinking as she stood there. Her gaze moved around her apartment. She'd been lucky to find this place. It was in a highly sought-after neighborhood, and while the place wasn't large, it fit her needs perfectly. Even if the rent was a little more than she should spend. Since she didn't have a car to pay for, she justified the cost.

Her salary was good. Good enough that a huge chunk went into savings each pay period. She'd never been one to have a lot of debt. That stemmed from a father who thought it was his duty to rack up as much debt as he possibly could and never pay for it. Just the thought of creditors calling her made Eden break out in hives. Her father had just never answered the phone or allowed anyone else to answer it, just in case it was a creditor. Having their car repossessed while she was at a volleyball game with a friend who was supposed to be coming home with her was a particular embarrassment that Eden still hadn't gotten over.

Which was why even with credit cards, she didn't buy anything that she couldn't pay cash for. She set a strict budget for herself that included trips like Prague. The trains were an economical way to travel around Europe, and even with farther destinations, the flights weren't too terrible. She wasn't cheap by any means, but she definitely knew how to be frugal when it was necessary. If she lost her job tomorrow, she had enough in savings to cover her for an entire year without a job.

Eden set down the now-empty glass and made her way to the sofa. She turned on the TV, but she couldn't find anything to watch. Promising herself that she would only book her trip, she rose and went to her computer. As she sat, she tapped the keyboard and waited for the login screen to come up.

Just as she was about to type in her password, her gaze landed on the words there. Her heart leapt into her throat as her blood froze in her veins. She pushed the chair back so hard that it rolled away from her and banged into the wall. Her heart slammed into her ribs as she looked for some kind of weapon.

Without a doubt, she knew that someone had been in her apartment. She rushed to the door and checked the locks. Everything was in place. Had they come before she'd gotten home after lunch? Or while she was sleeping?

It was unnerving to know that someone had been in her home. And they could still be here.

She walked to the kitchen and grabbed a knife before she checked every corner of her flat, making sure that the windows were locked, as well. Thankfully, there was no one there, but that didn't calm her in the least. *Someone* had been in her home.

Her gaze went back to her computer. What did THE SAINTS mean? Why had whoever it was typed it into that box? She set down the knife and poured herself a shot of vodka to help calm her nerves. Then she brought her chair back to the desk and sat. Her fingers hovered over the keyboard. There was no denying what she saw there. It wasn't something she would've typed into the password box. Which meant that someone else had to have put it there.

Did the person know what she did for a living?

If so, why not just contact her and ask her to look into whatever this was?

"Because they couldn't let anyone know about it," she whispered aloud.

Eden deleted the words and typed in her password. Once logged on, everything about Maks came up from the night before. If someone had asked her right in that moment, she would have said she was positive she'd seen him earlier. Maybe she was wrong.

Perhaps she wasn't.

Was it a coincidence that she'd been looking into Maks, saw him, and then someone broke into her flat? Eden had learned a long time ago that there were no such thing as coincidences. With that in mind, she typed the word *Saints* into a search engine. As she expected, everything that came up was about religion or football.

But as an information broker, she knew that you had to look deep into search engine pages, not the first ten. Not even the first twenty. She was scrolling down the forty-second page when she found *Saints* capitalized. Immediately, she clicked on the hyperlink. Unfortunately, the link no longer worked, so she couldn't read what was said.

She went back to the search page but there was nothing for her to gain there either. She kept scrolling through pages. On the seventy-ninth page, she found *The Saints*, just as it had been written in her password box, albeit not in all capitals. Her hands shook as she clicked the link. This time, the article came up, but no sooner had it filled her screen than it went blank.

Now completely unsettled, Eden stared at the

computer screen, trying to think of a way to find out about the Saints without alerting anyone. The first thing she had to do was think about throwing someone off her trail. If those words were being tracked by a government or security agency, then she had to make them think it was just some kind of fluke that she'd clicked on both of those results.

She was so focused on thinking about all of it that when the buzzer from the front door sounded, she jumped and froze. Her mind raced, wondering who it could be. She decided to ignore it when there was another buzz. That's when she remembered that she had ordered food.

Eden went to the mic. "Yes?"

"Your food delivery," said a young woman.

"I'll buzz you in, but leave the food at my door, please."

"Whatever you want, lady," came the terse reply.

Eden allowed the girl in and stared out the peephole to watch the delivery girl get off the elevator. She walked to Eden's door, bent to place the food, then straightened and got back on the lift. Eden waited for several minutes to see if there was any other movement in the hallway. When she deemed it safe, she opened the door and grabbed her delivery.

No longer hungry, she put it on the counter and returned to her desk to finish what she had begun. Eden began searching all kinds of things about the Catholic religion and saints. She tied that into her trip to Prague and some of the cathedrals there. For the next two hours, she did everything she could to make sure that it wouldn't look as if she were searching for something called *the Saints*. And she hoped she succeeded. If someone came knocking on her door, she'd have her answer.

Now she was really curious about what the Saints were. Maybe it was just some elaborate joke, but she didn't think so. Someone wanted her to find out about the Saints, but she needed to be careful. In her time as an IB, she'd never had to watch her back as she felt like she had to now. But she knew some others who had. That meant she would have to call in a favor. Thankfully, the provider of that favor happened to reside in Europe.

Eden sent the text and waited for a reply. It came almost immediately and gave only a location.

"What am I doing?" she asked herself, but she knew the answer.

After purchasing tickets online for the first train out to Budapest the next morning, she began packing.

8

It wasn't even dawn when Eden exited her flat. Maks kept to the shadows across the street as he noted her tight expression and the way she looked around nervously. She had replaced her tote with a backpack and a crossbody purse. Her steps were quick as she began walking.

Maks had wondered all night if she had found his message. It had been hours after he left her flat before a light had come on. And it and more had remained on until just a few minutes before she left. From his spot across the street, he saw that no one had come into the building aside from the delivery woman earlier. He waited, his gaze searching the shadows. If anyone was watching her, now would be the time they made their move to trail her.

Sure enough, two men fell into step behind her at different places. Maks looked in the opposite direction, but there was no sign of anyone else. He discreetly peeled himself from the shadows and started walking in the same direction as Eden and the two men.

When he realized her direction, Maks became curious as to where she was going via train. She didn't stop to purchase a ticket once inside the terminal. Instead, she went straight to the platform for the trains heading to Budapest.

Both men following her hurried to buy tickets. Maks didn't have that kind of time. He got next to someone going toward the platform with their voucher out to scan and bumped into them, taking their ticket at the same time. He dropped some money into the man's coat pocket to make up for the theft. With his cap pulled down low, Maks used his travel document and got through before the other two men had even received their tickets.

Maks moved in behind Eden. He kept one eye on her and the other on anyone who looked suspicious. Just as the 5:47 a.m. train arrived, the men rushed onto the platform. They hadn't seen him yet, which meant that they weren't looking for him. Their mission was Eden. Maks wasn't sure if that indicated they were supposed to just follow her or kill her. Regardless, he was going to put an end to all of it soon.

The moment the doors of the train opened, Eden got on and headed toward the front of the third car. Maks stayed behind, letting others go before him. The two goons got on in separate cars. Maks left the one in Eden's car and went after the other. With long strides, he caught up with the man quickly enough.

Maks bumped into him roughly. "*Entschuldigung sie.* Excuse me," he said.

The man barely looked his way, his attention on trying to keep his focus on Eden. Maks used that to his advantage and elbowed him in the back of the head, slamming the man's face into a metal pole and knocking him out instantly.

Maks grabbed him before he could fall and said loud enough for others to hear, "You shouldn't have had that last drink."

The onlookers shook their heads and went back to doing what they had been doing before. Maks lugged the man to one of the seats in the back of the car and used the guy's scarf to bind his hands to the rail just as the train left the station. He took a few minutes to check the man's pockets and grabbed his wallet and mobile phone.

Maks then straightened, putting the items into his coat pocket before walking through the car and into the next one where Eden and the other goon were sitting. Eden was facing the front of the train, situated near the window. Her head was turned to look outside, her leg bouncing nervously up and down. The man sat diagonally to her across the aisle, his gaze locked on her. Eden was oblivious to it, as most would be. Only the trained knew what to look for in such situations.

Once more, the goon didn't look his way. It was as if his only target was Eden, and he believed nothing could stand in his way of completing a successful mission. Too bad for him and his buddy that Maks was involved.

Maks sat across from the man and waited for him to look his way. It didn't take long. It was just a glance, but the goon did a double-take and realized that Maks wasn't just any passenger. Maks smiled and raised his brows, inviting the man to make a move.

The goon didn't disappoint. He lunged, going straight for Maks' throat. Maks kicked the man's legs out from under him and used the downward momentum of the goon's body to punch him in the throat. The man went limp, gagging as he struggled for breath. Maks then knocked him out with a quick punch to the goon's jaw.

Across the aisle, Eden stared at him with wide eyes and a shocked expression. He ignored her for the moment and propped the man back up in his seat. Maks looked around, but no one seemed to be paying attention since everyone was on some kind of electronic gadget.

Maks then moved into the spot next to Eden. She squished herself as small as she could against the window. He didn't look her way. "If I wanted you dead, I would've done it last night in your flat while you slept."

There was a beat of silence as anger mixed with fear in her expression. "That was you?"

"You obviously did a search like I wanted. Otherwise, two men wouldn't have been following you."

"Two? What?"

He turned his face to her then, noting her confused and wary expression. "They've been on your tail since you walked from your flat, where I was also watching. The other one is in the car behind us."

"Are...are they dead?" she asked in a whisper.

"No."

She swallowed, the sound loud even on the high-speed train. "Is Maks your real name?"

"Yes."

"You sound American."

He looked forward then and released a breath. "Because I am."

"How did you find me? Why did you come into my apartment? What are the Saints? Why are you still following me?"

With every question, her body uncurled, muscles going tight with annoyance and indignation. He looked at her once more. "I followed you from the office yesterday. I wanted to find out who you were. The Saints are a secret organization that has infiltrated every government, military, and security agency in the world. And I knew if you looked into them, they'd send someone. And...I need your help."

She turned her head away to look out the window. She was silent for several minutes. Maks had taken a risk by asking for her help. He wasn't sure why he'd done it. Maybe it was because of how he'd seen her yesterday—carefree and happy. If she was involved with the Saints, they wouldn't have sent men after her.

At least, that was his thought.

"It's not nice to break into someone's house," Eden stated before she looked at him.

He met her hazel eyes. "Extreme times call for extreme measures. I had to know what kind of person you were."

"So, the words you left on my computer were a test?" she asked, her eyes narrowing in anger.

Max shrugged. "Call it whatever you want."

"You wanted me to prove that you can trust me?" She rolled her eyes, snorting. "You're the one who should be gaining *my* trust. Not the other way around."

Without a doubt, she intrigued him. Eden wasn't used to his way of life. Her reactions since the night before proved that. And yet she had spunk despite her fear. She might have a bright outlook on life, but she wasn't one to be taken advantage of either.

"All right," he said. "You have a point. However, you're the one who has been doing research on me."

She settled more comfortably in the chair. "That's actually not true. My coworkers are, as well. Though it's difficult to do when you don't exist."

"How good are you at your job?"

"Good enough that SynTech offered me a package to work for them—including moving me to Vienna—that nearly doubled what I was making on my own. And I was making a very good living working for myself."

Maks bit back a smile. Yeah, she had pluck in spades. Which was a good thing because she was going to need it.

"The entire floor of IBs were looking for anything and everything on you," she continued. "What did you do to get someone so riled up?"

Maks decided not to answer that for the moment. He might want her help, but that didn't mean he trusted her. Not with the information that he was a spy. "You found something. In Amsterdam."

She froze, once more taken off guard. Her visible reactions helped for him to put more trust in her, because reactions like that couldn't be faked. Not to someone like him, who had been trained to look for anything that wasn't genuine.

"How could you possibly know about that?" she demanded.

He lifted a shoulder in a shrug. "I saw you at your desk through my scope. You were watching footage of me in the train station."

"Damn," she mumbled and looked forward. "I never expected that."

Maks took pity on her when he saw the amount of stress she was under. "I shouldn't have gotten you to look into the Saints."

Her head snapped to him. "Why did you pick me?"

A lie filled his head, but he didn't say the words. "I saw you yesterday. People aren't usually that cheerful going into work, but you were. I then did some recon on the building and spotted you again."

"I saw you yesterday at lunch. Twice," she said with a firm nod.

Maks didn't confirm or deny that.

"I thought I was losing my mind," she said more to herself than to him.

He tilted his head to the side. "Why didn't you report me to your boss? I'm sure you handed over the train station footage."

She cut her eyes to him and twisted her lips. "Actually, I didn't. Another coworker of mine, Kyle, was the one who used his special algorithm to locate where you'd been. I kinda stole that information from him and used it myself."

He couldn't help but smile at her *kinda stole*

comment. "That still doesn't explain why you didn't turn over the information."

"I don't know," she said with a half-hearted shrug. "From the moment they gave us the picture of you, there was something about you that pulled at me. At first, I thought it was because finding information on you was a challenge, but,"—she paused, a frown creasing her brow—"it's more than that. Yet I can't explain it."

Maks knew precisely what she was talking about because he'd felt the same thing about her from the moment he first laid eyes on her. "I'm glad you didn't tell anyone about that."

"I didn't tell anyone that I thought I saw you yesterday, either." She rolled her eyes, chuckling softly. "I'd stayed up the night before doing more digging on you from my home computer, so I chalked it up to me being tired."

Now he knew why she'd slept for so long. "Did Kyle find me?"

"Yeah. He was in the office with the suits yesterday when I left for lunch. I'm not sure how much he found. My guess is that he didn't see the footage of you jumping in front of the train, though."

Maks was even more impressed that she'd found that. "I was being tailed and had to run."

"Tailed? How did they find you?"

"They knew I was in Amsterdam since I'd been found earlier that night. It made sense to watch public transportation."

She licked her lips. "I got a decent look at your face on the CCTV from the station. You did good keeping yourself from being seen, but after you got to the other platform and walked with the crowd up the steps to the main floor, they got a good shot of three-quarters of your face."

Shit. He couldn't make mistakes like that. While he couldn't account for every camera—because some were hidden on purpose—he should've expected one to be in that spot to catch those coming up from the trains below.

"How did you know who was looking into you?" Eden asked in puzzlement.

"I have a friend who is a hacker. She found the company that was hired to dig up information about me."

Eden glanced away. "I see. Did you intend to pick someone to help you?"

"No," he admitted. "I wasn't sure what I was going to do. I needed to look at the building, learn more about the company and their employees, and go from there."

"You don't seem concerned that someone is looking for you."

Maks drew in a deep breath and slowly released it. "It comes with the territory, I suppose."

"How do you live like this?"

"I suppose you get used to it."

She looked out the window, nodding absently. Then she faced him. "Are you a spy?"

He stared into her hazel eyes, a dozen lies coming to mind. Whoever was looking for him had already blown his cover. So what if someone knew his profession? He was going down, and he was going to take anyone and everyone associated with the Saints down with him.

"Yes," he replied.

Her eyes widened briefly. "I didn't expect you to admit it."

"I usually don't."

"Why tell me, then?"

He smiled, chuckling softly. "Damned if I know."

Her lips softened into a grin. "I'm glad you did."

9

W as this really happening? No matter how much Eden wanted to deny it, there was no way she could. She'd seen firsthand how quickly—and easily—Maks had subdued the man. It had been done in such a way that no one even noticed. She hadn't realized that people actually had skills like that. In movies and books, yes, but not in real life.

When she looked over and saw him, her heart had skipped a beat before pounding at a furious pace. She hadn't been sure whether to run or pretend that she didn't know who he was. She was out of her element, and it showed because she had done nothing but sit there stupidly.

She was still a bit peeved that he'd been in her flat while she slept, but she was beginning to understand why he'd done it. Especially if she could believe him. And why wouldn't she? She knew better than anyone that there was nothing out there on Maks Volkov. What she did know was that he had skills only someone who had been highly trained could have.

And he'd just told her that he was a spy. Weren't operatives supposed to keep that to themselves? Then again, what did he have to lose? If he doubted she could keep his secret, he could end her in a heartbeat.

"You doing okay?"

His question surprised her. She jerked her head to him. "Considering everything? I suppose."

"You're in shock."

Was that what this was? She couldn't be sure. All she knew was that she felt safer with Maks around.

"Why Budapest?" he asked.

She filled her lungs with a big breath and released it. "I have a friend who owes me a favor. After I did a quick search on the Saints last night, I found two instances with the word as an entity, not a holy person or an American football team. The first page was no longer up, and the second came up and then disappeared before I even got to see what it was about."

"What else did you do to have men after you?"

Eden blinked, shrugging. "I knew that something wasn't right, so I spent the next couple of hours doing research on different churches in Prague since I planned to go there for the weekend to do some sightseeing anyway. I thought I'd done enough to throw anyone looking off my trail."

"I admit, it was a good try, but they keep their eyes open."

"You should've warned me," she admonished.

To her surprise, he grinned. "I suppose I should have. But I was watching you."

"I didn't know that. What if someone had gotten into the building like you did?"

His face went hard. "That wouldn't have happened."

She believed him, even though she had no proof. "Are you CIA?"

"It might be better if you didn't know who I work for."

"You involved me in...whatever this is. Don't you think I'm owed an explanation?"

His bright blue eyes stared back at her for a long moment. Then he sighed and looked away. "I was in the military, Delta Force. The CIA recruited me to serve as an undercover spy in the FSB."

She hadn't thought she could be shocked any more, but she was. She glanced around nervously and then whispered, "The FSB? You can't be serious."

"It's where I've been for the last few years. They think I work for them. The CIA believes I work for them."

"So, who *do* you work for?" The moment the words were out, she wasn't sure she wanted to know.

He smiled as his head swung to her. "Myself."

She held his gaze, her mind going through everything she now knew. Then it dawned on her. "This is about the Saints."

"Yes."

"They're the reason I'm going to Budapest. I wanted to know what it was I was supposed to find but couldn't."

His brows drew together in a frown. "You know someone there?"

"An old colleague who owes me a favor. I'm meeting him."

Maks shook his head, the baseball cap covering most of his blond locks. "You can't. They'll know exactly who it is you texted, and they'll be watching that person, waiting for you to get there. They'll also have every public transportation hub watched."

"In other words, they'll be at the train station looking for me. What am I supposed to do then?"

"Trust me," he stated calmly. "I can get you off this train undetected."

She glanced around, knowing she didn't have a chance on her own. She didn't know the first thing about escaping anyone's notice, much less that of the authorities. "Then what? I'm supposed to run for the rest of my life because I looked up the Saints?"

"I can give you the information you want. I have a ton of it, though I've not dug through it all."

She frowned at him. "Why would you get information and not look through it?"

"Time. I gathered what I could, when I could, and stored it for the day when I could look through it."

Eden bit her lip, thinking about what she was up against. If what Maks said about the Saints was true, if she didn't go with him, they would likely have her in a matter of minutes. And she had no trouble thinking of all the different ways they could hurt her. She had, after all, seen numerous movies depicting just that.

"Or..." Maks said. "You can get off the train in Budapest and pretend that you're there to see an old friend. Make up a valid reason for why you texted him last night and changed travel plans."

"That's easy," she said with a shrug. "We were once together romantically."

"When whoever it is comes for you, just go with it. Act confused and concerned but follow through with exactly what you did last night by looking up churches because you had planned to go to Prague. Tell them that you then thought about your ex and sent off a text to see if he was free. It's simple, and I'm pretty sure that after some lengthy interrogations, they'll let you go."

Eden drew in a breath. "Then what? Will they continue watching me?"

"Most likely for the rest of your life. Or until I can expose them and take them down."

She couldn't believe that he was so cavalier about such a statement. "You told me they're worldwide."

"They are. They infiltrate at the top and work their way down, be it governments, militaries, or companies. They are everywhere."

She glanced behind them. "They could be on the train."

"No doubt, they are."

"And they've seen me talking to you."

Maks gave a single nod of his head. "Tell them you feared for your life. That you remained because I terrified you."

"You're missing the point. If you're right, then the Saints are all around us. How do you think you, one person, can take down such an organization?"

"Because I have to," he stated in a soft voice.

Eden looked out the window, digesting their

conversation. She liked facts. It was part of her job to find facts and gather evidence against others. But there was another part of her who fell into those classified as conspiracy theorists. She considered herself intelligent enough to get the facts about things, and yes, her secret addiction was ancient aliens.

The naked truth about extraterrestrials was out in the world, even though so many discounted it for one reason or another. But if they just opened their minds to the possibility, they would see the truth for themselves.

Were the Saints the same thing? Was she purposefully trying not to see what Maks was attempting to tell her because she didn't want to believe it?

"Tell me something they've done," she implored as she looked at him.

Maks didn't hesitate when he said, "They developed a bioweapon called Ragnarök that they intended to deliver all over the world to control the population. It was designed to make women sterile without an antidote, only given to those they deemed to have the genes necessary to continue our species."

Eden felt as if the ground had been yanked out from under her. She had asked, but she hadn't expected...this. Though she wasn't sure what she *had* expected. Obviously, something less extreme.

"I have no proof to give you," Maks continued. "Another group of people in Texas stumbled upon all of that and stopped it from happening. I joined in at the last moment when there was a battle on their ranch."

Her eyes widened. "A battle? Like...a *battle*?"

"Of course. It didn't make the papers or any news, but there is footage of it. I can get it to you if you want to see it. To check my facts."

"I'm not sure I do," she admitted.

He shrugged. "You might need to."

"Possibly." Was she really getting into this? Did she really want to?

Eden faced forward again, her mind running through the two paths before her. She could take the out that Maks had given her. She would be detained and questioned for hours, if not days, and it would mean that she would be watched for the rest of her life. But she could be free of the fear that currently knotted her stomach.

Or would she? When catastrophes happened, wouldn't she always wonder if it was the Saints? She would, without a doubt.

So...that left her with the other path. One that meant constantly looking over her shoulder, hiding, and worrying that anyone she interacted with might be a Saint. However, she could be a part of taking them down.

The world wasn't a perfect place. Nothing could be. But *no one* had the right to choose if someone was allowed to become pregnant or not. No one should be able to dictate who was elected for public office, or who won wars. Humans were supposed to have free will. Many people had given blood, sweat, and tears for their countries to be democratic and have the right to vote on who they wanted in office.

All of that was being threatened on a scale that was bigger than she could fathom. And yet, very few knew what was happening. The fact that it was all done behind the scenes terrified Eden because that meant the changes happening could be done with an ulterior motive.

Out of the corner of her eye, Eden saw Maks take out his cell phone and text someone. She didn't think anything of it as her mind continued down a spiral of anxiety that made her realize that she had no other choice but to go with Maks and see if what he said was the truth.

If it wasn't, then she'd still take the other path. If he was a liar, then she wouldn't hesitate to throw his handsome ass under the bus to save her own skin.

But if he was telling the truth, then she had a responsibility to help him. To sit idly by and hope that someone else would take a stand was not what America had been founded on. Hundreds of thousands had lost their lives for her to live in a free world. As a woman, she stood on the shoulders of others who had come before her and fought for her right to vote and have a voice. How could she, as a woman and a human, not take a stand? How would she ever look at herself in the mirror again?

"Here," Maks said and handed her his phone.

She briefly met his vibrant blue eyes and took the cell. His face gave nothing away, but her curiosity was already piqued. She looked down at the screen to see a video that was paused, overlooking a fenced-in, rolling field. There were small groves of trees, and she spotted what looked like several men hunkered down together, holding rifles and getting ready to shoot.

Her hand shook as she raised her finger to press

play. The volume was turned down, but she still jerked at the sound of rapid gunfire from a rifle. She couldn't look away as she watched the battle playing out on the screen. There were explosions, screams of pain, and the spray of blood that was clearly not fake.

It was raw, gritty.

Chilling.

Eden didn't know how long the video played. She saw the different camera angles looking out over the field, towards a barn, and even the area between a house and an outbuilding. She wanted to think this was some part of a movie, but the moment she spotted Maks, she knew she couldn't.

Her gaze was riveted on him. He moved like someone used to finding himself in such situations. He was calm, methodical, and determined. When the video ended, she sat there in silence before handing the phone back to him.

"That was several months ago," he said.

She blinked, unsure what to say.

He switched to something else on the phone and handed it back to her. "Here is the information on the Ragnarök virus. You don't have to read it, but it's here if you want to know more. You're a smart woman. I shouldn't have pulled you into this. For that, I'm sorry. But we need people like you. Those who are appalled at what's happening right under everyone's noses."

"I've seen movies with such storylines." She met his gaze. "Do you know how many times the woman who helps out is killed?"

"I won't let anything happen to you."

She twisted her lips and snorted. "You can't promise that."

"I can, and I am. I'm very good at what I do."

"Spying?" she retorted. She wasn't angry at him, and she shouldn't be taking it out on Maks.

He briefly lowered his gaze. "I was an elite soldier who went to work for the CIA because I had an encounter with the Saints. I saw for myself what the organization was about and knew it had to be stopped. I'd thought I would have to do it on my own, but then I discovered that I wasn't alone in this. I have people I can trust, friends and allies who have my back. And I have theirs. I'll continue having theirs. No matter if you help me or not, we'll watch over you and do everything we can to throw the Saints off your trail."

Eden hadn't expected such words from him, and they affected her deeply. More deeply than she wanted to admit. She took the phone from his hand once more. "Let me see this."

On the first screen, she found herself reading the components of a virus. When she got to the bottom and saw that the desired outcome was indeed to control the world's population by preventing women from getting pregnant, her gut clenched. She scrolled back to the top of the page and saw the seal of the office of the president in Russia.

"It's not faked," Maks said.

She nodded slowly. "I know. I did research on a couple of people in the Russian government not too long ago." Her head swiveled to him. "Why was Russia developing this?"

"It's one of the headquarters of the Saints."

Now it all came together. "You're part Russian, aren't you? That's why you went to the CIA, because you knew they'd use you to get to Russia, and it would allow you to gather intel."

His mouth curved into a smile that made her blood quicken. "I knew you were smart."

10

"We lost contact with our agents on the train."
Janice stared at the screens that filled the wall before her, each one depicting a different point within the Wien Hauptbahnhof train station. Those working in this room had been locked on tracking Eden Fontaine since she left her flat that morning.

With one agent having gone missing not long after Eden left her flat, and the other two silent since the train had taken off, there was only one answer: someone was helping Eden.

Janice had been the one to recruit her from the States. Eden was good at her job. So good, in fact, that the Saints wanted to make sure they could control what she saw and who she dug into. It hadn't taken long for Eden to agree to the job offer, making Janice's job that much easier. And everything had gone exactly as planned from the moment Eden arrived in Vienna.

Every employee working for SynTech was monitored daily. Their whereabouts, who they spoke with, their communications, and anyone they interacted with. Only a few had been upgraded to having their homes bugged with audio and video. Eden had never gotten to that point, and Janice now realized that had been to their detriment. Had the surveillance equipment been in place, they could've known what she had done in her flat after she left work the previous day.

"Ma'am?" the technician nearest her asked.

Janice looked down at the skinny white male that would forever be classified as a dork no matter what clothes he wore or the position he held. It was in his bearing, his very essence. He'd told her his name a dozen times, but she'd never remember it. And it was him and others like him in the office that allowed the Saints to stay ahead of their enemies. At least, for the most part.

"Walk me through it all again," she ordered him.

He swallowed and cleared his throat. "Put video 2C on the main screen," he told someone.

In a blink, the monitors shifted. Janice crossed her arms over her chest as the CCTV footage began to play.

"This is the south entrance of the station," he told her. "In four seconds, our target will come on screen." Once that happened, he snapped his fingers, and the next video popped up. "From there, she walks through the station and to the terminal with the train headed for Budapest."

"Does she stop and talk to anyone?" Janice asked.

The guy shook his head of brown hair parted to the side and slicked back. "No one. We have clear shots of her here,"—he clicked a button—"here,"—

he clicked another button—"and here. No one bumps into her, stops her, and she doesn't speak to anyone."

"That we know of." Janice said it more to herself than to anyone else. "Next."

He shifted in his chair. "We pick her up right as she enters the terminal. The train is just getting there, so there's little time for her to interact with anyone."

Janice's gaze took in every face around Eden to see if she recognized any of them. As explained, the train got there seconds after Eden, and she quickly boarded. "And our agents?"

"One is a few people behind her," the nerd said.

She nodded when she spotted him. "And the second?"

"We picked him up two cars behind her, here," he said as the screen changed to show the second agent.

Janice barked, "Stop. Back up the recording a little." Her instructions were immediately followed. She peered closer at a man who bumped into her agent. It seemed harmless enough, but at this point, she couldn't take the chance. "Can we see the man's face? The one who ran into our agent?"

The nerd began issuing orders, and the room hurried to comply, each doing their best to give her what she wanted. Minutes passed as she watched and rewatched the footage of the man jostling her agent.

"Sorry, ma'am," the nerd finally answered. "The guy is wearing a cap, and none of the cameras can get a good angle of his face. Not even using the windows as a mirror."

"I see mobile phones out," she said. "Check social media and see if anyone got a hit on his face."

Once more, the room erupted in a flurry. There was a really good chance that she was chasing nothing. But there was also a chance that this could be something.

"Got it!" a female shouted a few minutes later.

Janice jerked her head to the side at the sound of the voice. The large screen in the middle of the room was filled with a profile that she recognized instantly. Maks Volkov. She'd had a feeling that someone was helping Eden, and now she knew for sure.

She leaned over the nerd and typed in Maks' name, pulling up and image of his face. "Go back to our target leaving her flat and check all cameras for any sign of this man, Maks Volkov."

But despite her request, they found nothing. There were too many streets without cameras to see everything. However, the train station was a different story. Maks was seen following about thirty feet behind Eden. There could be an argument that they were working together. Maks wasn't seen leaving her apartment, but that didn't mean he hadn't been there.

Janice spun around and left the room. Once outside, she dialed a number and brought her mobile to her ear. "I need a team at Fontaine's house immediately. Take prints. If there's a sign that anyone but her has been in that flat, I want to know who it was."

She hung up and made her way to the lift to head back up to the top floor. Kyle had found footage of Maks in Amsterdam, but no one had been able to find another trace of him until now. And had Eden not done a search on the Saints, they might never have found another sign of Maks for several weeks.

He was good at what he did. Very good.

And she should know. They'd briefly been lovers.

11

M aks was torn about involving Eden in his fight against the Saints. On one hand, he believed that anyone who didn't know who the Saints really were should be informed and pick a side. On the other, the fight brewing between him and the Saints was one that could potentially be catastrophic to anyone associated with him.

He was prepared to give his life, but he couldn't say the same for anyone else. Especially Eden. And his promise to protect her was one that he took seriously. No matter what, he would do everything in his power to ensure that the Saints didn't touch her.

Maks knew from firsthand experience how ruthless and merciless the Saints could be when they went after someone they believed was a threat to them. He was more than a threat. He was the very thing they had feared for years. To compound matters, they had helped to create him and develop his skills. And he was going to use every one of them on the Saints.

"Are you sure they didn't release this bioweapon?" Eden asked.

Maks looked at his watch to check the time. It took two and a half hours to reach Budapest from Vienna. They still had a little over an hour before the train pulled into the station. "I'm sure. The Loughmans helped to kill the scientist who engineered it. On top of that, Orrin Loughman, the father, was responsible for stealing the only vial of it after a mission into Russia. He was meant to be a scapegoat, but Orrin is smart and realized that something was up almost immediately. He managed to escape his team that turned on him."

"I gather they were Saints."

Maks nodded. "Orrin sent the vial to Mia for safekeeping, which was a good thing because he was taken prisoner by Yuri."

"The general you worked for."

To say Maks was impressed at how she was keeping up with names was an understatement. "That's right. I didn't know then that the Loughmans were waging a war on the Saints, but as soon as I did, I helped out as I could. The FSB had been worried about Yuri and whether he would come on board as a Saint. The CIA wanted to know where Orrin was."

Her brows shot up in her forehead. "I'm guessing you didn't turn over any information to either agency?"

"I gave them enough to keep them happy. The CIA knew we were in the States, but I told them Yuri kept us moving. In fact, we stayed in one spot. As for the FSB, I told them Yuri was after Orrin, wanting to get retribution on an American who'd invaded his homeland. It worked because it was the truth."

"Did you not know Yuri would join Orrin in the fight?"

"I had an idea that he might. Yuri didn't trust anyone, not even those closest to him. He kept his feelings and thoughts close to the vest. People like that usually have a plan, and Yuri seemed the type. Besides, he had the opportunity to kill Orrin and he didn't take it. They had a feud that went back decades, each believing the other had betrayed him. Turned out, they'd both been betrayed. When they figured that out, they joined forces."

Eden tucked a strand of her dark blond locks behind her ear. "If this virus was made once, it can be created again."

"It can be, but it'll take some time. I plan on dismantling the Saints before that happens."

"That's a lot for one man to do."

He grinned at her. "I'm not alone. I've got the Loughmans, and then there's a mob boss I helped out not too long ago. Lev is with us, and so is his woman. And she was undercover in the Saints for five years."

"Sounds like you have a plan."

"Not a plan so much as hope. Because the Saints are everywhere and embedded so deeply in communities, we need to make sure that the information gets out to the right people before anyone can stop it. But first, I need to ensure that what I have is enough. I'd hoped to get more, but my cover was blown the day before yesterday."

Eden frowned, her brows drawing together. "What happened?"

"I had a burner phone that no one knew about. At least, I didn't think anyone knew. Somehow a high-ranking FSB official that I'd had limited contact with sent me a text on that burner phone minutes before he was killed."

She blinked, startled. "What did the text say?"

"Watch yourself."

"I don't understand," Eden replied, puzzlement filling her expression.

Maks glanced at the goon to make sure he was still knocked out. "My theory is that he found out something about the Saints. He was on a train out of St. Petersburg. I don't know if he was leaving the country, but my guess is that he was. Whatever happened, he was spooked enough to contact me."

"Which put the heat on you."

He shrugged. "It did. I've been expecting something like this for a while, though, so I wasn't taken completely off guard."

"Where is the information you have?"

"In a safe place."

She gave him a flat look. "Do you not trust me now?"

"If I didn't trust you, I wouldn't have told you everything I already did. Part of this is to make sure that you have nothing to tell anyone if you're captured."

"Oh." Eden swallowed and licked her lips. "I've never done anything like this before."

He saw the goon begin to twitch as he regained consciousness. "I'll guide you. Now, grab your things. We need to go."

Without question, she got her backpack and slung it over a shoulder as she stood. Maks glanced behind them to make sure that no one was coming, then he stepped into the aisle and waited for the sliding door to open so they could go into the next car. Eden remained in step with him.

"Act calmly," he whispered over his shoulder.

He heard a snort behind him, then she said, "That's a tall order, but I'll do my best."

That made him smile. He walked to the middle of the car and found two seats facing each other. He motioned her into the one facing forward, then he took the one looking back the way they'd come.

The man next to her was in a heated conversation on his phone, which meant he wasn't paying attention to them. Across the aisle were two lovers that were making out in such a heated fashion that Maks was surprised one of them wasn't naked yet.

"What now?" Eden whispered.

Maks took a deep, steadying breath. "We make it to the station without being seen."

Her hazel eyes widened. "You've got to be kidding. There are only so many places we can go while it's moving. Forward or backward."

"Backward is where two of the men are."

"Forward it is," she said.

He twisted his lips. "If we go too far, then we won't leave ourselves room for escape. Besides, we don't have first-class tickets. We've gone about as far as we can go."

She pulled out her phone and looked at the time. "We still have forty minutes."

"That's right."

"How can you be so calm?" she asked, her voice rising as hysteria took hold.

He met her gaze and held it. "I need you to breathe. All you have to do is trust me and do what I say. Everything will be all right."

"You're asking a lot."

"I know, but if you want to live, you'll do it."

She flattened her lips. "Of course, I will. I'll give you shit about it, but I'll do it."

Maks fought not to chuckle at her sarcasm. He liked that she wasn't afraid to speak her mind or give him an earful despite the situation. She didn't have to trust him, and he wasn't sure she did, at least not completely. He'd given her a lot to digest in a short period of time. It wouldn't be until she went through everything that he had that she'd truly understand the depth and scope of who the Saints where.

Maybe then she'd trust him without reservation.

He wasn't offended that she kept a wall up. It was the smart thing to do, and Eden was sharp. If she had blindly trusted from the beginning, he'd have been wary and wondered if she was a Saint. There was still a chance that she was with the organization. He was putting everything he had on his instincts that said she could be trusted.

But he was going to make sure that Callie had a link to what he planned to show Eden. That way, if he was betrayed, at least the Loughmans would have the intel he'd worked so hard for over the years.

"Focus on your breathing," he told her.

Little by little, her hands unclenched in her lap as she started to calm. She closed her eyes as if meditating. He used that time to look around them, noting the emergency exits and how many people stood between them and each doorway. With every minute that passed, neither of the goons he'd knocked out came at them, and they got closer to Budapest.

The outside was a blur as the bullet train sped down the railway. Maks looked at his watch. Thirty minutes had passed. They only had ten more before they reached the station. He was beginning to think they might actually make it when he saw movement through the doors to the car behind them.

Maks leaned forward and tapped Eden's knee. Her eyes snapped open. "Do you have a hat or a scarf?"

"For my hair?" she asked.

He nodded, his gaze going to the door again.

She unzipped her pack and pulled out a scarf that she hastily draped over her hair just as the doors opened and the two goons walked in, their gazes scanning faces.

"Remain calm," Maks said, keeping his head down and his focus on the men.

One of Eden's hands clenched the ends of the scarf together to keep it from falling off. The other hand gripped her backpack strap, ready to jump up at a moment's notice. As the men approached, the man beside Eden began to yell in German into his phone. He jumped up and continued spewing profanities at the caller. The goons barely glanced at Maks and Eden as they tried to get as far from the loud man as possible. When they were gone, Eden smiled while the man next to her ended the phone conversation.

Maks really hated to burst her bubble, but he had no choice. "They'll come back through when they don't find you."

"Oh," she said, the smile disappearing.

Then Maks had an idea. "Go to the toilet."

"What?" she asked in confusion.

He looked over his shoulder, knowing the men would be back soon. "Go to the toilet. Stay there until I come and get you."

"Okay," she said nervously. Then she rose and took her pack with her as she walked to the back of the car and the restroom there. It wasn't long after the door closed behind her that the men returned. And just as Maks had suspected, they took their time looking at each individual.

The goon that stopped next to him was the one he'd knocked unconscious first. He hadn't seen Maks' face. "Excuse me. Wasn't there a woman sitting here?"

Maks shrugged and answered with a German accent to his English. "I think she went to another car."

"*Danka*, thank you."

If things went his way, then the second goon wouldn't stop.

But luck wasn't on his side because the second guy halted beside Maks and asked in German, "Were you with the woman that was sitting here?"

Maks shook his head and looked out the window. He used the window like a mirror to see the goon studying him. The moment the man recognized who he was, Maks rose up and slammed his elbow into the man's face. The sound of bone crunching was followed by a spray of blood from the man's nose.

At the sound of the scuffle, the first goon spun around. Maks shoved the Saint he was fighting backwards, right into his partner so that both went down. Maks landed on top of them, punching the first so his head slammed back into the second. All around him, people were screaming and trying to get away.

The moment Maks felt the train slowing as they neared the station, he threw two more quick jabs into the men and jumped over them, rushing toward the toilet area. He reached it as the train came to a stop and said Eden's name. She opened the door, and he took her hand and waited for the crowd to come around them before they disembarked.

"Keep your head down," he told her. "In five steps, we're going to separate. Find a group of people and stick with them until you clear the north entrance. I'll find you there. Don't talk to anyone. Don't stop for anything. Can you do that?"

"Yes," she said.

He gave her a reassuring smile, and then they parted ways. He wanted to glance back at her to see how she was doing, but he didn't. There were cameras everywhere, and he made sure to keep his cap low and his head down. When he was able, he took off his coat and tossed it onto a chair as he passed. That way, if anyone was looking for him by that, it would throw them off. Not for long, but enough that it would give him and Eden more time.

12

Nothing in her life could've prepared Eden for any of this. She knew that someone could point at her and shout her name at any moment as she walked through the station. Sweat covered her brow and ran down her back. Her legs wobbled uncontrollably, and her heart thumped wildly, threatening to burst from her chest at any second.

She knew why Maks had separated them, but she didn't like it. At least with him, he knew what to look for as far as their enemies went. To her, hell, *everyone* was a potential enemy. And that was probably the smartest thing she could put in her mind. She had a habit of trusting people too easily, of taking their word for stuff. She'd been burned so many times that she should've learned her lesson by now, but somehow, that wasn't the case.

Eden tried to swallow, but her mouth was dry. She kept her head down like Maks had told her to do and refused to look up. She was so terrified. The fight or flight thing was going into effect, and she was all about the flight.

It was easy for her to stay with a group and appear as if she were one of them when the train station was so crowded. As they neared the exit, that became more difficult. She did her best, which had so far gotten her through most of the building. When she saw the exit signs ahead, relief loosened the tight hold that fear had on her.

Then she spotted the police officers at the entrance, looking at everyone. Eden froze in place. In her head, she screamed at herself to keep moving like Maks had told her. But her legs simply refused to obey. Her fingers grew numb, and she loosened the hold she had on the scarf, remembering only then that she still had it on. A woman with a fedora walked in front of her, chatting on the phone with someone. Eden's gaze followed her into the toilet.

Even though Maks had told her not to stop, something had prodded her to change her appearance. Eden pivoted and made her way to the toilet area. Oddly, there weren't many women inside. The woman with the fedora went into a stall and locked the door. Eden remained at the sink. She looked at herself in the mirror and removed the scarf. Next, she took off the backpack and unzipped it to take out her thickest sweater.

Eden shimmied her shoulder to remove the jacket and fold it up to put into the pack, leaving her in a thin, long-sleeved tee. She put the sweater over the tee and straightened to run her fingers through her hair. Her gaze slid to the scarf sitting by the sink. She quickly folded it and put it away, but she still needed something to cover her head.

It wasn't as if she could stop in a shop and buy

something. And she'd never stolen anything in her life, so that wasn't an option.

Your life is at stake. Do what needs to be done.

At that moment, the woman walked out of the stall. Eden kept her gaze lowered as she put her hands beneath the faucet to run water over them as if rinsing them from washing. The woman stopped two sinks away and removed the fedora to comb her short hair. Eden knew now was the time. They were the only two in the restroom. She could just take it, wrestling it from the woman if need be.

That would be stupid. Yeah, let's cause a ruckus so the authorities are called.

Okay. So she had to think of something else. But her mind was blank. Then she thought about Maks. What would he do?

And then it came to her.

Eden dried her hands and put her pack over her shoulder. She opened her mouth, but the words came out as a squeak. Clearing her throat, she tried again. "Excuse me. Is that yours?" Eden asked and pointed to the side.

The moment the woman turned, Eden grabbed the hat. The woman kept walking towards the place Eden had pointed, which gave her the time she needed to leave the toilet. She didn't immediately put on the fedora in case the woman came running out to look for her. Though she did find another group to fall into step with.

Eden maneuvered herself into the middle of the crowd to hide herself even more. As they approached the exits, she placed the hat on her head and smiled at one of the men next to her. He returned her smile and asked in German how she was. She used the opportunity to reply to him as they walked through the doors and out of the station so that it appeared as if they were together.

When no one tried to stop her or call her name, she kept going, wanting to be as far from the station as she could. The air hit her face, cooling her. She made herself stop and take a couple of calming breaths. Then she turned around and looked at the train station. It wasn't her first time in Budapest, and she had spent time exploring the architecture of the station before, but now she looked at it differently.

She looked at *everything* differently.

Seconds felt like an eternity. She scanned faces, looking for Maks. The longer she went without seeing him, the more worried she became that he had arrived while she had been otherwise occupied in the toilets. Maybe he'd left.

He wouldn't leave you.

Eden snorted. Why wouldn't he? She was doing nothing but weighing him down. If he knew a hacker, then they could look through the intel he had. He didn't need her for anything. She couldn't protect herself. She didn't know the first thing about going undetected through a city, and she certainly didn't know enough about the Saints to know what to look for.

"For fuck's sake," she said and closed her eyes in frustration.

"What's wrong?"

The sound of Maks' voice next to her had her eyes flying open. She threw her arms around him, holding him tight. "I thought you'd left me."

"I wouldn't do that," he said, his arms coming

around her.

That's when she realized what she'd done. Eden loosened her hold and stepped back. "Sorry. I sometimes let my imagination get away from me. Actually," she grimaced, "it's not sometimes, it's all the time."

One side of Maks' mouth lifted in a smoldering grin. "That could come in handy. It'll keep you on your toes so you don't trust anyone."

"Eh. I trust too easily. I mean, look at you. I took your word for everything."

His blue eyes were intense as they stared at her. "Actually, you asked questions and wanted proof. You've had no reason not to trust people before now. Some people believe everything."

"Like me," she interjected.

"And some believe nothing."

She raised a brow. "Like you?"

He chuckled softly. "Like me. Ready to get out of here?"

"Please."

They turned right and started walking. She felt his gaze rake over her, and she took the opportunity to do the same. She just now realized that he no longer wore his jacket.

"I thought I told you not to stop," he said.

She shrugged and pointed at him. "You seem to have lost your coat."

"I got rid of it, but I didn't stop." He jerked his chin to the hat. "You seem to have picked up something yourself."

Eden raised her eyes to the fedora and shrugged. "I know what you said, but something told me to change my appearance."

"While I don't disagree with what you did, next time, I need you to do exactly as I say. Because it might mean your life."

"I understand."

"Changing your appearance was smart."

She lengthened her strides to keep up with him. "I just took off my jacket and replaced it with a sweater. The hat, well, I stole that. It's the first time I've ever stolen anything in my life."

He glanced at her. "How did it feel?"

"I'm not sure. I'm alternating between knowing I had to do it and wanting to run back and give the woman some money."

Maks smiled and shook his head. "You have a good heart. There's nothing wrong with that. However, you also have a strong will to survive, which means you'll do what needs to be done to ensure that. It's a good combination."

"If you say so."

"Well, you're about to get another dose of knowledge because I'm going to steal a car."

The toe of her shoe caught on the lip of the sidewalk, causing her to stumble. Maks had his hand on her arm immediately, steadying her. She flashed him a reassuring smile, but his frown said that it did anything but that. "I'm good."

They walked in silence, Maks taking them deeper and deeper into the city. The streets became narrower, and the people thinned out so that the tourists were left behind. Eden hadn't seen this part of the city before. She tended to stay close to main attractions the first few times she visited a city, then slowly worked her way outward to take in as much as she could. Living in Vienna had made that possible. Otherwise, if she had made it to Europe, she wouldn't have been able to spend nearly the amount of time in each city as she had.

"Stay here," Maks said before he suddenly walked between two parked cars.

She watched as he made his way down the line of vehicles along the street until he found the one he wanted. Eden was shocked at how easily he got into the car. He motioned for her to join him as he got behind the wheel. She got inside and closed the door in time to see him twist two wires together as the engine roared to life. In the next second, he pulled out onto the road.

"Whew," she said and fastened her seat belt. "I wasn't sure we'd make it."

Maks didn't look at her as his gaze scanned the streets. "We've not made it out of anything yet."

"But we got out of the train station and are now in a car heading...I don't know where. But there are no border checkpoints, so we're good."

"Just because there are no checkpoints in place doesn't mean they can't spring them up for some special reason while looking for us."

Eden was deflated. "Oh."

"That doesn't mean what we've done is diminished. You did good."

"What happens now?"

He glanced at her. "Get some sleep if you can. We've got a bit of a drive."

Eden wasn't sure she could sleep, but she would take the time to rest her eyes and meditate. At the rate things were going, she was going to need all the meditation she could get to keep from expiring from fear.

The car was old and smelled like someone had left rotten food in it. Or vomited. Either way, it wasn't a good smell. But beggars couldn't be choosers. She would deal with the stench if it got them where they needed to go.

Despite wanting to meditate, she couldn't keep her eyes shut. She looked out the passenger window as the city fell away. Without meaning to, she was going to see another part of Hungary that she hadn't gotten the opportunity to see before. She found herself grinning, because she was doing what her mom always had, finding the silver lining in any situation. It had worked for the most part until her father had left them with no money, no home, and no place to go. That's when her mom finally had enough and left her dad.

"You're smiling. That's good," Maks said.

She turned her head to him and shrugged. "I was thinking about my mom."

"Did she want to visit here?"

"She had a list a mile long of places she wanted to go. When I was a little girl, she got a map and put colored pins in all the places she wanted to visit. She bought another color to change them out to show everywhere she had been."

Maks briefly met her gaze. "How many places did she get to see?"

"Two. And only because she finally divorced my father and was actually able to save money and travel. The two of us went together. We were just about to leave for our third trip when she died."

"I'm sorry."

Eden smiled, her heart full of love for her mother. "Thank you. She was a good woman, who always found a way to make any situation suit her. It's what I just did, thinking about how I'd never seen this part of Hungary before and now had the opportunity to do so."

"You two have a rare gift. Most people see the negative in everything."

"Do you?"

He seemed to think about that for a moment. "I think I see the reality of any situation. My training and years in the military taught me that."

"In your line of work, that's to your advantage."

"Maybe. But in the real world? I'm not sure it is."

She twisted her lips and looked through the windshield to the road before them. "I don't know. People take advantage of me all the time. It might be nice not to let that happen. Maybe I can pick up a few tricks from you," she finished with a smile, her gaze returning to him.

"The worst thing that has happened to you is me coming into your life. You're a rare treasure, Eden. I wouldn't change anything about you. I'm sorry I pulled you into this."

"I'm not," she replied honestly.

His blue eyes met hers for a heartbeat. "You won't be saying that in the end. You'll be cursing the day we met. Everyone does."

"I won't." She lifted her chin, daring him to argue the point.

Despite now running for her life, she knew that what they were doing was for the greater good of the world. How many people had the opportunity to take such a stand? It had come to her, and she had the right, no, an obligation to do her part.

She wasn't going to let Maks or anyone else down.

13

F our hours later, after crossing into Romania, Maks turned off the road onto a narrow drive. The house looked like any other in the countryside, but it was anything but. Sometime during the trip, Eden had finally fallen asleep. Her head lolled to the side, her lips parted as she breathed evenly.

He slowed the car and put it into park. Maks didn't want to wake her. Things could go south quickly, and this might be the only peace and calm they got for days or even weeks. He wouldn't change anything that had led them to this place, but that didn't mean he didn't feel bad about involving her. Eden's world had been simple and happy before. He'd upended that without a second's hesitation. He hadn't had a choice.

Before he knew what he was doing, Maks reached over and moved a lock of her dark blond hair from her face. The sun chose that moment to break through the clouds and shine on her. He stared in amazement at the array of different-colored strands in her hair. They ranged from bronze to gold and every color in between.

Until that moment, he'd never thought much about the color of someone's hair. Maybe it was just Eden. His thoughts took him to when she'd thrown herself into his arms. It had been wholly unexpected and amazingly delightful.

With his job, he didn't let anyone close to him. Ever. He had women he visited in different cities when the need arose, but he hadn't had a relationship since... Well, a long time. It had been better that way. Maks couldn't let his guard down, couldn't let anyone into his life.

What would you call Eden then?

Lovely. Pure.

Good.

He'd run across all kinds of people in the years he'd been a spy, and he could say with certainty that those like Eden were unusual. Some pretended to be sweet and giving, but it was all for show. They did what they thought others expected of them in order to get praise. That wasn't Eden. She did what she wanted.

Maks thought about the last time he'd done what he wanted to do, without caring how it affected his job or anyone else. It was so long ago that it almost felt like a dream. As if that life had never existed. He'd reconciled himself to the knowledge that he would never have a normal life. He wasn't meant to have a wife, a home, or children. How could he after the things he'd done?

He was a trained killer, an assassin that two governments thought they controlled. He'd taken so many lives, some because he had to in order to survive. Others because it was his job. Not once had he taken pleasure in it. Even when he took out a Saint. A life was a life, no matter whose it was. The moment he started enjoying killing was the time he needed to fade away and disappear into some jungle to be forgotten.

His hand slowly lowered. Maks hadn't realized he'd been touching Eden's hair the entire time. It was soft as silk. His gaze moved over her face, taking in the contours and her smooth skin. She wasn't made for this kind of life, but she was strong enough to get through it. And she would make it out. If Maks did nothing else, he would see to that.

With a sigh, he found himself thinking of her body against his. How her arms had held him tightly, how her breasts had pressed against his chest. The warmth of her body that had surrounded him. He'd become instantly, painfully hard. For her.

Even now, he throbbed with need.

The longer he sat there and thought about what it would feel like to press his lips against Eden's, to run his hands over her naked flesh, the harder it was for him to think of anything else. Finally, he gave himself a mental shake. If he didn't wake her now, he wasn't sure he ever would.

Maks touched her arm lightly. The moment he made contact, she startled awake. Her head lifted as her eyes opened, blinking as she took in the house before them. Then her head swung to the side, and hazel eyes met his. She smiled as if she were glad that he was there. It warmed the place in his chest where his heart used to be. He'd never expected to feel anything like that again, and yet...here it was.

He put it to memory because he knew it wouldn't last. And that was okay. He knew what to expect and what was coming. It was his job to shield her from it. He was more than willing. Because she was worth it.

Actually, she was more than worth it.

Eden stifled a yawn. "Where are we?"

"A small village in west Romania."

Her gaze slid back to the house. "Are we visiting someone?"

"I own the house."

"Oh." She looked at him. "I'm guessing no one knows about it."

He glanced at the older house. It was at least forty years old, but it was well maintained and had good bones. "No one should. I bought it years ago under a false name and paid cash to the old man who was selling it."

"When was the last time you were here?"

"Over eighteen months ago. I pay for the property to be maintained. They believe I'm a hermit and don't want visitors."

Her lips lifted in a grin. "You think of everything, don't you?"

"Why don't you wait here? I want to look around the house first."

He opened the door after she nodded and then stepped out. Maks looked inside the car and met Eden's gaze before he shut the door and started toward the dwelling. Damn, there was something about that woman that made him want to stay with her all the time. And that was dangerous.

Maks made a round of the house, checking windows and doors as he walked the perimeter to see if they were still locked. Then he went to the shed and opened the wooden double doors. When he returned to the front of the building, he headed to the car and got in.

"Everything good?" she asked.

"Yep. There's a shed in the back where I'll park the car to keep it hidden."

With the car in the shed, they both got out. Maks shut and locked the shed doors as Eden waited for him. Together, they walked to the back door of the home. There was a normal lock that a key fit in, but that wasn't what would open the door. He shifted it to the side to show the keypad beneath. With the seven-digit code, the lock slid open.

"Make yourself at home," he said as he opened the door for her and stood aside for Eden to enter.

She cautiously walked in, her gaze moving around the house. Maks shut the door behind them and removed the baseball cap to toss on a table near the back entrance. While the outside of the house looked old but maintained, the inside was a different story. He had completely redone the home as if he had built it from scratch.

"Wow," Eden murmured as she slowly faced him. "This place is beautiful."

He stood in the kitchen and leaned his hands on the island. "It was meant to be a safe house, which it is. However, it's also a place I come to when I want to get away. There's a vibe to this house that feels..." He paused, looking for the right word.

"Comfortable."

Maks smiled. "Yes. Comfortable. It's a quiet village, and that appeals to me when I want to get away."

"I can see why."

"There won't be much food in the fridge, but the pantry is stocked with nonperishable items. There are three bedrooms upstairs. Pick whichever one you want. I suspect we'll be here for a couple of days."

She bit her lip. "Thank you."

"For what?"

"Getting me out alive. For taking out the men on the train. For showing me what is really going on in the world."

He blinked. "I'm not sure you should be thanking me for that."

"I should. And I am." With that, she walked to the stairs and made her way up.

Maks watched her go, wondering how in the world someone like her had found their way into his existence. He should get her to the Loughmans and walk out of her life. But he wasn't sure he could.

And, if he were honest, he didn't want to.

He heard her moving around upstairs. Maks wondered what she was doing. He looked around the kitchen, trying to find something to do. But again and again, his gaze was drawn to the stairs. No longer could he hear her moving. If he couldn't get his desire under control, it was going to be a very long few days.

It could be longer.

Maks hoped it was. He'd only spent a few hours with Eden, but she had changed... everything for him. No one had ever had that effect on him before, and quite frankly, he wasn't sure what to do about it. He feared that if he was around her too much, he would never want to leave.

That wouldn't be bad at all. There are certainly worse things.

He had to stop thinking like that. If he continued down this path, then it would only cause problems that he didn't need. He had enough to deal with right now. He turned his back to the stairs and opened the pantry doors. Inside were various food items, but that wasn't what he was hungry for now. He wanted the woman upstairs.

"Enough," he whispered to himself.

"Are you all right?"

Maks couldn't remember the last time someone had snuck up on him. He drew in a breath and turned to face her. "Talking to myself."

"I do that all the time." She twisted her lips, frowning briefly. "Not sure I listen to myself. Do you?"

"Rarely."

She smiled, and damn if he didn't return it.

"You settled?" he asked.

Eden nodded while shifting her feet nervously. "We're safe here?"

"For a bit. I've got cameras all over the property and monitors in the house. We'll be notified if anyone gets close. You worried?"

She lifted one shoulder. "I've never run from the authorities before. I've never run from anything or anyone before."

"You must be starving. How about some food?"

"I'm surprised you don't want to get started on the intel."

He scratched his cheek. "I do, but I'd be a bad host if I didn't at least feed you."

Eden's laugh was a sound that reminded him of his childhood. It brought him back to a time when the world had been simple. He could only stare at her, wanting to hear more of it.

"I've lived alone for so long that I'm used to fending for myself. You don't need to worry about me. I'll let you know if I'm hungry. And, oh, by the way, I'm hungry."

He smiled as he held open his arm to the pantry. "Help yourself. I can have some fresh food delivered, too."

"Don't do it on my account," she said as she walked past him.

Maks watched as she shifted through the cans of soup. "I'd prefer not to have anyone come here that isn't supposed to, but I want to make sure there's food to eat."

She lifted a can of tomato basil soup. "Like I said, I'm good at fending for myself. When this is all over, you can take me to dinner."

"Deal."

She raised her brows and eyed him. "I'm going to hold you to that."

"I'm the one who'll be holding you to going with me. The bowls are on your left."

He also chose soup and poured it into a bowl as she heated hers in the microwave. It wasn't until his was done, and he was sitting beside her at the island that she said, "You seem very comfortable in this life."

"I'm not sure I'd say comfortable. It's more you get used to it."

She thought about that for a moment. "Yes, I can understand that. I saw it with my parents for a long time. When my mom finally left my dad, I asked her what had taken her so long. She said she'd gotten used to things."

"Was he abusive?"

"No. At least, not how you're thinking. He came from a family where the men decided everything and had control of everything. My mother was a very passive person. She didn't need to have that control, and she trusted him. That was her mistake. You see, my father was a banker, but despite that, he didn't know how to handle money. As soon as he had it, he spent it on things we didn't need instead of paying bills."

Maks was surprised that there were still men like that in this day and age, but he guessed it was partly because of the dynamic of the parents.

Eden took a bite and swallowed, rolling her eyes. "Mom had an allowance every week. She didn't have access to the actual bank account where his money was. Only he had that. Instead, he opened her an account and would transfer money each week so she could buy groceries. Everything else, including filling her car with gas, had to be done through him. I don't know how, but he was able to get a lot of credit cards, and as soon as he did, he racked up the debt. We could never answer the phone because there were always creditors calling. He filed for bankruptcy twice."

"That had to be hard on all of you."

"It was just me, Mom, and Dad. He didn't see a problem with any of it, but it caused a lot of stress for Mom. Especially when he wouldn't have enough to give her for groceries. That's when she took a stand. Not that it did any good. She didn't leave him until I was out of the house, and he'd been fired from his job. The cars were repossessed, the house was foreclosed on, and they barely had money for anything. I sent Mom funds for food. She never asked, but I wasn't going to let her starve. Dad asked me for money all the time, but I refused to give it to him since I knew he wouldn't do the right things with it."

Maks watched Eden, noting the lines of stress around her mouth as she talked about her father. He didn't know how many years had passed since she'd left home, but she still carried a lot of that around with her. That much was clear. "At least your mom left. I hope she got on her feet."

Instantly, Eden's face curved into a smile. "She did. My mom was an amazing woman. I gave her a little to get an apartment and a few things, but she paid me back. When I tried to refuse the money, she told me that I was the one who gave her the strength to start again, even in her early fifties. Those few years we had together were some of the best of my life. She really came into her own then. She could always make the best out of any situation, but I could tell she was genuinely happy."

"A good ending to the story," he said and stirred his soup before he took a spoonful into his mouth.

Eden looked into her bowl, still smiling. "She used to tell me that as much as I gripe about my father, it was how we lived and the mistakes he made that showed me what *not* to be."

"Your mom sounds like she had the right thought."

Hazel eyes met his. "I know she did. I didn't think of it that way until she said it. Even now, when I think of my dad, I still get angry at what he put us through."

Maks took two bites of soup before he looked at her. "Do you have any contact with him?"

"After he asked for money and I wouldn't give it, he told me I was no longer his daughter. He stopped calling, which was a relief. Mom and I never really discussed him. It was like we both wanted to put him out of our lives. After she died, I realized I only had one parent left, but I didn't really consider him a parent. He was selfish and egotistical and a slew of other things. It always felt as if he sucked all the good out whenever I thought about him. I knew it was better if we didn't have a relationship. Besides, he knew where I was. He could have called at any time."

"Did he?" Maks usually didn't prod into people's personal lives like he was, but he couldn't seem to help himself when it came to Eden.

She shook her head. "I received a letter six months ago from a hospital in Oklahoma. They wanted to let me know that my father had died, and as his next of kin, they wanted to know what I wanted them to do with his body."

"What did you do?"

"I found the mortuary closest to the hospital and had him sent there to be cremated. And, no, I didn't go for the funeral. I told the state to do whatever they wanted with his ashes. I suppose I should feel guilty about it, but I don't."

Maks shook his head. "You shouldn't feel guilty. Your father made his decisions and lived with the consequences. It cost him his wife, his family, his job, and everything else. He shoulders all of that. Not you."

"Thank you," Eden said with a soft smile.

They went back to eating, the silence easy between them. Maks was comfortable with her, and he was rarely comfortable around anyone. He always had his guard up, searching for any tell, any word that would alert him that someone was being untruthful.

"I'm sorry," Eden suddenly said. "I didn't mean to blurt out all my family drama."

He glanced at her as he swallowed his soup. "No need. I like hearing about your life."

She had just taken a bite and laughed, quickly covering her mouth with her hand. After she swallowed, she met his gaze, shaking her head. "You like learning about my catastrophe of a family?"

"It's what made you who you are. Why wouldn't I want to know? No one has a perfect life. Each of us has problems. Just when you solve one, another arises. That's life."

"I don't think I've ever thought of it like that. It's...eye-opening."

Warmth spread through him at her smile. He quickly returned his gaze to his soup and spooned several bites into his mouth. When it came to Eden, he suddenly became philosophical. What was it about this woman that made him say and do such things?

"What about your family? Was it as crazy as mine?"

The minute her words reached him, he froze.

"I'm sorry," Eden hastily said. "I shouldn't have asked."

His soup now finished, he set down his spoon. "It's fine."

Her face wrinkled with regret. "It's not. Forget I said anything."

He watched as she rose and went to the sink to rinse out her bowl. Maks waited until she shut off the water before he said, "I had a great family. My parents are still married and will celebrate their thirty-seventh anniversary this year. I have two sisters and two brothers. They all have kids of their own. Both of my sisters are divorced, one of my brothers is married, and the other has a woman he's been with for over twelve years. Neither of them wants to get married. It's a big family, so get-togethers are loud and chaotic, and of course, we bicker. Because that's what families do. I've not seen them in over a decade, though. They think I'm dead."

14

Eden was utterly gutted. She had been listening to Maks' description of his family with interest. Right up until he said the last part.

They think I'm dead.

Her brain couldn't comprehend the words. She stood there, unable to think of how to respond. What did someone say to something like that? Was there anything *to* say? Her gaze followed him as he rose from the stool, walked around the island, and came to the sink beside her. There was no sorrow in his eyes, only acceptance.

"You're confused," Maks stated.

She blinked and got out of his way so he could reach the faucet. "A little."

He said nothing as he began to wash both the bowls and spoons. Eden made herself busy by throwing away the cans and cleaning up the area where they had eaten. She needed to remember that Maks had lived a much different life than she had. How could she possibly understand any of what he'd done?

I don't care. I want to know.

She did want to know. He might be a badass and able to take on the world, but she caught a glimpse of misery. She didn't think he even realized it. Maks was good at hiding his emotions, but talking about his family had opened up something inside him and allowed her a brief peek.

"I had a choice to make."

His voice behind her halted her. She slowly turned to face him. He stood at the sink, his hands on the edges as his chin hung to his chest, his eyes closed. She wanted to tell him to stop, that he didn't need to go down whatever road he was on to tell her this. Obviously, he had shut it away for good reason. She had no right to open old wounds.

"Don't."

At the same time, he said, "I was in Delta Force for four years. My family was used to me being away. They didn't like it, but they understood my need to serve my country the best way I could." He lifted his head and looked at her. "It just started out as me wanting to do my part with the Army. It didn't take long for me to realize that military life suited me. I moved up through the ranks quickly and got some notice from the higher-ups. I turned my sights on the Rangers. I did well enough that I was chosen to join Delta Force. It was an opportunity I wasn't going to pass up. Do you know what Delta Force is?"

She shook her head, unable to find words.

"They, like the SEALs and the 24th Special Tactics Squadron of the Air Force, are the US military's primary Tier 1 special operations units tasked with performing the most classified, dangerous, and complex missions."

"Oh." Her voice came out as a squeak.

Maks shifted so one hip rested against the counter. "During my time there, I met someone. She had no idea about military life or what it was like to be with one of us. Yet, we managed. Being a Tier 1 operator means that you leave on a moment's notice sometimes, and there's no telling how long you'll be gone. It's why so many marriages break up. I was determined to make it work somehow."

Eden's heart hurt for him. She didn't need to ask if he'd gotten his wish. If he had, he wouldn't be here with her now.

His gaze slid to the side for a heartbeat before he drew in a quick breath and looked at her. "I was on a mission with my team, which included Wyatt Loughman, when we were sent into Columbia. The mission went to shit quickly. We had a leak somewhere because our enemies knew exactly where we were and split us up. We'd trained for such things, so we didn't let it rattle us. We kept going, pursuing the target to bring him in. The government wanted him alive, which meant that we had to be careful about who we were shooting at."

She swallowed hard. The sound loud even to her ears.

"Wyatt was shouting orders through the COMs when they suddenly went out. My teammates and I were cornered and pinned down. We had nowhere to go, and no way to let the others know where we were, much less get to them if they needed help. I had the best line of sight out of the four of us, so I covered them as the other three took off to find another spot to take out the enemy. It would've worked, too. That mission..." he said with a shake of his head. "You don't forget ones like that."

Unable to help herself, Eden asked, "What happened?"

"What I'm about to tell you is classified. Two of my teammates were killed. I was trying to get to the third one who had been shot when a woman walked out and stood over him with the barrel of a rifle pointed at his heart. At first, I couldn't believe what I was seeing. Because I thought she was back home in the States, waiting on me. The leak we had was none other than my girlfriend, Stacy."

Eden's mouth went slack at the news.

"The woman I'd fallen in love with had been recruited by the Saints. After Stacy killed my teammate, she walked to me and told me that it was my destiny to join the Saints, who were making the world a better place. I had no idea who she was talking about. I kept asking her why she'd betrayed me, and she said that she'd done it to protect me. I knew I had no way of getting to Wyatt and the others, so I stayed where I was. Besides, she was leading the men who had pinned us down. So, I did the only thing I could."

"You got information from her," Eden guessed.

Maks raked a hand through his blond hair. "She told me it was a general in the Army who had approached her. Others within the military had made contact with her, giving her information and showing her how they could protect me if she would help them convince me to join them."

"Dear God."

"The entire time, she was kissing me as if she hadn't just murdered my team, as if none of what she'd done would change us. I'm not sure how long we sat there as she kept saying it would be the best thing for me. I wasn't sure I had a choice then. I understood that if I didn't agree, I'd be killed. I wasn't afraid to die, but the more I listened to her talk about the Saints and their network, the more I realized that this was a huge operation that had been going on right under my nose. Then, the COMs began working, and I heard Wyatt. He was close to me. I didn't hesitate to tell him where I was and that I was surrounded by enemies. The look on her face was one of confusion and anger. Then, she lifted the rifle. I took the shot before she could. Then I turned and went to find the rest of my team."

Eden walked to him and put a hand on his arm while gazing into his blue eyes. "I'm so sorry. No one should have to be betrayed, but especially not by someone they're in love with."

Maks shifted his arm so that his hand came in contact with hers. "I've never told anyone that story. Not even my team. They assumed that the enemies had gotten her and brought her there to use against us. Me. I let them think she died as a casualty of war."

"Because you didn't want to tell them that you shot her?"

"Because I didn't know who might be part of the Saints. I wanted to believe that they could be trusted, but I was no longer sure of anything anymore. I kept what happened to myself. Even when command interviewed me multiple times when we got home, I never told a single person. The team was put on leave because of what happened, and we needed to fill slots. I was given more time than the others since..." He paused and then shrugged.

Eden liked that their fingers were linked. She didn't know why, but having their palms together eased some of the turmoil within her. "Understandable."

"I attended the funeral with her family and grieved as was expected of me because I knew I was being watched. And I was right. Just a day after the funeral, I was approached by the CIA. The woman was tall, stunning, and most definitely a killer. She shot me a smile, gave me a manila envelope, and told me that she'd get back in touch in a couple of days."

Eden frowned, taken aback. "What? They didn't talk to you? They just gave you a packet?"

"Yep."

"What was inside?"

He glanced down at their linked hands. "An offer for employment. They listed out my credits, things they shouldn't have been aware of but were. The job was similar to what I'd been doing with Delta Force, but I'd be working alone, or I could have a team that I would pick."

"You chose to be alone."

"Damn straight. I didn't trust anyone."

"Then why join the CIA at all?"

He briefly raised his brows. "Because I needed to get information on the Saints. Like I said on the train, I knew if the CIA had my stats from the military, then whoever had chosen me was most likely working for the Saints. They had made several references to my being of Russian descent and speaking the language fluently. There was one stipulation in the offer. I couldn't tell anyone. I said that I refused to lie to my family. Besides, I didn't want the Saints to use anyone I cared about against me again. I was the one who suggested that I be sent on a mission and reported killed in action."

"I would've done the same. But to give up your family to take down the Saints? How were you even sure you could?"

Maks shrugged. "I didn't know, only that I would figure it out along the way. I'm doing this *for* my family because I love them. I couldn't return to my life and forget what had happened or what I'd learned. I had to do something."

She couldn't blame him for that. Not when she felt the same way. "That's why I'm here. Because I have to do something, too."

"Yes," he said as he looked deep into her eyes. "I think I knew that from the first. It's why I chose you."

Eden tightened her fingers around his and smiled. "I'm ready to kick some ass. Let's take down the Saints."

His grin was slow, but it pulled at his lips until it filled his face. "Come with me."

Eden followed him after he released her hand. He took her into a room at the front of the house. A desk and a chair sat in the center of the room. Behind it was a table with a printer, and on either side of the table were bookshelves filled with various titles. The right-hand side held a comfy leather chair and a floor lamp. On the other side of the room sat a small leather sofa with end tables on either side of it.

No matter where she went in the house, Eden liked what she saw. There was no clutter, something she detested. If anything, she would call it a minimalistic style. And she liked it a lot. Maks had the comforts, but there wasn't a lot of extra stuff around.

She watched as Maks went to the right-hand bookcase and moved some books out of the way. To her surprise, there was a small safe hidden there. He punched in the code, then used his fingerprint to open it. He withdrew a laptop, two pen drives, and several file folders that he put on the table.

"Is that all you have?" she asked as she came over to investigate.

Maks chuckled. "It doesn't look like much, but, trust me, it is."

"Oh, I'm sure it is."

He held up the two drives. "The majority of the items is on these. I made copies of everything I could to digitize it, but I didn't always have that opportunity."

"These aren't the originals, I hope. Please tell me you kept them somewhere else so if the Saints came and destroyed it, you wouldn't have to start again." When he didn't answer, Eden looked at him to find him watching her curiously. "What?"

He shrugged. "I find it odd that I was ready to give you that answer when, with anyone else, I wouldn't have answered it one way or another."

"Because you wouldn't be sure if you could trust me." She nodded, shrugging. "I can understand. So, don't answer me. I'm just thinking, as you told me I should."

"These aren't the only copies. I tell you that

because I trust you. I'll also tell you that there are two other sets. One is in Texas with the Loughmans."

She didn't mention the fact that he hadn't told her where the second set was. In reality, she didn't need to know. "Thank you."

"Where do you want to start?"

Eden looked at everything and then said, "At the beginning. Is there an order?"

"In a way. Make yourself comfortable. Desk, sofa, chair. It doesn't matter."

She turned and pulled out the chair from the desk then sat facing the table. "How about here."

Maks chuckled as he opened a file and put it in front of her. "This is the offer the CIA gave me."

15

Maks was awed by how Eden filtered through the information. She certainly knew how to delve into something and find the hidden gems. There were piles of papers on the table around her. He didn't know what each was, and it didn't matter at the moment. She had begun by describing everything to him and what she was doing, but it was slowing down her process. So he told her to work now and explain later.

He took the empty glass of water to refill it. When he returned, he had it, along with some tea in case she might want that.

"Oh, you're a mind reader," she said and flashed him a smile before putting some honey into the hot liquid and stirring.

Maks noted that she was coming close to finishing with the pile of papers. Every once in a while, she'd turn to the laptop and type something into a document she'd begun. It looked like some kind of shorthand, which he deduced were notes for herself.

Eden took a sip of the tea and sat back after she

finished reading the paper. "Well. That was quite a bit."

"Anything good?"

She raised her brows at him, then barked in laughter. "I think it's safe to say that the majority of it is good."

"Really?" He hadn't expected that at all. "I was hoping there might be one or two things in all of it."

Eden shook her head and held the mug between both hands. "Did you look at any of this?"

"Some of it. Others I just copied and got here. Why?"

"Because you've got some very important pieces of information with names, locations, and dates on them."

Maks thought about that for a moment. "All right. Information like that is always good if you can connect the dots."

"You most certainly can connect them. I may not have figured it out as quickly as I did if I didn't know about August 12, 2017."

"What date is that?"

"The day that a prominent history professor at Cambridge University was found dead in his home. The authorities ruled it a suicide almost immediately, but someone in the department leaked evidence that proved it was a homicide."

Maks couldn't believe it. "Are you sure?"

In answer, Eden switched to the internet and entered the information into a search engine. Just before she hit ENTER, she looked at him and asked, "I gather this is encrypted?"

"It's why it's stored in the safe."

She pressed the button and various news

articles filled the screen. Maks moved to get a better angle and read the many headlines. One after the other taking off with the story that the Cambridge professor's murder was a coverup of some kind, and everyone trying to figure out how deep in the British government it went.

"While this is great, how do we know it has anything to do with the Saints?" he asked.

Eden's lips turned down in a frown. "Unfortunately, two weeks later, four cops were killed. I did a little digging and discovered their names were linked to the original investigation of the professor."

"You think they leaked the information?"

"I think there's a really good chance of it. The fact they were killed in some random act of violence makes it pretty sketchy to me. Especially when one of them was off-duty at the time but had been called to the scene."

Maks had to admit it did look as if someone was trying to get rid of those who went against policy.

"That's not all, either. Two days later, one of the detective chief inspectors resigned, and two others above her were moved to other departments," Eden told him.

He turned his head to her. "Did you look into this for some client?"

"No. I did it because something sounded off to me. It died pretty quickly, though, which also didn't sit well with me. It wasn't long before some other big story came through."

"Maybe by design," he said.

She snorted. "Maybe. I didn't think about that."

Maks straightened and crossed his arms over his chest. "I think it's time to check those other dates."

"That's what I'm about to do. It might take some time. If it is something similar, I'll get all the information I can, including anything that could be connected."

"In other words, I shouldn't hover?" he asked with a grin.

She laughed as she tilted her head to look at him. "Hover all you want. I'll be happy to tell you what I'm doing as I'm doing it."

"There's no need. I'll leave you to it. There are woods behind the house. I'll go hunting and get us some meat for dinner. You do eat meat, right?"

Her chuckle caused her eyes to twinkle with merriment. "Most definitely. And while I'm not usually one to want to hunt for my food, I'm also aware of the situation. What I'm trying to tell you is that I'm not picky. You bring back food, and I'll eat it."

"I'll lock the door on my way out. No one can see through the windows, and no one can get into the house. You'll be safe."

She stared at him for a moment. "I'll be fine."

He started to turn away then reached under the table near her and pulled out the gun he'd hidden there. He laid it near her. "Do you know how to shoot?"

"Some. It's been a few years since I fired a weapon."

"It's already loaded." He lifted it and pulled back the slide. "Just point and shoot. It has a kick, so hold it securely. Aim for center mass. Don't try to scare anyone away. If someone tries to get in and it's not me, assume they're a Saint."

Eden nodded solemnly. "I got it."

"I'll be back as soon as I can."

"I'll be fine. You've made sure of that."

He hesitated, wondering if he should wait. But they needed fresh food, and he didn't want to go into town. Finally, he turned on his heel and walked to the back of the house. The closet looked like any other until he pushed on a board, and the wall shifted, opening another door to a room. Overhead lights flickered on to show the many and various guns, rifles, knives, grenades and ammunition at his disposal. It had taken him years to accumulate the weapons, and this wasn't his only stash. He had three other houses just like this one in various parts of the world that he could get to if he were in trouble.

Maks chose the 30/30 hunting rifle and loaded the weapon. He then walked out, closing the hidden door behind him. After a glance to the front of the house where Eden was typing on the keyboard, he walked to the back door and let himself out. He locked it and turned to face the woods.

Part of him didn't want to leave Eden, but another part of him knew that she was safe in the house. It's why he had set it up. He'd bought—and installed himself—each window with bulletproof glass. The walls were also lined with fiberglass to help stop projectiles. He'd done everything he could to make the house as impenetrable as possible.

He stepped off the porch and headed into the woods.

Maks had learned to hunt at an early age. His father had wanted all of his children to know how to fend for themselves if there was ever a need for it. As soon as the woods swallowed him, Maks was transported back in time to memories of hunting with his father. Sometimes, his father would take him out on his own. Other times, it was with the others. The one thing Maks could never say was that his parents didn't spend quality time with all five of their children.

Talking about his family with Eden had made him homesick in a way he hadn't been in years. He longed to hear his mother's laugh and smell her cooking. He wished he could sit with his father as they grilled something and shared a beer. How he missed the times he and his siblings would play card games late into the night.

He'd given all of that up to make the world a better place. But had he actually succeeded? He hadn't. He wasn't even sure he stood a remote chance of taking out the Saints. But he had to try. For his family. For Eden. For everyone else in the world.

Maks didn't stray too far from his house. It might be on a moderately trafficked road, but its location set against the forest was prime real estate for him. Being in the woods and with nature helped to center him, to ground him. His father said that in order to be a human, one had to know, respect, and love nature and the Earth.

It was something that had resonated with Maks. To this day, he made an effort to get out into nature the moment he felt like he needed to be centered again. Even just walking in a park and listening to the birds could do it. Sitting next to a stream, standing on a beach as the waves crashed on the shore. There was never a place where he didn't take the opportunity to soak in nature.

Unfortunately, now wasn't the time he could do that. Eden might have told him that she was fine, but he didn't like leaving her alone. He knew for a fact how difficult it would be to get into that house, and if anyone came, he'd hear them before they ever got through. That didn't seem to ease his mind, however.

For two hours, Maks searched for any sign of animals. He spotted boar tracks. Found week-old deer tracks, and just when he thought he might not be able to find one, he came across a Roe deer. Maks raised his rifle, sighted down the barrel. As he breathed out, he pulled the trigger. The deer collapsed where it stood.

He hurried to it and kneeled beside the beast, putting his hand on the animal's head. "Thank you."

In quick order, Maks slung the small, reddish deer over his shoulders. He grasped his rifle and straightened before he turned and made his way back to the house. As he approached, he slowed, his gaze moving about, searching for anything that seemed out of the ordinary. None of the sensors had gone off to alert him on his phone, but he didn't rely on only technology. It was nice to have, but he'd been burned too many times not to trust his own eyes and senses.

Only when he deemed that no one had come

near the house did he leave the forest. At the back porch, he lowered the deer to the ground and went to the door. He punched in the code and wiped his feet on the mat before entering the house.

The first thing he heard was music coming from the office. He smiled as the strings of Godsmack's *When Legends Rise* song reached him. He never would've thought Eden was a hard rock girl. He made his way to the front of the house and peeked inside the office to see her head moving to the beat of the music as she gazed at the computer screen.

Not wanting to scare her, he tapped on the door. Her head snapped around to him. Maks lifted his hands. "Just wanted to let you know I'm back."

"I see you got something. Or did you shoot yourself?"

He frowned, blinking. "What?"

Eden pointed to his shirt. "There's blood."

"Oh." He glanced at the stain. "I'll be right outside, cleaning the deer."

She flashed him a bright smile. "Okay."

Without waiting, she turned back to the computer and began typing something. Maks backed away and went to the kitchen, where he had freezer bags. He grabbed the box and returned to the carcass. With sure strokes, he gutted the dear before removing the coat. After that, he began cutting the meat into pieces before putting them into the bags.

Once that was finished, he took the bags inside, putting all but two in the freezer. Then he gathered the remnants of the deer and tossed them into the forest to be eaten by scavengers. There was no need to waste anything.

Maks then washed off the blood that had gotten onto the back porch. He made sure that everything was just as it had been before he arrived. Then he went inside and removed his clothes in the laundry room. There might not be any hope of getting all the blood out, but they needed to be washed anyway. He started the washing machine and walked from the room to go upstairs. With one foot on the bottom step, he paused at the music.

He hadn't thought about Eden seeing him naked when he removed his clothes. But now that he had, he wished she had been out here. Though, he wasn't sure what he would've done if she were. This wasn't the time for anything romantic. Even if he did desire her.

"Stop it," he ordered himself and proceeded up the stairs to take a shower.

16

"Holy shit," Eden said as she slowly lowered herself into the chair.

She had gone out to get some more water when she caught a glimpse of Maks in the laundry room. Naked. She hadn't known a man's back could have that many muscles in it. His broad shoulders tapered to narrow hips, and he had a fine ass. His legs were long and lean. Whether he got that body from the gym or his lifestyle, she didn't know.

What she wanted was to see the front of him. If his back looked that good, then his front had to be amazing.

Eden shook her head, trying to dislodge the image of Maks' nude body from her brain. But it wasn't going anywhere. She was beginning to think that there wasn't anything he couldn't do. Not only was he handsome as sin, a superb fighter, massively intelligent, and honorable. He was also a guardian.

Her mother used to tell her that there were special people out in the world who were guardians. It was their job to look out for others, to protect them and save them in times of danger. Without a doubt, Maks was a guardian.

At the sound of water above her, Eden's gaze looked to the ceiling. She wished now that she had stayed in the kitchen when Maks had turned around from the laundry. Not only would she have gotten to see the front of him, but she might be in that shower with him.

Her eyes returned to the computer. "Now isn't the time for such things. Not when so much is at stake."

It didn't take long for her to get back into the work. Every lead she chased down netted information. To the untrained eye, it was easy to overlook stuff or dismiss things as inconsequential, but she was searching for anything and everything. And there was a lot out there. Eden was floored at how far the Saints had gone to rid themselves of what they considered people who might stand in their way.

The smell of something delicious pulled her from the work. She blinked, not realizing the sun had begun to set, and the room was now bathed in light from the desk lamp and lights overhead. She stretched her neck and paused her music before she rose and did more stretches for her back, shoulders, and legs.

She'd learned that she could become absorbed in her work to the point where it became detrimental to her health. She'd forget to move her body or drink enough fluids. Like she'd done today. That couldn't happen again. She had to be cognizant of those things and take the time to care for herself. And she knew that wanting to do it didn't always mean she'd remember. So, she was going to have to set timers.

When she walked out of the office, it was to see Maks in the kitchen, cooking. She stopped and stared as he moved from the stove to the island to chop mushrooms. He glanced up and met her eyes.

"That smells delicious," she said as she walked to the island and took one of the stools.

He scooped up the mushrooms but stopped short of putting them in the pan. "Do you eat mushrooms?"

"I do."

After dumping the fungi in the pot and stirring, he glanced her way. "I didn't disturb you, did I?"

"Not at all, but I think you should have." She turned her neck, feeling her muscles tightening. "I have a habit of not taking breaks when I'm working. I suffer after."

One side of his mouth lifted in a grin. "Then I'll be sure to interrupt every couple of hours next time."

"Please do. Can I help?"

"Nope," he said as he tossed in some salt and pepper. "You're doing all the hard work."

At that, she laughed. "I wouldn't say that."

"I couldn't find what you have."

"You haven't even looked at it, so you don't know. Besides, I'm pretty sure you could have, but your other skills are more important. I can handle this part."

He glanced at her again and covered the pot before he came to stand at the island across from her. "I gather you're finding a lot?"

"More than I'd like." She shrugged, her lips

twisting. "I know what to look for. It isn't too hard when you're trained to look for the words or phrases others use when they want to throw someone off a trail or hide something. I've got a lot to show you, and I've even started on the pen drives."

Maks released a slow breath. "That's good. I know there's valuable information on the drives. I took those from a computer of some high-ranking Russian in the FSB that I know is part of the Saints."

"How did you not get caught?"

He shrugged. "I'm trained for such things."

"Yeah, but I'd be so terrified that someone would see me that I couldn't do it."

"Sometimes, I am caught. You have to be able to think quickly and come up with a couple of excuses in case someone walks in."

Eden hadn't considered that before. "Good advice. Not that I foresee myself in such a situation, but if I ever am, now I'll be prepared."

He turned back to the stove and lifted the lid. Steam billowed out. Her gaze roamed over his back. The dark green tee covered his muscles but not the width of his shoulders or the thickness of his arms. The dark denim hung low on his hips. When he stepped to the side, she just now noticed that he wasn't wearing shoes or socks. There was something very homey about him being barefoot.

"What are we having?" she asked.

He covered the dish again and turned to her only to pick up the knife and began to chop some long herbs. "I'm panfrying some deer steaks. I found some wild rosemary, onions, and mushrooms."

"Sounds simple and delicious. Do you like to cook?"

Maks finished chopping. "I don't hate it. My mom made sure we all knew how. We were always in the kitchen with her, learning something or other. Dad also taught us how to grill various meats. When we got old enough, Mom made us take turns picking out a meal and cooking it each week."

"Now that's an idea."

"Yeah," he said with a shrug. "It's just fine until you attempt to eat something my oldest sister cooks. She can't even boil water."

Eden threw back her head and laughed. "You're just making that up."

"I'm not," Maks said with a smile. "It's the truth. It became so bad that Mom stopped asking her to make anything. We used to think she did it on purpose, but that's not what it was. She really was trying, but she just can't do it. On the days she was scheduled to cook, one of us kids would rotate that week and pick up the slack."

"That means your mom only had to make two meals a week."

Maks snorted and turned to check the meat. "One. Dad cooked the other. He was a good cook himself, and while he could prepare any meal, he preferred using the grill."

She watched him for a minute and waited until he faced her once more. "Do you think you'll ever see them again?"

"No."

There was no hesitation in his words. No hope.

Nothing. She didn't understand that at all, because sometimes, hope was the only thing that kept her going at all.

"Why not? If we win this thing with the Saints, you can go home."

Maks walked to the wine stacked on the counter and pulled out a bottle. Without looking at her as he began to open it, he said, "Because I won't be alive. I know that facing the Saints with all of this will mean my life. I accepted that a long time ago."

"You don't have to die." And she was appalled that he would think he had to.

Bright blue eyes met hers. "You live in a world I see every day, but it's one I'm not a part of. People like me have no place in such a world. We're the darkness in your eyes, the demons that should never see the light of day."

"You're not the darkness or a demon. You saved me."

He pulled out the cork and let the wine breathe as he got out two glasses. "I brought you into this fight without so much as a second thought. I knew if you weren't a Saint what it could do to you, and I didn't care."

"Because you're thinking about the bigger picture. I'm one person. I'm inconsequential."

"On the contrary, you are very important. I'm not a savior, Eden. I'm an assassin, a man who has done so many dirty things that I wouldn't be able to wash my hands of it in twenty lifetimes."

She got off the stool and walked to him, keeping her gaze locked with his. When she stood in front of him, she said, "I disagree. You're the one who saw the bigger picture from the beginning. You walked away from your friends and family, from a life, in order to take down the Saints. You've sacrificed your existence and any kind of normalcy you might have had to ensure that happened. You're not a demon, Maks. You're a goddamn hero."

"The worst thing you can do is make me into something I'm not."

"I know exactly what you are. You've shown it to me since you came into my life just this morning." My God. Had it just been that morning? It had been a long day, but so much had happened in that short time that it had altered her world forever.

He went to the stove and took the pan away before shutting off the burner. "I have to be rational about all of this. I have to deal in reality, not hopes and wishes."

"There's nothing wrong with hoping for a good outcome and wishing to see your family."

"It takes my focus off what I'm doing." He looked at her. "I warned you I'm not a typical guy."

She took out two plates and set them on the counter. "It's a good thing you aren't, or I'd most likely be dead now. But I understand what you're telling me. I just want you to know there's nothing wrong with looking ahead and hoping for the best. There have been instances where that's the only thing that kept me going."

Maks brought the pan to the plates and dished out the steaks and mushrooms. He set aside the pan and took her hand in his. "Thank you. For trusting me, for reminding me of what it is to be normal, and...for being you."

"There's nothing special about me."

"I disagree."

She glanced down at the floor and smiled before looking at him. "You're welcome."

"Come. Let's eat."

The conversation during the meal was an easy one. They stayed away from topics of family and the Saints, and instead just talked. Eden found herself telling him about how she got into being an information broker. It was a boring story, but he genuinely appeared interested. No matter how many times she tried to turn the conversation to him, he had a knack for bringing it back to her.

By the time she finished the steak, which had to be one of the best meals in her life, and was sipping the last of her wine, she realized that she didn't want the night to end. Despite the severity of the situation and how she'd come to be there, it had been a day she'd never forget.

"What is it?" Maks asked.

She shook her head and took a drink of wine. "I'm just marveling at how glad I am that I'm here. With you."

"I'm glad you're here, too."

For the first time, an awkward silence fell between them. Eden finished off her wine because she didn't know what to say next. Then she stood and reached for the plates, but Maks was quicker.

"I got them."

She frowned and took the wine glasses as she followed him to the sink. "You hunted our food, cleaned it, and cooked it. I think I'm due to wash the dishes."

"Afraid I can't let you do that. You had an early morning, had unusual stressors today, and worked the entire afternoon. There's a big tub upstairs. You can go soak for a bit and relax. I'll even open another bottle of wine if you want."

A bath did sound great. Her neck and back were killing her. "Fine. I'll relent this time, but next time, I'm doing the dishes."

He chuckled, the corners of his eyes crinkling. "If I don't beat you to the sink first."

"Not gonna happen," she said confidently before she started toward the stairs. "I won't be long. I am going to loosen the knots in my muscles, then I'll be back down to show you what I found."

"It can wait."

She halted and looked at him. "I don't think it can. And neither do you."

"You're right." Maks let out a sigh. "Take your time with your bath. You've earned it."

They shared a smile before Eden ascended the stairs. At the top, she looked into the guest bath but only saw a walk-in shower. The tub must be in the master. She hesitated, then decided not to go in there.

"It's in my bathroom," Maks shouted from below. "And you better use it."

She laughed as she gathered her pack and brought it through the master bedroom to the bath. When they first arrived, she had taken a look at all three bedrooms upstairs. Each was done in a neutral tone. One was beige, and the one she'd chosen was white. The master was done in shades of pale blue to deep navy. Utterly masculine. Yet she really liked it.

It felt odd to be in his room. She hurriedly made her way to the bathroom and sighed as she took in the detail there. The freestanding white tub sat on white and gray marble tile that was also used in the large shower. There was a long, white vanity with two rectangular sinks and ultra-modern faucets that matched the tub and shower fixtures. Even the toilet was modern-looking. Nothing like the regular toilets she was used to seeing.

Eden set her pack down and turned on the water for the tub. Hot water came almost instantly. After she set the temperature she wanted, she straightened and closed the door to the bathroom. Then she pulled out fresh clothes and got out of hers. In so many ways, it felt as if she had left her flat a week ago, not just that morning. Being on the run tended to shift time. Or rather, it amped up the stress level so that time felt warped and extended.

The moment she dipped her toe into the tub, she sighed. She didn't waste any time lowering herself into the hot water. When it covered her body, she turned off the water and simply sat there. She was just thinking about getting up and finding her phone to turn on some soothing music when the first strings of a song reached her.

Eden's eyes snapped open at the sound of the cello. She had a particular love for the instrument. She didn't know how or why, but the sounds of it touched her in a way that nothing else did. She loved music period, but a cello could take her to another level. And what she was hearing now wasn't from some station on a radio or phone. It was the instrument itself below her. That could only mean that Maks was playing it.

A smile pulled at her lips. This was a side of him she hadn't expected. In all her imaginings, she never would've guessed that as a spy, he would also play the cello. And he was *good*. Very good, in fact. She'd been to a lot of symphonies over the years, and she was able to recognize when someone was good enough to make their living at a craft. And Maks certainly would've been able to.

It made her think about how different his life would've been had he followed that path instead of entering the military. She wouldn't be here now, and she never would've met him. That made her frown because while she didn't want to be on the run, fearing for her life, Maks had made a difference. He'd forced her to look at the world differently, to look at herself differently. She liked that. She'd *needed* that, even if she'd believed she was content with the way things were.

How odd that a single person could change her life so drastically. But Maks was different and special like that. It might be how he'd lived for the past years as a double agent, or it might just be who he was. It didn't matter. She was thankful that he had opened her eyes.

Eden let her mind drift as the music continued. The song wasn't one she recognized, but it was soothing and lulled her into relaxation. She felt the tension ease out of her muscles. Her eyes closed, and she focused on her breathing as she did during meditation. When she finally lifted her lids, it was to find that the water had cooled, and her skin was pruney.

She let out the water and stood. After stepping out of the tub, she got into the shower and washed herself thoroughly. In short order, she was drying off and cleaning up her mess in the bathroom. Eden put on some sweats and a loose shirt and fluffy socks. Then she combed out her hair and left it wet before packing up her things and returning them to her bedroom. All the while, Maks still played.

Her steps were light and soft when she made her way downstairs. She didn't want him to stop. When she reached the bottom, the music led her to the office, where he sat off to the side, playing with his eyes closed. He was relaxed, his head tilted to the side as he listened. The music had utterly taken him. Each note seemed to fall from his fingers effortlessly. She rested her shoulder against the doorjamb and watched him.

When he drew the bow along the strings of the instrument, drawing out the last note, she found her gaze locked on his handsome face. When the note faded, he drew in a deep breath and opened his eyes. Slowly, his gaze slid to her. For several moments, they stared silently at each other.

"That was the most beautiful thing I've ever heard," she said.

"I don't get to play as much as I would like." He stood and lifted the cello, taking it back to its case.

"You don't have to stop on my account."

There was a soft smile on his face as he said, "I didn't."

"You're very good. You could've made a good living at playing."

He shrugged as he closed the case and gathered it as he straightened. His gaze didn't shift her way as he set it in the back corner. "My mother would've loved that. She had all of us pick an instrument to play. She believed that music was something everyone needed. My father also loved music, so there was no getting out of it for us." He then turned to her. "We all put up a fuss, but secretly, we loved it."

"That's a great story." She fidgeted when he merely stared at her. Finally, she cleared her throat. "Are you ready to get started?"

"Whenever you are."

D id she have any idea how beautiful she was? How tempting? Maks really didn't think so, and that was a good thing. Because if Eden wanted to seduce him, she could've had him on his knees in seconds.

He'd known she was standing there, listening to him play. It had been years since anyone had heard him. He'd thought he would be finished before she came down from her bath, but once he'd begun playing, he hadn't been able to stop. The look on her face proved that she had enjoyed it immensely.

Maks hadn't known what to say because there hadn't been any words. All he'd wanted to do was go to her and pull her into his arms. Her wet hair hung around her face that was still flushed from the heat of the water. She wore comfortable clothes and seemed at ease. Either she didn't know the full threat of the Saints, or she was at ease with him.

Eden wasn't a fool. She was learning for herself just who the Saints were. That meant she felt secure with him. And that only made his hunger for her flare higher.

He watched her as she walked to the back table and opened the laptop. He followed her but was careful not to get too close. At one touch, he might lose all control. No one had ever made him feel like this. What was it that undid him?

Her beauty? Maybe.

Her intelligence? Possibly.

Her complete trust in him? Probably.

The way she looked at him as if she found him fascinating? Hell, yes.

Fuck. He was in trouble. Trouble in a bad, bad way. There was no way he could give in to what he was feeling, for a number of reasons. The first was that if the Saints ever found out, they would do everything in their considerable power to take Eden and torture her, prolonging her pain. Second, he wouldn't be able to do what needed to be done if he allowed himself to feel the emotions rising up inside him.

All these years, he'd been able to keep his distance from people, rarely forming any kind of attachments. And those romantic attachments he *did* have might look serious from the outside looking in, but they meant nothing to him. It was all for show for anyone who might be watching him.

But he was alone now. Alone in a cabin with Eden. No one was here but the two of them. No one was watching. No one would know what he did.

I would.

Maks knew that if he gave in, for even a heartbeat, there would be no pulling himself out of the depths of whatever it was he had begun to feel each time he was near Eden. He wouldn't even go into the emotions that consumed him when he merely *thought* about her. And damn if that wasn't most of the day.

He watched as she pulled up different tabs on the laptop. He'd told himself that he thought about her because she was his problem now. He'd drug her into this shitstorm, and he'd promised to keep her safe. But he knew that for the bald-faced lie that was.

He wanted her.

No. *Wanted* didn't describe the wanton depths of his desire.

He craved her. Yearned. He *hungered*.

Her head swiveled around to him as her hazel eyes blinked up at him. Her lips were moving. Maks registered that bit too late. He attempted to hear what she was saying, but he couldn't. He was too wrapped up in imagining what it would be like to have her against him. To strip her bare and lay her on his bed as his hands and mouth learned every inch of her body. To hear her moan with need.

And scream in pleasure.

"Maks?"

His lungs seized. He tried to draw in a breath, but nothing worked but his cock, that was now as hard as granite. Finally, he was able to swallow. Eventually, he made his body relax so his lungs could expand and take in air. But nothing stopped the fine sheen of sweat that covered him. All he could pray for now was that she didn't lower her gaze and see the bulge in his pants.

"Yes?"

Her brows drew together in a frown. "Are you all right?"

"Never better." *Fucking liar.*

But it wasn't as if he could tell her the truth.

The doubt in her eyes told him she didn't believe a word he said. "As I mentioned, all the dates from before coincided with a death."

"All of them?"

"Every last one," she said and turned back to the monitor. She clicked a button, and a page filled with all the dates. Beside them were names.

Maks ran through the list, but none of them looked or sounded familiar. "I don't know any of these people."

"You wouldn't. They're relative unknowns."

"So why kill them?"

Eden clicked another tab. "This."

Maks put one hand on the back of her chair and the other on the table as he leaned down. Without meaning to, he drew in the scent of her hair. It was his shampoo. Nothing special there. But somehow, mixed with her natural fragrance, it was an aphrodisiac that made his balls tighten, and blood roar in his ears.

He had to get himself under control. He wasn't some randy teenager who got hard every time the wind blew. He was a grown man who made sure his needs were satisfied regularly. He shouldn't have such a reaction to her.

Shouldn't. But he certainly was.

"Well?" she asked as she glanced at him. "I thought you'd react more."

Her face was scant millimeters from his. All he had to do was lean slightly to the side and he could press his face to hers. For fuck's sake. *Enough already.*

Inwardly giving himself a hard shake, he focused on the screen and saw that each of them was somehow linked to a government or military. Now that was of interest. "Any way to tell what these people were working on when they were killed?"

"If I was a hacker, I probably could. I assume that what most of these people were doing would be considered classified. Even some of the low-level people still had access to classified documents."

"Do you think there's a chance they saw something about the Saints?"

She shrugged her slim shoulders. "I'd be guessing right now. I did some searches randomly through the group, and all of them were model citizens. I think the worst I found was a DUI."

As he continued looking at each individual and their job description and employer, the more he realized that the only one who could get him what he needed was Callie. The problem was that each time she got into a system, she opened herself—and everyone at the ranch—to another attack.

"You're thinking of sending this to the hacker you know. Callie?" Eden asked.

Maks nodded as he straightened. "She can get the information."

"But you're worried about them."

He blew out a breath and crossed his arms over his chest. "I am. I'm still not sure how we won against the Saints last time, but I know the organization well enough to know that they're not going to take that lying down. They'll retaliate. And it's going to be big."

Eden tucked a leg beneath her in the chair and shifted to look at him. "Wouldn't they have already done that?"

"They're waiting for the Loughmans to let their guard down." He lifted one shoulder in a shrug. "The Saints came close to killing each of the brothers individually. If they weren't as good as they are, or have strong women with them, they'd probably be dead. Look at the list before you. I've been sent after enough people to know that if anyone angers the Saints, they're removed. And quickly."

"But who makes the decision? Is it run by just one person?"

Maks dropped his arms to his sides. "From what little I've been able to discern, it's a small group of people. Think of them like elders of a village. They're the ones who make the decisions."

"I don't suppose these Elders happen to all live in the same place?"

"If only. Actually, I don't know who any of them are, so I can't tell you where they live. I believe I was getting close to learning of one in Russia, but I can't be certain of that."

Eden's hair swung out as she turned her head to the monitor. She stared at it for a long moment. "Someone has to notify them about anyone against the Saints."

"Undoubtedly. And others take that information and decide if it's a credible threat or not."

"Exactly."

He frowned as she turned to face him with a grin. "What's that look for?"

"An idea. Maybe," she said with some hesitation. "If we had enough time, we could seed different threads of information in different places and see which one works. We could then decipher who gave the information over and who might be an Elder."

"A sound idea. One I thought about a few times. Unfortunately, that takes manpower and time. Neither of which I've had."

Her lips twisted. "And we don't have it now."

"A list of sixty-seven dates directly connected to deaths isn't something I've had before."

"I can find more information. I didn't dig deep on any one person because I wanted to see how much I could find on all of them."

"You did great. More than I could've hoped."

"But I'm not finished," she told him. "This is just from a few pages in the file. I'm not finished with it, nor have I dug into the pen drives."

This was going to take more time than he'd imagined. Maks hadn't realized just how much information he'd gathered in the years he'd been gathering it. Maybe he should've been looking at it during that time. Most likely, he would've found a few things, but nothing like Eden was uncovering.

"Let me do some more digging on these people," she asked. "I want to find out more. Besides, I can tell you're leery about asking Callie to do anything."

He mentally calculated how long they could remain at the house. They had another handful of days. And Eden was right. He didn't want to ask the Loughmans. They'd do it, especially Callie, but they needed to focus on things coming at them, not have their attention divided. When the attack did come at them, they needed to be prepared.

Maks gave a nod. "All right."

"We can stay here, right?"

"For the time being. We've got a few days before I think we'll need to move."

"I'll work fast," she promised and turned back to the computer.

He touched her arm. "Why not rest tonight? You can start fresh in the morning."

"I'd like to work now. I need to do something, and this is me contributing. I'll be fine. I promise."

Maks dropped his hand. Eden went back to work as if he didn't exist. Not that he blamed her. He did the same thing when he was working. Maks walked quietly from the room. With a few clicks, she had music playing from the computer. With one last look at her, he walked out to check the perimeter of the house.

18

Janice stared out at the city from the window in her office. Her people had been searching for any trace of Maks and Eden since the train station in Budapest and had gotten nothing. The Elders weren't at all happy, and if she didn't get some results soon, she wasn't sure what would happen to her.

Her people had everything at their disposal to locate Maks and Eden. If it had been anyone else, they likely would've already found the couple. But Maks wasn't just anyone. He was better than any other spy. He'd been nicknamed *the ghost* because of how good he was. All this time, everyone at the Saints had assumed that they had control of him.

That was laughable. No one had ever had control of Maks Volkov. That much was painfully obvious. The fact that he'd duped not only the CIA and the FSB but also the Saints wasn't something anyone was taking lying down. In fact, heads were going to roll. Quite literally.

All she could do was pray that hers wasn't among them.

A knock on her door caused her to turn around as it opened. She stared into the brown eyes of the head nerd. Damn, but she really needed to try and remember his name. Eventually. "Yes?" she asked.

"You might want to come down. We might have something."

She frowned as she strode toward him. "You should've told me that as soon as you knocked. Come on."

Every second wasted was a second that might very well cost Janice her life. She used the code to get into the room as the nerd hurried past her and got into his chair.

"Show me what you found, people," she called out.

The nerd was the first to say, "Once we lost the two subjects in the station, we expanded our search outside of the building. Unfortunately, we didn't get anything."

Janice drew in a breath while trying to hold onto her patience. They wouldn't have brought her down here if they hadn't found *something*.

"We soon realized that they would've likely left the city. So, we began using the CCTV cameras, going grid-by-grid. That's when we found this."

An image of a man getting into a car and bending over to hotwire it filled the screen. A second later, a woman joined him in the vehicle. All the while, their faces were obscured. Right until the car drove away, and the woman's head turned to the side. There, filling the large screen on the wall, was none other than Eden Fontaine.

"Where did they go?" Janice demanded, hope filling her.

There was a beat of silence before the nerd said, "We lost them."

Her gaze snapped to him. "Again?"

"There aren't cameras on every corner of the city."

"But you know what they're driving. Look for that."

The nerd visibly swallowed. "We did. And nothing. Until just a few minutes ago. One of the new cameras set up at the border of Hungary and Romania caught this."

Janice looked at the screen to see the same car Maks and Eden had stolen in Budapest, now leaving Hungary and heading into Romania. "Where did they go?" When no one answered, she sighed loudly. "Let me guess, you lost them again."

"We'll keep looking," the nerd hastily replied.

"I want every border crossing out of Romania watched. Send teams of men to Romania for when Maks is found. I want boots on the ground within two hours," she barked.

Fingers flew over keyboards, and voices filled the room as calls were put in to carry out her orders. She stared at the screen. Why would Maks take Eden to Romania? What was there for him? Nothing, at least as far as Janice knew. But Maks wasn't stupid. If he went to Romania, then he had a reason. In order to figure out what he was up to, she needed to know what was in that country for him.

Janice turned on her heel and left the room, confident that her orders would be carried out. Once in her office again, she picked up the phone and dialed. Her call was answered on the second ring. The American male voice wobbled with age and often fooled people into underestimating the intelligence still there.

"He's in Romania," she said.

There was a beat of silence. "Interesting. Do we know what's there?"

"Not yet."

"Do you know where he is exactly?"

She pressed her lips together. "Not yet. My team just found footage of him crossing into the country."

"How many hours ago?"

"Lunchtime yesterday."

There was a snort through the receiver. "So he could've already left Romania and gone somewhere else. Don't call again until you have him. And, Janice? You better find him. Alive. We want answers."

"Yes, sir," she said as the line went dead.

Janice drew in a breath, hating that her hand shook as she lowered the receiver to the base. There was no way she was going to let someone like Maks Volkov ruin her career. He was nothing but a speck on the road she'd been on. But if she wasn't careful, he could spin her out of control and have her rolling downhill to end in a fiery crash.

"Not going to happen," she told herself. "He's merely a spy who has forgotten what it means to give someone loyalty. He needs to be reminded."

And if that meant taking his life, she wouldn't hesitate.

19

Eden woke to the smell of coffee and bacon. Her stomach rumbled in response. She stretched her arms overhead and yawned. Her eyes opened, and she realized that she was still in the office, but she wasn't at the table anymore. Instead, she was on the sofa. She didn't remember getting there or finding a throw to cover herself with.

She was frowning when she sat up and swung her legs over the side. Her neck was tense, as were her shoulders and upper back, which meant that she had spent considerable time on the computer without stretching. Usually, she woke bent over her desk, not on a couch.

While trying to figure out when she'd finally passed out from exhaustion last night, she rose to her feet and folded the blanket. Then she walked out of the office to see Maks in the kitchen once more. There were plates on the island, as well as two coffee mugs that had steam rising from them.

He glanced up as she walked toward him and grinned. "Morning."

"Morning," she replied.

"You really need to be more careful. I've no idea how long you were asleep hunched over the laptop, but that can do serious damage to your back."

She bit the side of her lip. "I know. How did you get me to move to the sofa?"

"I didn't get you to do anything. I carried you to it so you could sleep properly."

At this bit of news, she winced. "I'm sorry. When I work that late, I'm pretty out of it. Not sure you could've woken me if you tried."

"I didn't try," he said with a chuckle.

"But thank you. I appreciate you moving me. I would be in worse pain if I'd stayed hunched over all night."

Maks lifted the pan and transferred the bacon onto a plate to drain. "Why not just go to bed if you knew you were getting that tired?"

"Usually, it's because I'm on the trail of something and don't want to stop. I've done that before and wasn't able to remember what I'd been looking for the day before."

"Ah. Makes sense, I suppose. Hungry?"

"Famished." She took a seat at the island and quickly dumped some cream into her coffee before moving a few slices of bacon onto her plate. "How do we have bacon? I wouldn't think that's something that lasts for months."

Maks shook his head. "It isn't. I walked to the store and bought a few items."

"Walked?" she asked, shocked. "How far away is it?"

"About five miles. I needed to get in a run anyway. I used the time to do that, get some items, and also check around the village to see if anything was amiss."

She raised her brows. "Wow. Well, thank you for the bacon. Did you find anything?"

"Nothing, thankfully."

"Weren't you worried about someone recognizing you?"

He shrugged. "I made sure I went early when there were few people about. The shopkeeper was more concerned with getting set up for the day than paying attention to me. I've done this many times before."

"Oh, I'm sure you have. I just know that if it was me, I would've been seen by everyone." She took a bit of bacon and chewed. "If we need to go, then we can go. I can work anywhere."

"This house has a secure connection to the internet. We won't have that if we leave, and if we get on the internet searching for anything about the Saints, we might as well paint a bullseye on us."

The fact that Eden hadn't thought of that proved just how ill-prepared she was for what was going on. "Of course."

"Don't beat yourself up for not thinking of these types of things. That's what I'm here for. It's what I do daily. You concentrate on doing what you do best."

She flashed him a smile. "That, I can do."

He finished off a piece of bacon. "Did you find anything interesting last night?"

"A few things that caught my attention. One of the women who was murdered happened to be in a relationship with a man that the papers went out of their way to hide."

"Did you find him?"

"I did," she replied with a nod. "He's in British parliament. He's been married for thirty-five years, has two kids, and five grandchildren. The interesting part is that when I dug into him, he was a nobody. His rise in politics was quick, and within just a few years, he had a seat in the House of Commons. That's when things *really* got interesting. He suddenly became someone everyone wanted on their side. From what I could learn about him, he has brought nothing significant to the table other than the fact that he could take a fish out of its scales."

Maks swallowed his bite and drank some coffee. He lowered the cup back to the island before he said, "That is interesting, and I wish I could say that was something odd, but it isn't. Things like that do happen."

"When he was all but homeless just two years before he was first elected into parliament?"

"Some might say he had a windfall."

She chuckled. "It was something like that for sure. I managed to find an early interview with him where he let it slip that someone had come into his life and helped him to get back on his feet. You could see it on his face that as soon as the words were out, he regretted them. He never mentioned anything like that again, and no one ever asked him that question again. At least that I could find."

"Hmm," Maks said. "This could certainly be an intervention by the Saints. But why him?"

"That's what I wondered. It took some time, but I learned that his great-great-grandfather happened to invest in a British company that did work in both Russia and Europe."

"Okay..." Maks said with a shrug.

Eden couldn't hold back her smile. "The company was actually owned by a Russian, who was known to have been a part of the KGB."

Maks slowly nodded his head. "The dots are connecting."

"Little by little. It's not a slam dunk, but there are too many coincidences, and I don't believe in them."

"Neither do I. And this is just from looking into the murder of one woman?"

Eden nodded and grabbed another piece of bacon. "That's right. Her death was ruled natural since the medical examiner said she had a heart attack, but if that date was on the sheet you gave me, then she was likely killed by the Saints."

"I agree. And if she was having an affair with this man in the British parliament, who the Saints helped to get into his position, then the woman must have stumbled across something she shouldn't have."

"Or was about to say something she shouldn't," Eden offered.

Maks' lips twisted. "Either way, she's dead."

"Sadly, yes."

Eden finished her bacon and coffee and slid off the stool to begin cleaning up.

"You don't have to do that," he told her.

She didn't even glance his way as she washed their plates. "I know."

The kitchen got quiet as the water ran and she cleaned. She dried her hand on a towel when she finished and turned around to find herself alone. Eden walked upstairs to get changed for the day and spotted the door to Maks' room closed, and heard the water running from the sink in the bathroom.

Eden hesitated, though she wasn't sure why. It wasn't as if she'd knock on the door and tell him that she'd like for him to remove his clothes so she could see a full frontal. Instead, she continued on to her room and softly clicked the door into place. She stripped out of the clothes she'd slept in and put them and yesterday's clothes in a pile. Then she found her spare pair of jeans and a long-sleeved shirt. She opted to put on socks and her shoes, just in case they had to leave quickly.

After washing her face, brushing her teeth, and getting the tangles out of her hair, she took the dirty clothes downstairs and started a load of laundry. Might as well take advantage while she could. There was no telling when they'd have to leave, or if she'd be in the same clothes for days at a time. Although, when running for your life, no one really cared what they were wearing or how long they'd been in it. Needs changed quickly in such instances.

Eden made her way to the office and began working once more. It wasn't long before she was lost in the search again, going down one rabbit hole after another. Sometimes, nothing came out of it, but she did uncover a few gems along the way. She made sure to put everything in a document for easy access, and then she copied it multiple times. There was no way she was going to go through all of this work and have it lost if the Saints took it.

For the next three days, she worked, finding more and more information while Maks continued cooking and hunting and even cleaning. He brought her water to keep her hydrated, which reminded her to get up and walk around, stretching her muscles. They would chat for a few seconds, but he always left quickly so she could get back to work.

Lunches were nice. They were simple meals of sandwiches or soup, but she came out of the office and let her brain rest for a little while. Her favorite meals were dinner. Every evening, Maks had something for them to eat. There was also always a bottle of wine for them to share. This was the time when they really talked.

Usually, it was her speaking about her family, but Maks didn't hold back. He told her more and more about himself and the time before he joined the Army. And the more she learned, the more she found him incredibly interesting. And the more she wanted to know.

It was only after the wine had been drunk and the kitchen cleaned that they went back to the office and she would show him what she'd found that day. She was always ready to tell him, but he was patient that way. Something she'd never been able to conquer. For an hour, they'd sit on the sofa together while she went through everything.

Sometimes he took notes, sometimes he gave clues to things she hadn't known, which helped her search and uncover even more. On the third day, she finally got to the first pen drive. It was loaded with information. So much, that she knew she was going to need a few days just to sift through all of it and put it in some kind of order before she could even determine where to start searching.

"I wish I had more to show you," she said as he scrolled through the documents and images on the pen drive.

After a moment, he said, "I've seen this man before."

Eden peered closer at the older man bent with age with thick eyebrows that had been carefully cut. What was left of his hair was white and wispy, with only a few strands atop his head. He was impeccably dressed in a suit as he got into the back of a black Jaguar.

"Do you know his name?" she asked.

Maks shook his head.

She shifted the computer and opened another screen to see if she could match the man's face to a photo somewhere else to perhaps get a name. "William Holder," she said when several photos popped up of the American business owner with ties to Hollywood investments.

The frown Maks wore grew deeper the longer he looked at the photo. "I saw him in the CIA building when I first joined. He was in an office with other suits. There were men like him everywhere. But...I'm certain I saw him about two years ago at the FSB headquarters."

"There's a real possibility that William Holder could be a Saint. Maybe even one of the Elders you spoke of," she offered.

Maks moved the laptop completely onto her lap and got to his feet. "I can't shake the feeling that I've seen him somewhere else, as well."

"Don't force it. It'll come to you eventually."

"We don't have that kind of time. There's something about his face that I recognize, something from long ago that I should remember."

Eden opened her lips to speak, but Maks walked out. She stared at the doorway long after he'd gone, thinking of what he'd said. Then she turned her attention to the computer and began doing a deep dive on William Holder.

20

He knew the face. But no matter how hard Maks tried to place William Holder in his life, he couldn't. Maks had always had a way with faces. It was a huge asset as a spy. One that he had used multiple times.

Now, when he needed it most, his memory failed him. Maks couldn't figure out why. Or determine why the face of the man seemed to register more than the name. The name *William Holder* meant absolutely nothing to him. But the face? It meant *everything*.

Maks paced his room, his mind sorting through dozens of faces, going back to his earliest years. Yet he kept coming up empty. The more that happened, the more frustrated he became. Then, all of a sudden, he stilled. Every instinct inside him said that he and Eden needed to leave. Immediately.

He had no idea how long his gut had been yelling at him. If he hadn't been so damned focused on trying to recall William's face, he might have heard it sooner. Maks ran from his room and down the stairs. He didn't yell for Eden to gather her things. Instead, he went to the back room where the monitors were located, the ones connected to the sensors around the property. All was clear.

For now.

He spun on his heel and stalked to the office. Eden turned to him. There must have been something on his face, because she immediately closed the laptop, gathered the papers and the pen drives, and stood.

"Do we have company?" she asked.

He shook his head. "But we need to go."

"Do we take the car?"

"They'll have figured out we took it by now. We'll have to go through the woods."

She didn't bat an eye as she said, "All right."

"Give me all of that. Get your things together quickly."

"I'll be right down."

Maks looked at the file and pen drive in one hand and the laptop in the other. Eden had made great headway here. He hated to leave it all behind. He had copies, but they wouldn't contain her notes or anything else. No, it was better if it all came with them. They would just have to be doubly careful about internet connections because the Saints would be scouring the Net for them.

Eden was down much sooner than he'd expected. "Take the laptop," he told her.

She immediately put it into her backpack as he went to find a pack for himself. He put the folders inside, but the pen drives he stuffed into the front pocket of his jeans. Then he went to the pantry and got as much food and water as he could hold and carry for them. When he turned around, Eden was waiting for him with her jacket zipped and her scarf in place.

He hesitated, because going into the wild in such weather was hazardous at any time, but especially with someone who wasn't used to it. He took in her jacket. It wasn't thick enough, but it would keep her warm.

"I'll be fine," she said, lifting her chin as if daring him to call her a liar.

"It's going to get cold."

She nodded, her gaze never breaking from his. "I know. I can handle it."

"We'll be moving fast."

"I'll keep up."

He wanted to believe her, but he couldn't help but worry about her. "You could remain behind. Tell them I kidnapped you."

She walked past him to the back door, then turned to face him. "I know too much now. Besides, I chose my side."

"This is real now."

"It was real before. Stop arguing and let's get moving."

He strode to her and took her hand to get her attention. There might be time for him to steal another car, but Maks didn't want to leave Eden behind. So much could happen to her while he was gone.

Finally, he set his mouth because he realized that he didn't want her to leave his side. "It's night, so we'll have to move as quietly as we can. I won't leave you behind."

"If you do and I die, I'll haunt you," she replied with a cheeky grin.

Maks smiled despite himself. "Ready?"

"As I'll ever be."

He punched in the code to unlock the doors and ushered Eden outside after grabbing some weapons from his stash. Maks then set another code, one that would blow up the house if someone tried to force themselves in. He didn't want to lose the house, but it was better that than their lives.

"Let's go," he said as he spun around.

He sprinted to the forest, Eden right on his heels. It was already dark outside. The Romanian countryside was pitch black. Once inside the cover of the trees, Maks slowed to a walk. There were predators in the woods, and he wasn't sure there weren't Saints, as well. He glanced behind him and saw the outline of Eden's head. Breath billowed from her lips in the cold.

One of the things he'd done after purchasing the house was to learn routes through the forest. There were two different spots he could get to in order to hide out. One was farther than the other, and unfortunately, that's the one he was going to. The farther from the house they got, the better at this point. He'd hoped they could stay at least one more day, but they had been on borrowed time from the moment they got off the train in Romania.

The snow crunched beneath their boots as they slowly made their way. Maks stopped every few minutes and listened to the forest. So far, the sounds were normal. The moment it got quiet was when he knew someone was near.

He looked up through the snow-laden branches

above him to the night sky. The thick clouds were moving quickly and hiding the moon. Still, it shone brightly enough that it illuminated the ground from behind the clouds. Any other night, he would've been happy to stare at the sky for hours. The tall conifers loomed around them, providing shelter. But they also hid unseen enemies.

Maks looked at Eden, who smiled at him, letting him know that she was fine. More snow was on the way, and he wanted them to be sheltered before then. The odds of them getting there before the snow started falling were slim, though. It all depended on how quickly they could move.

He started walking again. Because they sank into the deep snow, they expended more energy. Maks stopped often to let Eden catch her breath. She had kept up with him thus far, and even though she was breathing heavily, she hadn't said anything. He was cognizant of the fact that he might be used to moving in such conditions, but she wasn't. Between the winter conditions and the Saints, everything was stacked against them.

Maks wasn't one to give up, however.

And he was coming to learn that neither was Eden.

After nearly forty minutes, he removed his pack when he paused and took out a bottle of water to hand to Eden. She waved it away as she sucked in huge mouthfuls of air. He pushed the water at her again. "You're going to need it. It may not feel like it, but you do," he whispered.

Without question, she took it. Then drank it down to the last drop. She winced when she handed it back to him. "Sorry."

"Don't be. You needed it."

He gave them another two minutes before they started moving again. There were very deep sections of snow that Maks had to help Eden through. It would've been easier to find another route, but the one he was on kept them hidden, and right now, that was more important.

Just as he was pulling Eden toward him, her leg gave out, and she fell forward into the snow. Maks quickly got her on her feet. She was past exhausted. He could see it in her face and feel it in her muscles that shook from the prolonged exertion. He glanced over his shoulder to the destination.

"I can make it," she whispered and pushed away from him to stand on her own.

His head swung back to her. "Let's get out of this and into the group of trees up ahead. The ground is higher, so the snow shouldn't be as deep."

She nodded and started walking, not bothering to wait for him. Maks stayed beside her instead of walking in front of her. Eden kept putting one foot in front of the other, and each time she wobbled, he was there to keep her upright. Once they reached the trees he'd pointed out, she leaned against one and closed her eyes.

At that moment, the snow started falling.

So far, the ground they'd covered had been relatively flat. In just a few, they would be headed downhill. And after that, everything would be upward, making it even more difficult. He thought about telling Eden beforehand, but he realized it wouldn't make a difference. She was on autopilot now. And maybe that was a good thing.

He gave her another bottle of water as well as

half of a protein bar. When she wrinkled her nose, he raised a brow. "You're burning a lot of calories. Your body needs fuel."

With gloved fingers, Eden took her portion and brought it to her mouth. She ate with her eyes closed. Maks had done this trail many times in all conditions. He knew how long it would take him to reach the shelter in any situation. But he'd never thought to have someone with him. That was the one thing he hadn't factored in.

His instincts pushed him to get moving, but he was keenly aware that Eden couldn't handle the pace he wanted to set. He had to slow things down. Otherwise, he might be carrying her. Not that he couldn't do it. Frankly, he had been expecting that to happen. The fear of being chased, knowing her life was on the line, had her adrenaline pumping. But that only lasted so long before the body just gave out—and Eden was close to shutting down.

"Don't look at me like that," she said.

He frowned as he stared at her closed eyes. "Excuse me?"

"You're looking at me, clearly wondering how we're going to get to wherever we're headed. I can do it. I'm stronger than I look."

That made him grin. "You might have the mental fitness to get through this, but there is only so much a body can handle."

"I knew I should've gone to the gym more," she said with a sigh. "But coffee ice cream is just too good to pass up when you've had a bad day."

Maks turned his head away as he fought not to laugh. "No one is going to say anything about your ice cream preferences or habits."

Her eyes opened as her brows drew together. "Coffee ice cream is mana from the gods."

"Gotcha," he said and briefly held up his hands in surrender.

She nodded once. "That's what I thought. And my body isn't going to let me down. However, I will be making sure I'm more fit for the future. You know, in case I'm ever chased in the dead of night through the woods in Romania in winter. I bet you thought of that. Of course, you did," she said with a roll of her eyes.

"I did, yes."

"How much farther do we have?"

He hesitated. "Do you really want to know?"

"I don't think I do. It might be better if I believe it's just over the next hill."

They stood in silence while both finished eating. Maks kept his gaze moving, searching for any kind of movement that seemed out of the ordinary. Though with the dense trees and the darkness, it was difficult to see much of anything. He couldn't even say that was an advantage since the same could be said for the Saints coming for them because they'd most likely have night vision gear.

After one more look around, Maks took Eden's hand, and they continued on. There were easy sections that Maks had chosen when he planned this route that would allow him to put some distance between himself and whoever might be after him. They were on such a section now.

He maneuvered them through the trees, and the steep slopes that followed. Eden caught a second wind, and they were making good progress.

The night was quiet as the snow fell. The only sound was their movements. Eden actually made it up a small, sharp incline onto a bluff before he saw that she was tiring.

Maks tugged on her hand to let her know that they were taking a break. She bent over, her hands on her knees as she tried to catch her breath. He was surveying the terrain ahead of them when something snapped behind them, the sound echoing in the silence. His head jerked around. Eden straightened, her gaze following his.

His mind raced with possibilities. It could be an animal. Or it could be the Saints. There were still packs of wolves in Romania, as well as bears and lynx. He didn't want to be cornered by any of them. They weren't in the best location to stay still for a bit while he determined what had made that sound. But to move now would definitely draw attention to them.

Yet, they couldn't remain here either.

He looked at Eden and waited until her gaze met his. He leaned close to her and whispered, "Keep going. Straight up. Don't deviate from the line we're on. Don't wait for me. I'll catch up with you."

"Maks," she replied, concern and fear in her gaze.

"I'll be fine. We can't stay here. And I need to see what's behind us. Just be mindful of where you're putting your feet. You can do this."

Eden slowly nodded her head and forced a grin. "I can do it."

He shot her a smile of encouragement. "I'll be right behind you. Go."

Despite the trepidation he saw in her, Eden did as directed. He watched as she started up the hill, moving steadily and taking her time so she didn't fall. Once he knew she was doing as he'd asked, Maks turned his attention behind him. He squatted down to make himself as small as possible, less of a target. Then he scanned the darkness, waiting for something to move.

This was Hell. Without a doubt, Hell wasn't some fiery pit. It was ice and snow and frigid temperatures.

Eden kept moving her toes in her boots, but it didn't matter. They were as numb as her fingers. She couldn't believe how much heat Maks put off, she had been warmer just being near him. Now that he was gone, it felt ten degrees cooler.

Or it could just be her mind freaking out because she was now alone.

Yeah. That was probably it. Though she should stop thinking that way because there might be a real chance she could lose her mind. That made her pause. Could she go nuts from being in the cold? She'd never thought to ask something like that.

"Oh, God. Stop," she chastised herself.

One foot in front of the other. It took her twice as long to pull her feet from the deep snow as when Maks had been there to pull her out. She then groaned aloud because she realized that he'd been expending much more energy helping her than if he'd been on his own. She hated being a burden in any situation, but this one was even worse.

I'm not going to fail. I'm not going to fail. I'm not going to fail.

Eden repeated that over and over in her mind, her resolve growing. She was cold, yes. Actually, she was fucking freezing and never wanted to see snow again, but that was beside the point. She wasn't in the hands of the Saints, and that was all because of Maks. He had gotten her this far, and she was a capable woman who had lived alone for many years. She could take care of herself, and even though she didn't know the first thing about surviving in the wild, she was a fast learner.

With her lungs burning, she paused. Each breath felt as if icicles were scraping her esophagus and nasal passages. She put a hand on a tree to steady herself and not fall backward. Thinking about that had her looking back the way she'd come. Eden was shocked to see that the incline was as steep as it had felt. There was no sign of Maks, but she wasn't worried. No doubt he was hiding someplace.

Eden tried to even her breathing. She could already feel what little energy she'd had draining fast. It wasn't just the altitude or the climbing, it was the extra effort just to walk in the snow. All of that, combined with the frigid temperatures, was zapping her strength at an alarming rate.

She looked around, really taking in the sights. She might admire how the snow glowed in the night. Or how one side of the trees was covered with snow, showing how the wind had driven it against the bark. Or that the snow flurries hovering against the backdrop of the darkness was stunning.

That is if she could stop her teeth from chattering long enough to appreciate it.

With a deep breath, Eden pushed away from the tree and continued up the path. The farther up the mountain she went, the more difficult it became. She had to stop frequently just to catch her breath. She glanced behind her often, hoping to see Maks and praying that there wasn't an animal—or worse, a Saint—coming after her.

The only thing helping her at the moment was the knowledge that she would most likely be a popsicle soon, which would make for difficult eating for an animal. Or would it? Something else she didn't know and should've thought to ask.

She rolled her eyes at herself. The thoughts that went through her brain at times were disturbing. Why should she care if it was hard for an animal to eat someone who was frozen? She didn't want to be eaten *or* end up frozen.

Eden paused to catch her breath for just a moment. She went to take a step when something out of the corner of her eye caught her attention. Her eyes rounded when she found herself staring into the yellow eyes of a Eurasian lynx. Its winter fur was thick and a silvery beige-gray with black spots. It's belly and neck were white. She took in the black-tipped, bobbed tail and the long tufts of black fur on its ears. It was a beautiful animal, even with its really long, powerful legs.

She knew from her love of animals that the lynx was a shy creature who liked to stay away from other animals and humans. With as much noise as she'd made on her trek up, no doubt it had heard her. However, it was half-hidden, so perhaps it thought she wouldn't see it. And she wouldn't have, had it not twitched an ear.

"You are a beauty," she whispered to the animal before giving it a wide berth and continuing on.

When she glanced behind her, the lynx was gone. She spotted it going to the east as if giving chase to something. Eden was happy the lynx hadn't been some other kind of predator that could've made a meal of her.

She was beginning to think that she would never reach the top of the mountain when she heard something behind her. A look back confirmed that there was indeed someone coming, and it was Maks. She wanted to shout for joy. He was moving quickly, so she kept a steady pace, knowing he would catch her soon.

When he did, she fought not to give him a hug. "I knew you'd make it."

"Did you?" he asked with a grin.

"Of course. Did you see anything?"

"A bear."

"I saw a lynx," she said excitedly while continue to walk. "He was stunning."

Maks slowed to stay with her. "How are you doing?"

"I could be worse." She smiled when he chuckled.

"Things could always be worse."

They continued on in silence until they got to the top of the mountain. Eden hoped this was their destination, but she had a feeling she was wrong.

And when Maks kept going, it was all she could do to hold in her groan of disappointment.

"Not much farther," he told her.

At least they would be going downhill again. Or she believed that until Maks shifted from their path and went to the left, which took them up another part of a mountain. Time no longer mattered. All Eden could focus on was walking and staying upright. She didn't try to carry on a conversation with Maks or even herself. Her brain couldn't handle that at the moment.

She walked when he told her. She stopped when he told her. She drank and ate when he told her. And it was a good thing he was there because she was sure she would've stopped a long way back and just sat in the snow, waiting for the elements to finish her off. She just didn't have any kind of energy or will to do anything herself.

Whether it was the cold, the fear, the altitude, or simply utter lack of drive, she didn't know. What she *did* know was that she wasn't cut out for this kind of stuff. Hiking in the summer was vastly different than in the winter. There was a reason she declined such things when it was cold. She'd instinctively known that she couldn't cope.

Eden didn't even care what Maks might think of that. He hadn't left her behind, and that was saying something. Nor was he carrying her. She might not be moving very fast, but she was moving and on her own. There was no telling how long that would last, but she would wring every last drop of it before she let him carry her.

A giggle escaped her at the thought, causing Maks to look at her with a frown. As if she could stop him from carrying her. She was only on her feet now because falling would take too much effort. And each time she did start to lean one way or the other, he was there to right her. The simple fact was, she had no idea how she was still going. Sheer will, it seemed. Odd how much that could get you when you really needed it.

She was aware of the many times Maks looked over his shoulders to check behind them. He was always very careful to keep his face devoid of expression, but she knew he was worried. Not once had he told her to hurry or speed up. He didn't need to. She knew for herself that they were being hunted.

"There's an easy spot up ahead," Maks told her. "We're going to need to run. Can you do that?"

"Yes." *Damn, I really hope I can.*

He didn't question her, which she was thankful for. She'd given him the answer he needed, the answer *she* needed. Whether she could actually do it or not was something altogether different.

"Here it comes."

Maks grabbed her hand. Before she'd been on her own, that gesture would've warmed her significantly because he put off so much heat. But she was too cold to feel anything. She was glad he had a hold of her, though. She tried to squeeze his hand, but her fingers were too numb.

"Run, Eden. As fast as you can," he urged in a low whisper.

She pulled her foot out of the snow and stepped down to find there was rock beneath her. The snow on this section was only a few inches thick, allowing her to move freely. It felt like she had shaken off five hundred pounds of weight. In fact, if she tried, she was pretty sure she could fly.

Despite that thought, she still couldn't keep up with Maks. He was half pulling her behind him. She wanted to look over her shoulder, but she didn't dare. To do that meant she would certainly fall on her face. A glance to the side showed that they were inches from a sheer drop-off. If she fell, there was no doubt she'd tumble off the side of the mountain and disappear into the darkness below into who knew what.

All too soon, the easy section ended, and Eden found herself back in snow that was up to her knees. She choked back a sob. It had felt so good to be free of it, and now that she was back in the snow, it felt heavier than before, as if it were pulling her down.

Suddenly, Maks stopped and faced her. His hands grabbed her upper arms, and his bright blue eyes met hers. "Listen closely."

"Don't leave me again." She'd barely survived on her own the first time. She couldn't do it again.

Maks's lips softened. "You're a strong woman. One of the strongest I've ever met. Look what you've done."

"It's because you were here."

"You could've done it on your own. I know that. So do you."

Maybe she did. She was just so tired. She wanted to lie down and close her eyes. They were so heavy.

"Eden," he said sharply and gave her a little shake.

Her eyes snapped open. "What?"

"If you keep on this heading, you'll find a cave entrance. It's covered so no animals can use it. You'll have to look closely for it, but you can do it. It's only another few kilometers away."

Anything more than a foot was too far right now. Did he really expect her to walk that by herself? On top of the mountain. Oh, God. Then there was the cliff she'd have to worry about falling from.

"I caught up with you the first time," he continued. "I'll do it again. I give you my word, and I never break a vow."

Eden swallowed, tears threatening. "I'll try."

"That's all I ask of you. Just don't stop moving. Go as slow as you need, but don't stop. Do you understand?"

She nodded, emotion choking her. She was more terrified now than when they'd left the house. The cold had permeated every inch of her. Warmth was a distant memory she feared would never return.

"You can do it," he told her with a smile. "I know you can."

Eden sniffed and lifted her chin. "Of course, I will."

One side of his lips curved into a heart-melting smile. "I'll catch up soon. Remember, don't stop. No matter what you hear behind you, keep moving."

She tried to look down the slope, but his fingers on her chin prevented her from turning her head.

"You need to go. Now," he said and gave her a little push.

Eden turned and started walking. She wanted

to look over her shoulder and see Maks once more, but she didn't. She had to stay focused, needed to concentrate on what was before her so she didn't bust her ass and maybe even die.

The cold was turning her into a pessimist. That had to be it. Obviously, she was suited to warmer weather. Modern conveniences made people forget how damn cold it really was. It wasn't something she would ever take for granted again, that was for sure. She even tried thinking of sitting in front of a fire, or taking a hot shower to warm herself, but it did nothing. Kudos to those who could think such thoughts and shift their internal temperatures. She didn't have that skill.

Step by step, she plodded ahead. When the silence of the night was broken by the sound of a gunshot, she jerked, pausing for a heartbeat before she started moving again. She didn't want to think that it was Maks who might have gotten hit. She would continue thinking that he'd either fired the gun or that whoever had fired on him had missed. There weren't any more gunshots, but she wasn't sure if that was a good thing or not.

Her mind raced with all kinds of possibilities. It wasn't until she went over what Maks had told her to look for that she realized she hadn't been looking for a covered cave entrance. Nor did she know how far she'd walked. Not that she was ever very good at gauging distance on a flat road, much less going over mountainous terrain.

She stopped caring about the cave and instead concentrated on walking. If she had to go all night, she would. She'd have to stumble across a house or village sometime. Right? If she was lucky, maybe.

Eden began to keep a lookout for anything that might be a hidden cave. She tried several spots that her fuzzy brain thought might be a covered entrance, but so far, she'd come up empty. It became harder and harder to even lift her feet. She refused to stop, though. Maks had told her to keep going, and that's what she would do. No matter what, she would keep going. She wasn't going to let him down. He'd made a promise to her, and she was going to keep her side of the bargain and continue on.

"Don't stop," she said to herself. "Just don't stop."

Maks stood over the corpses, his breathing ragged. He looked down at the blood-splattered snow. It wasn't going to take long for wolves to make their way there. They would dispose of the bodies better than anything Maks could do.

He flexed his hands as he turned and started up the mountain. From the moment he'd left Eden, he'd been worried about her. He hadn't wanted to let her go alone, but he hadn't had a choice. The Saints had gotten closer than he would have liked. Too damn close, actually. One had been taking aim at Eden. If Maks hadn't gotten there in time...

His thoughts trailed off. It was better for everyone if he didn't complete that thought. The four-man team hadn't been expecting him. That gave Maks an advantage, and he'd needed it because the team was good. Very good. He'd encountered all manner of trained fighters in his life, and these were some of the best he'd seen. The Saints must be upping their game.

Perhaps he'd been a fool to think they'd kept

recruiting others like they had with him. Maybe after their run-in with the Loughmans, they'd changed tactics and began training their own men. If that was the case, there were only a few select people in all the world who could train others like that.

Maks didn't stop his ascent while his mind turned over this new information. The thing he hated about the Saints was that he didn't know what was fact, what was a guess, and what was completely wrong. All he could do was put the information he had together with the facts he'd experienced and seen firsthand. So far, he'd been pretty spot-on in his guestimates. How long would that last, though?

His body urged him to rest, but he couldn't. Finding Eden was his top priority because he couldn't be sure that none of the Saints had gone around him to follow her. Maks tracked her footsteps in the powder. They were quickly being covered by the snowfall. The deeper impressions told him where she had stopped to rest before continuing.

Maks plowed through the deep snow, his gaze moving all around, searching for enemies, predators, and Eden. When the cave finally came into sight, he moved quicker, hoping that Eden was there. But as he drew closer, he could tell that the cover hadn't been moved. No longer were her footsteps visible either. He halted and turned in a circle, hoping for some sight of her.

He'd told her to keep moving. Maybe she'd been so focused on staying upright that she hadn't seen the cave. It wasn't easy to find in general, and the fact that she was exhausted and cold only made things worse. There was no movement anywhere he looked. He wanted to shout her name, but he didn't dare. There were more Saints out there. If they hadn't already found her, then he needed to get Eden out of the weather and warm. Soon.

"Fuck," he murmured.

Maks turned back the way she'd been headed. He'd told her to keep moving in this direction, so he was going to look there first. She couldn't have gotten that far ahead. Maks plowed through the snow, ignoring the ache in his legs and lungs. Behind him, he heard the howl of a wolf, followed closely by several others. No doubt they were already at the bodies. The last thing he wanted was the pack to track him and Eden.

He hadn't gone very far before he spotted something through the trees. He stilled and watched, his gaze narrowed as he waited. The moment he saw Eden, relief poured through him. He hurried to her. As he came up behind her, he said her name softly so as not to startle her. She didn't appear to hear him, and that concerned him.

Maks put a hand on her arm, but once more, she didn't stop. He then moved in front of her and stood in her way. She stopped and blinked up at him. When her gaze finally registered him, her face crumpled. His arms came around her, bringing her against him.

"It's all right," he told her. While he wanted to stand there and comfort her, he didn't dare. "We've got to get to the cave."

She tried to walk forward. Maks stopped her and turned her around. Eden didn't say anything, just started walking. She stumbled twice, but he caught her each time. They weren't making as good of time as they needed to. Just as Maks was about to lift her into his arms, Eden dropped.

He checked her pulse to make sure she was still alive, then he gathered her in his arms and double-timed it to the cave. Once there, he set her down and removed the natural covering to check that no animal or person was inside waiting. When he saw that it was just as he'd left it, Maks got Eden inside and quickly covered the entrance again.

In short order, he had a fire going and pulled out blankets from an airtight box of supplies he'd left behind. The moment he pulled off Eden's gloves and felt her flesh, fear rushed through him. He moved faster than he'd ever moved in his life, putting a blanket down on the hard ground, then removing Eden's clothes down to her underwear. Finally, he covered her with another blanket before stripping himself and getting under the covers with her.

He kept his pack of food and weapons close, but right now, his worry was getting Eden through the night. She didn't so much as twitch when he pulled her against him. He rubbed his hands up and down her arms and back to get her blood pumping. Then he moved to her legs and feet and hands, repeating the process over and over again.

It felt like an eternity before he felt any warmth in her. Only then did he pause in his ministrations and simply wrap her in his arms. Maks kept having to force himself to loosen his hold. He closed his eyes and allowed himself to rest. They weren't out of the woods yet, but this respite could make all the difference in if they lived or not.

An hour later, he woke and got up to put more wood on the fire to keep it burning. He checked the entrance cover. He'd fashioned it so that no light could be seen from outside. On top of that, he'd created a latch on the inside so no one could just open the door if the cave was in use.

After checking Eden's fingers and toes for frostbite, he took a few minutes to eat a bag of nuts and drink some water. Only then did he climb back beside her. The moment he did, she turned toward him, seeking his warmth. The fact that he liked the action made his heart skip a beat. Growing up, he'd seen the love his parents shared, and he'd wanted that same kind of love.

It wasn't until he was older that he realized how rare such a love was. He'd still held out hope that he'd find it, right up until the Saints came into his life. Never did he imagine someone like Eden. Now that she was here, he didn't want her to leave. Ever. But he knew that was only wishful thinking. He might have been waiting for a woman like her his entire life, but these fleeting moments were all he could have. It didn't matter that he felt more alive with her than he ever had, or that, despite the seriousness of their situation, he didn't want to be anywhere else but with her.

Eden pressed her cheek against his chest. Maks wrapped his arms around her, holding her firmly as he pressed his lips to the top of her head. This moment, this short flash of time, would stay with him for the rest of his life. All he'd suffered, everything he'd endured, had been worth it to have a woman like Eden not only in his arms but also giving her trust completely to him. He wasn't sure he deserved any of it, but for her, he'd live up to it all.

No matter what he had to do in order to achieve it.

All the while, he tried to ignore the fact that he could feel all of her against him. He'd dreamed of her for three nights, wondering what it would be like to have her just as he did now. It was better than any fantasy. She fit against him perfectly, as if their bodies had been made together as a single unit and then taken apart.

It would be so easy for Maks to allow himself to believe that he could have Eden, that there weren't enemies around every corner waiting to kill her and to hurt him. That he hadn't lived a life of lies and blood and death. He was the monster people only half-heartedly believed was real because their brains couldn't comprehend how anyone could choose such a life.

It wasn't the life he'd wanted or the one he thought to have. But it was the one that had been handed to him. Sure, he could've walked away and let what he was doing fall to someone else, but that wasn't who he was. How could he be sure there would even *be* a next person? For all he'd known, there was no one else but him. Thankfully, there were people like the Loughmans, but it was sheer luck that he'd stumbled upon them.

And even then, he hadn't been entirely certain that he could trust them, not at first. That had come from fighting alongside them and seeing what the family and their friends were willing to sacrifice for the good of the world. It had been the same fight he'd been in. The relief that he wasn't doing it alone had been staggering.

He could've given them everything he had and walked away, leaving it up to them to take down the Saints. And they would've done it without question. He couldn't, however. It wasn't just because the Saints had forced their way into his life, taking the woman he'd believed he was going to marry. It was because of everything wrong with what the Saints stood for and were doing.

Maks lowered his gaze to Eden. The firelight danced across the walls of the cave and cast a red-orange glow over her hair and down the side of her face. If the Saints hadn't come into his life, he would never have met Eden. He didn't want to thank the organization for anything, but he couldn't help it. Eden was...amazing.

Intelligent. Brave. Beautiful. Strong.

Could he have been happy with his old life as a Ranger? Could he have loved his girlfriend and made her his wife? Yes, he could have. But it wasn't the same relationship his parents had. He knew that now. As much as he didn't want to admit it, a part of him had known, even back then, that she hadn't been right for him.

And Eden is?

He couldn't say for certain, nor would he even try. They weren't in a relationship. But he wanted her. Damn, did he want her. It wasn't just about desire and lust. It went deeper, to a place he didn't want to look at, a part of himself he'd thought long dead.

Eden chose that moment to inhale deeply and

slowly release the breath as she snuggled against him. She threw one leg over his, pressing her body against his. Maks closed his eyes, the temptation too much to resist. His balls tightened as his cock hardened. Only her bra and panties separated them. He'd left them on because he hadn't had the strength to remove them.

It had been sheer torture to see her full breasts covered in red lace and the black cotton panties with the red lace at her waist. His hands had actually shook when he'd taken off her clothes to discover her underwear. Just thinking about it now made his mouth go dry.

He lay there in exquisite torment with the woman he desired above all others draped over him as his body throbbed with a craving only she could quench. Maks didn't dare move. He barely breathed. His control was holding on by only a thin thread and even that was unraveling by the second. There were hours left before dawn, and he wasn't sure he could last that long.

All the times he'd been tortured, all the training he'd undergone to withstand the cruelest types of punishment, and all it took to break him was Eden half-naked in his arms. The irony didn't go unnoticed by him. Thankfully, she didn't seem to know the hold she had on him. But that was little comfort at the moment.

It was going to be a very, very long night. The fact that he was conflicted, torn between wanting it to hurry and end and *never* end, was almost laughable.

Never in his life did he think a mere slip of a woman would be what felled him.

Eden was floating on a cloud of heat. Something firm was beneath her cheek, but she didn't care. She never wanted to wake. She was finally warm again. Her fingers and toes no longer hurt, and the snow had stopped stinging her face as it fell.

She just hoped that Maks found somewhere to get out of the weather.

The moment that went through her head, her thoughts came to a halt. Maks. In that instant, she knew the firmness she was against, the heat that permeated every inch of her, was none other than Maks. She tried to think back to the last thing she remembered, but there was nothing but cold and snow. Obviously, he'd found her, but she couldn't remember locating the cave.

She opened her eyes and found herself looking at a cave wall doused in an orangish light. Behind her was the crackle and pop of a fire, and beneath her ear, the steady rhythm of his breathing. The fact that she was the most comfortable she'd been in her entire life certainly said something about using Maks as a pillow.

That made her grin.

"What are you smiling about?" he asked in a smooth voice.

Her heart dropped to her feet. She'd thought he was asleep. "I was thinking that you make an excellent pillow."

"Good." He drew in a deep breath and released it. "How do you feel?"

"Warm. I honestly didn't think I'd ever feel that way again."

She shifted her head to look up at him. She knew it was a mistake as soon as she did it, because she found herself staring into his bright blue eyes. Did he have any idea how gorgeous he was? She could get lost in those orbs, forget there was anyone other than the two of them in the entire world. They were in the middle of nowhere in Romania in a cave. Who would look for them here?

It was foolish for her heart to even think of going down the bumpy, dangerous road of love. She'd been down it enough times to know that it rarely worked out. Her heart had been broken so many times, that she'd given up on ever finding someone to spend her life with. She'd made up her mind to be done with relationships, and yet...none of that mattered with Maks. Because he was different.

She would gladly walk down that road with him, no matter how bumpy and dangerous it got. Which seemed odd since she hadn't known him for that long. Then again, it felt as if she'd known him her entire life. How was that even possible? She was comfortable with him, and she'd never felt safer in her life.

Even if she was running from the Saints.

Eden blinked, realizing that they'd been staring at each other this entire time. She swallowed and looked away, unsure of what to say now that all of that had gone through her head.

"Besides warm, how do you feel?" he asked.

About to answer, she suddenly realized that her clothes were gone. She was under a blanket, her body intertwined with Maks', and she was naked. Or almost naked at any rate. And she thought he might be fully naked. If this wasn't a prime opportunity for her to get a look at the front of him, she didn't know what was.

"Eden?" There was concern in his eyes as his brow began to furrow.

"I—" She started to answer, and then realized she hadn't fully taken stock of her body since comprehending who she was pressed up against. She mentally took note of things, feeling for anything that hurt or didn't seem right. Her fingers moved well, as did her toes. "I think I'm all right."

He glanced at the fire behind her. "I need to look at your fingers and toes again."

"For frostbite?" she murmured.

Maks nodded once. "You should be okay, but I'd rather be safe."

"Do you want to check now?"

"No."

The word was clipped, his tone harsh. Eden was taken aback by the brusqueness of it. She shifted her leg to move away from him when she felt his arousal against her thigh. Instantly, she stilled.

Neither said a word as the silence stretched between them. Eden couldn't decide if she should try to ignore it—which became a bigger issue the longer she didn't move or say anything. Or if she should just play it off and laugh.

There's another option.

She swallowed, thinking about reaching for his cock beneath the covers. She'd nearly died a few hours ago. Well, that might be a bit extreme, but she knew that the Saints were after them, which could mean death for her. Why shouldn't she throw caution to the wind and give in to the desire within her? Maks was a stunning specimen, and he hadn't once made a move on her. Some might think that was because he wasn't interested.

There could be an argument for that, but she didn't think so. Not after the way he'd watched over her and taken care of her. Not after the stories they'd shared with each other about their families and lives. The more she thought about it, the more she began to suspect that Maks hadn't done or said anything so she wouldn't be put in an awkward situation.

Eden drew in a breath and shifted her head to look at him. Bright blue eyes met hers, searching. She smiled at him and returned her leg to where it had been. Some of the tension left his body. Without a word to him, Eden reached between them and slid her hand along the hard length of his arousal.

Her heart was pounding, her blood running like fire through her veins and pooling between her legs to throb with need. At her touch, he sucked in a mouthful of air, his body going taut. They never broke eye contact. She slowly wrapped her fingers around him, stroking up and down firmly.

In the next instant, Maks had her on her back, his hands on either side of her head as he leaned over her. Her heart missed a beat at the sight of the blatant need that he allowed her to see. He must have hidden it before because there was no way she could've missed that. It made her knees weak and caused her entire body to shiver in excitement of what was to come.

He slowly lowered himself atop her until their lips were breaths apart. She looked down at his lips as hers parted. Then his mouth was pressed against hers. The kiss was soft but insistent, gentle but firm. Indulgent but unwavering.

The moment her arms wound around his neck, he released a moan. He settled between her legs, his cock pressed against her stomach as his tongue swept into her mouth. She ran her hands over the firm sinew of his shoulders, arms, and back to his tight ass while her feet moved up and down his legs.

She felt every movement of his body. He didn't just kiss with his mouth but with every part of him. And could the man kiss! She was beginning to think there wasn't anything Maks couldn't do to perfection.

Eden's thoughts came to a halt when the kiss deepened. He rocked her to her very soul. He was fire and passion, hunger and fierceness. It awoke something primal, something elemental within her. All that mattered was having him against her, in her. She'd never craved anyone as much as she did Maks.

When he finally lowered his full weight atop her, Eden groaned. It felt right that he was there, that they were together. As if Fate had chosen this moment for them.

One of his hands tangled in her hair, holding her head in place as he plundered her lips again and again. She grasped his hips, needing to feel him against her. Then he ground his cock into her, and her sex throbbed in response.

She shoved at his shoulder until he was on his back and then she straddled him. Eden sat up slowly, using her hands against his chest as his hands settled on her hips. Then she reached behind her and unclasped her bra. She tossed it aside, her gaze never leaving his.

"Damn, woman," he murmured. "You're...stunning."

She smiled and started to lean down for another kiss, but his hands moved up her hips to her stomach and then cupped her breasts. Eden gasped, her eyes rolling back in her head as he teased her already aching nipples. His fingers knew just what to do to send her spiraling out of control straight toward an orgasm.

Just as she was getting comfortable, Maks flipped her onto her back once again. This time, he removed her panties. His eyes were hungry as they followed his hands from her ankles up the outside of her legs and back down again. The next time his hands slid upward, he parted her legs, running his fingers inside her thighs to her sex.

He laid on his stomach, his mouth so close she could feel his warm breath on her skin. His gaze lifted, briefly meeting hers before his tongue lightly swirled around her clit. Eden clenched the blanket beneath her as her eyes rolled back in her head. The need he'd fanned with his kisses and touch roared to life.

He was thorough, tasting every part of her. He was soft, he was hard. He was relentless. Every lick of his tongue pushed her closer to climaxing. As if he knew, he doubled his efforts, gripping her hips with his big hands when she tried to get away from the pleasurable onslaught. Need spiraled within her, tightening with each heartbeat. She sought out the orgasm she knew would be amazing, but also wasn't ready for the pleasure to be over. Everything felt so...right.

With one flick of his tongue, Maks sent her tipping over the edge and into ecstasy like she'd never experienced before. The blissful waves wracked her body over and over. Time stopped. The world disappeared.

Leaving only her, the pleasure, and...Maks.

The climax went on for eternity. Or perhaps it only lasted a moment. When she finally came back to herself, she could barely remember her own name, much less anything else. All she knew was that she had felt something she hadn't known existed. And she wanted it again. In fact, she wanted it for the rest of her life.

It took Eden a moment to realize that Maks had moved. She opened her eyes and found him lying beside her, watching her with a curious expression on his face. Her lips curved into a smile when she met his gaze.

"That was...wow," she said in a hoarse voice.

One side of his mouth tilted in a sexy grin. "It was certainly beautiful to watch."

Eden looked away, a little embarrassed. "Was it?"

"It was."

She turned her head back to him, glancing down at his impressive cock. Her hands had felt him, but this was the first time she'd gotten to look at him. Eden turned onto her side and took in his thick length. Even after having such a mind-blowing orgasm, her body still hungered to have him inside her.

"Why did you stop?" she asked.

His stomach tightened, sending his many muscles moving and making her hands itch to run over his hard body. "I was too intent on watching you."

"You sure you just want to watch?"

"Hell, no," he replied with a grin.

Eden reached for his arousal at the same time he rolled her onto her back. She spread her legs and guided him to her entrance. The moment the blunt head of his cock touched her, he thrust his hips. She moaned at the feel of him sliding inside her, stretching her. Filling her. She wrapped her arms around him and gave in to the flames of desire that had only been tamped down and were now roaring once again.

He began an easy tempo that soon had them both gasping with pleasure. Sweat covered them both, allowing their bodies to glide against each other easily. Another orgasm began to build. She wrapped her legs around his waist, hooking her ankles together as he thrust deeper, harder. The feel of his muscles moving beneath her hands combined with their ragged breaths caused her senses to riot.

Her eyes rolled back in her head as his hips moved faster, propelling them both towards pleasure. The thought barely went through her mind before a tremor ran through Maks, right before he pulled out of her, spilling his seed on her stomach.

As his hips continued to thrust, she found herself having a second orgasm and wishing that she could've felt him inside her.

Nothing had ever felt so good.

Or so damn right.

Maks dimly realized that Eden had had another orgasm at the same time as he did. He wished he'd stayed inside her, and it was a miracle that he'd even remembered at the last second that he hadn't been wearing a condom.

He looked down to see Eden's face filled with pleasure. The first time he'd seen it, she had taken his breath away. It had been something utterly beautiful to behold, and now, he was getting to see it again. Instead of taking away from his own pleasure, it added to it.

A few moments later, she opened her eyes and smiled up at him. He returned the grin. Maks could've stayed like that for an eternity, but reality soon set in. He moved off her and used the edge of the blanket to clean his seed from her stomach. Then he reached for her, happy that she eagerly curled against him once more.

He lightly ran his fingers up and down her back, thinking about how light he felt. As if all the weight he'd been carrying around for years had suddenly vanished. He couldn't remember the last time he'd felt this...free.

"Thank you for pulling out," she said into the silence.

He turned and kissed her forehead. "Honestly, I barely remembered until the last minute. That's how much I wanted you."

"Same," she answered with a giggle. "At least one of us was in their right mind."

"I've never felt what I feel with you," he confessed. "It's amazing."

Her head shifted so she could look at him. "I'm afraid I have a confession."

His gut clenched. He'd opened up and said something he should've kept to himself. Was this when it all backfired on him? He really hoped not. Nothing he'd seen with Eden over the past few days alluded to that. "What's that?"

"I'm officially addicted to you. You'll never be rid of me. We'll have to have sex at least once a day. Maybe more."

Maks laughed and tightened his arm around her. "I definitely like the sound of that."

She was still smiling when she returned to her original position. "You really are something. If you couldn't tell by how quickly and easily you brought me to orgasm initially, then the second one should have told you that I've not experienced anything like this."

Neither had he. There was so much he wanted to say, but he wasn't sure how. For so long, he'd kept his true thoughts to himself, making sure never to get too close to anyone because it could mean his death or theirs. And yet, he'd ignored his rules and done the exact opposite with Eden. He knew better than that. Both of their lives were at stake. It shouldn't matter how much he craved her.

But it did.

"You got quiet," she said.

He blew out a breath. "Just thinking."

"Okay."

Maks closed his eyes. This was when normal people gave a little insight into what was going through their minds. Or they'd lie, just to make sure their partner didn't think the worst. What did he do? He didn't say anything.

And what was that accomplishing? Most likely putting all kinds of thoughts into Eden's head. He heard it in her voice. She was worried that he regretted what they'd done, when that wasn't it at all. He was worried about *her* and how he was going to get them out of this situation with the Saints.

"I'm not used to talking or carrying on meaningful conversations with people," he explained. "I've always said very little unless I needed information. I don't...*share*...things."

"It's all right. I understand."

"But it isn't fine," he insisted and opened his eyes to watch the firelight dancing on the ceiling of the cave. "We just shared our bodies and have been on the run from killers. You need more from me."

Eden propped herself up on her elbow and met his gaze. "I do, but I'm also cognizant of the fact that you've lived a very different life. You're focused on keeping us alive, and you've done an excellent job so far. I don't want you to change anything just because I want to talk."

"I appreciate all of that. However, I think I'm going to need to compromise. For both of us."

"Then I will, as well," she stated.

Maks smiled up at her. At every turn, she surprised him with her courage, wit, reasoning, and understanding. She tried to hide it, but he saw her terror. He wouldn't have blamed her if she wanted to complain about it, but she hadn't. Not once.

To that end, he pulled her back down against him and said, "I was thinking about you."

"Me?" she asked, surprise in her voice.

"It's been a long time since I let my guard down as I have with you. The last time didn't work out so well."

Eden was silent for a beat. "I know that shaped your world, and it should have. But on the other hand, you need to let that go. You can't continue to base all of your decisions and actions on the fact that one woman was swayed by evil people. I'm not sure you can even blame your girlfriend. You don't know what she was presented with. Obviously, she cared about you, and she did what she thought she needed to do to ensure your safety. Who says I wouldn't do the same? Or you, had you been in her position."

"I've thought about all of that, as well. I forgave her a long time ago. She didn't know what I did, hadn't been through the things I had. There was no way she could've known what to believe and what to ignore. I lay the entire blame on the Saints. They can be very persuasive."

"As you should. They recognized your girlfriend as a weak link to get to you."

Maks felt Eden shiver and pulled the blanket up higher to cover them both. "To allow anyone close to me is to invite death and destruction to both parties."

"The only thing I know about spies is what I've watched in movies."

"They get some of it right, but not all of it."

Eden yawned. "That's probably for the best so not all spy secrets are revealed."

"Lies are our commodity. We deal exclusively in them. I use different names, different jobs, live different lives. I can't remember the last time I told someone my true name."

"Not even the Loughmans?" she asked.

Maks shrugged. "Wyatt knew who I was before, so I never had to tell them. He did."

"How did it feel to be you again?"

He thought about that for a moment. "I wasn't really me. Not even then. Wyatt knew who I was, and while I joined them in the battle—as well as their fight against the Saints—I was still undercover."

"Because you've been fighting against everyone since you know the Saints are everywhere. If you hadn't seen Wyatt and the others fighting the Saints yourself, would you have believed them?"

"No," Maks answered immediately. "I would've feared it was a trap. The Saints do that to people."

"You've had to become the person you are in order to stand against the Saints. You've done what you had to do to survive. I will never judge you for that, and neither should anyone else. Few people could've done what you did. The strength of will and mind that must have taken staggers me. I couldn't have done it."

"I think out of all the people I know, you could have."

Eden chuckled softly. "Thank you for saying that. I fully embrace the wuss that I am."

Maks laughed at the unexpected comment. "I never know what's going to come out of your mouth."

"Good. I'd hate to be predictable."

There was no one else Maks would rather be with at this moment than Eden. She had an unusual and unique way of looking at any situation, no matter how dire. He viewed the world in all its various shades of gray. Eden saw it as it was, taking everything in stride and not judging herself, the situation, or anyone else.

"Alexander Maksim Petrov." He waited a moment as the words sunk in. "That's the name my parents gave me. I went by Alex growing up, but my family always called me Maks. My team members in the military also called me Maks."

"It suits you," Eden said.

"I've gone by so many names, I'm not sure anything sticks anymore."

She shifted her head to look at him. "You went by Maks again this time. Why?"

"It's a common Russian name. And it was easy. Perhaps that was my first mistake."

"That's what I don't understand. After so long working for both the US and Russia as well as the Saints, how did everything blow up in one day?"

He'd been wondering the same thing. "I don't have an answer."

"How close do you think you were to gaining the biggest secrets of the Saints?"

Maks snorted and gave a shake of his head. "I've no idea if it's one person or a group of people. The few times I've heard anything, it was made to sound as if there was a small group. The Elders. That could be something allowed out to throw people off looking for information about the Saints. They've done that before, and I know it for a fact because I was in on it."

"So, what can we believe?"

"That's just it, we can't believe anything we hear. It has to be facts. It's why I spent so long gathering as much intel as I did. The one fact I know is that the Saints have a firm grip on every country around the globe, and they're going to do anything and everything to ensure that it remains that way."

Eden pressed her lips together and looked away. "They won't ever stop coming for us, will they?"

"Not unless we stop them."

"Then I need to get somewhere with a secure internet connection. I've got to keep looking at the intel to find how and why you were targeted."

"And by who," he added.

Eden blew out a breath. "Then there's the text you got that seems to have set all of this off."

"It has to involve Luka somehow. I can't figure out how the old man got my private number or why he would text me."

"And you've no idea what *watch yourself* means?"

Maks used his free hand to scrub down his face. "It could mean any number of things. My first thought was the Saints, of course, but I quickly dismissed that."

"Why?"

"Because I don't think Luka knew about them."

"What if he did?" she pushed.

Maks thought about that for a second. "Everything I've dealt with has been about the Saints. I thought it was too easy to connect Luka to them."

"But you don't know what he was working on or looking into?"

"Not a clue."

"Before you rule out the possibility that he discovered something about the Saints, think about that for a moment."

Maks flattened his lips. "I've looked at Luka from every angle. There's no reason for him to have texted me."

"Unless he knew you had some kind of connection to the Saints."

"If he was looking into the group and he thought I worked for them, then I'd be the last person he reached out to."

Eden rose up on her elbow and said, "Unless he knew you *weren't* working for them."

Maks' mind went blank. He'd believed he was so far undercover that no one would know what he was doing. Obviously, he'd been wrong. Shit. He needed to go back over everything starting...well, starting at the beginning.

He felt Eden's eyes on him, and he met her hazel gaze. "If Luka knew I wasn't working for the Saints, then his message could mean only one thing."

"And what's that?" she pushed.

"I'm in danger."

25

Eden shifted to an upright position, not bothering to hide her nakedness as Maks sat up. The look on his face said that he hadn't considered any of what they'd just discussed. He swung his head to her and raised his brows before looking away. She didn't say anything else, just gave him time to process whatever thoughts were going through his head.

"It seemed too easy to think that Luka connected me to the Saints," Maks said after a few minutes.

"He must have found something that linked you to them. And then somehow unraveled the truth."

Maks turned to her so they faced each other. "You have to understand. Everything I've done over the last years has been to make everyone believe I was doing exactly what they wanted. The CIA believed I was fine spying on Russia. The FSB thought they had turned me into a double agent, and the Saints believed they were controlling me."

"I've no doubt you were great at your

deceptions, but need I point out that you helped the Loughmans?"

He frowned briefly. "Everyone there was killed. Even if I was seen, they couldn't have reported it to anyone."

"Are you sure no one got away?"

Maks opened his mouth to reply, then closed it. "I was sure enough that I went back to my position."

"That's what doesn't make sense. You work for the CIA, the FSB, and the Saints. Who really determines what you're doing?"

"I have handlers I check in with for the CIA and the FSB. The Saints have long stood in the shadows, but I've always known they were there. I did what they wanted, so they left me alone."

Eden twisted her lips. "You slipped away to fight with the Loughmans. Don't you think your absence was noted?"

"I'm often out of contact when I'm undercover on missions."

That gave her pause. "Let me get this straight. You've been undercover for both the CIA and FSB since you joined them. And then, working for both agencies, you went undercover from there to do whatever assignment they wanted you to do?"

"Now do you understand why I said I don't know who I am anymore? There are lies on top of lies on top of lies. Everyone is an enemy. I have to plan a dozen steps ahead in every situation. I'm closely watched, which is why I learned how to disappear when I needed to have some time, gather intel, or help out the Loughmans. I always came back before anyone got concerned that I'd be gone for good."

"Because you knew they'd go after your family."

Maks swallowed and nodded once. "Exactly. When you're a spy like I am, your life isn't your own. The country owns you. For me, I have two countries dictating my life, and a maniacal organization that wants to control me. There are only two ways to get out of this."

"Take down the Saints."

"Or die," he told her.

Eden licked her lips. "I'm going to have to work on the run, and that's fine. I can shift through documents on the computer once they've downloaded, but I need to get everything off the pen drives."

"What about searches on the internet? Won't you need that?"

"Yes, but I'll try to limit that as much as I can. This place would be perfect for getting some work done, there isn't a secure connection."

Maks ran a hand through his blond locks. "We're going to need to get to a city for that."

That meant leaving the safety of the cave and going back out into the snow. Eden wasn't looking forward to that in the least. But if she wanted to have any kind of life, that meant they had to leave the cave.

"We'll wait here until the day after tomorrow. We'll set out at dawn then," he told her.

Eden's insides melted at the idea of having all that time alone with Maks. It was a nice break in the hectic speed with which they'd been moving since he came into her life. The knowledge that every day she couldn't get to the intel he'd collected was another day that the Saints ruled was always in the back of her mind, though.

Maks rose and added more logs to the fire. He'd stacked them neatly in a pile, and by the look of them, they had been there for some time. Which meant he'd had this place ready and waiting for just such an event. She glanced at the pile and knew they would have enough for at least another day.

He kneeled on the other side of the fire and looked over the flames at her. "The snow covered your tracks, which means they'll cover mine for anyone looking for us. We're safe here."

For now, went unsaid.

"I know," she told him and let her gaze move over his gorgeous body. The front of him was just as muscular and defined as his back. More so, actually.

"You should rest."

She lifted one shoulder, noting that his gaze dropped to her bare breasts. "I'm not sleepy."

One blond brow quirked at her statement.

"I didn't say I wasn't exhausted. I said I wasn't sleepy. There's a difference. There's too much going on for my brain to shut down enough for me to sleep. At least, for the moment."

He straightened, the movement purposeful and slow. The more she watched him, the more she realized that he wasted no energy. Everything he did, every move he made, had a reason and justification. She was curious about how he'd trained his brain to look at the world. Or perhaps he hadn't trained it. Maybe he'd been born that way. Either way, it astounded her.

"What?" he asked with a tilt of his head.

She grinned and said, "I was just wondering how your brain works. You know, how you see things and make decisions. It's much different than mine."

"There is no doubt in that." He walked around the fire and joined her back on the blanket. "I look for danger and enemies everywhere, and based on that, I can determine how to react and what actions are needed."

"I understand that when we've been running from the Saints. But in everyday life, as well?"

Maks nodded. "Absolutely. Even when I'm not on assignment and have some free time, I never let my guard down. That's when spies are killed. They believe they can forget for a little while. That's not the case. It's how I was able to determine that I had men following me in Amsterdam."

"When this is over, do you plan on staying a spy?"

A nondescript sound came from the back of his throat. "You mean if I make it out of this alive."

"You will. You're a survivor. I've learned that about you."

He lifted one shoulder in a shrug and looked away. "*If* I survive, I plan on disappearing to a remote region of the world to live out my days."

That shocked her. "You wouldn't go back to your family?"

"It's better for them if they think I'm dead."

"Not if the threat is over."

"But it won't ever be over. Not really. The CIA will be upset that I want out. They don't just readily give up their agents. Then there's the FSB.

You think they're going to freely let me go? Both agencies will worry about what I might tell the other country."

Eden hadn't thought about that part. "After all you've done, you're the one person who deserves a happy ending."

His gaze slid back to her. "I'm the last person who does. After all the lives I've taken, all the horrible deeds I've done?"

"You did it for a greater purpose."

"There are arguments against that very statement."

"I don't give a shit about everyone else. I'm talking about you. You risked your life for me. Granted, you wanted something from me, but even after that, you could've walked away. You didn't. You're a guardian. You always have been, and you always will be." She reached over and put her hand on his.

He turned his hand so their palms met, and then he slipped his fingers between hers. "You can be very convincing. Do you know that?"

"When I want someone to know the truth, yes," she stated with a bright smile.

Maks tugged her against him as they stretched out once more. She found a comfortable spot with her head resting on his chest. They stayed there for a long time in silence. Her eyes closed, and she was more relaxed than she had been in days. It didn't matter that it was freezing outside or that they were in a cave with no modern amenities. She was in the arms of a man who made her feel special. That was priceless and worth everything she'd endured.

Suddenly, his voice filled the cave. "It's not that I don't want a life after this. I do. Very much."

"Then don't give up on it."

"The moment I set out on this path, I knew that it would likely mean my death. But if it frees the world from the Saints, then it's worth the cost."

His words made her heart hurt. Not because she didn't understand why he said what he did, but because she didn't want to think of a world without him. "You've survived this long. You might survive it all."

"That would be nice."

"And if you could have the life you want? Do you know what you'd do? Where you'd go?"

His chest rose as he drew in a deep breath. "I'd go home to my family. If I were really lucky, I might find someone to spend my life with."

It was crazy that Eden hoped that was her. She barely knew Maks, but she could actually envision a life with him. That's usually how she made decisions. If she could envision whatever it was—be it a person or a thing—in her life, then she took the leap. She'd forced many, many relationships, thinking that just because she couldn't see herself with someone, it didn't mean it wouldn't work.

When she thought about the future, she could see Maks and her together. Maybe it was the fact that her body was still floating from the intense pleasure it had received. Or perhaps it was because the truth was right before her.

"We should all be so lucky," Eden finally responded.

"You don't think you will?"

She chuckled and reached for the blanket to

cover her feet that were getting chilled. "I don't exactly have a good history when it comes to dating."

"And long relationships?"

"Three. I dated a guy for two years in high school, but it didn't last once we graduated. I met a guy my junior year of college, and we dated for a year and a half, but he really wanted a wife who stayed home and took care of the kids. That wasn't me. Then I was with another guy for three years. I really thought that would work, but we realized that we were better as friends than lovers."

Maks made a sound in the back of his throat. "Do you regret any of the relationships ending."

"Nope. Was I hurt? Of course. There's always hurt, but part of being in relationships is learning what you like, what you need, what you hate, and what you know you can and can't do without."

"I think I'm going to need to relearn all of that."

She chuckled and glanced up at him. "I can safely say you're on the right track."

"Well, that's good news," he said with a wide grin.

The wind whistled outside the cave as the fire popped. Who would've thought she'd be in a cave in Romania with a hot-as-fuck spy while on the run from evil people?

Certainly not her.

26

"What do you mean, you lost them?" Janice demanded through the mobile phone.

The agent on the other end of the line began giving excuse after excuse.

"I don't want to hear about snow or the fucking conditions," she told him, cutting him off. "You were sent out there with a team of our best men, and you can't track down two people?"

"Ma'am, one of them is as trained as we are," he stated.

She rolled her eyes. "And? The woman isn't. She'll slow him down."

"She may not be trained, but she's capable because we've not found any sign of her either."

Janice squeezed the phone as rage filled her. "They can't have gone far if the weather is as bad as you say it is. It's winter in Romania."

"We'll keep looking," he replied in a testing tone.

"You bet your ass, you will. If you see them, kill them."

There was a beat before he said, "We were told to bring them in alive."

"Who told you that?" she demanded. "You're taking orders from me, and I never said that."

"The order came after we arrived here. And no, ma'am, it didn't come from you."

Janice's gut clenched. The only people who knew she'd been told to bring Maks in alive were the Elders. That meant they'd contacted the team that she'd sent out. Did they do it because they didn't think she'd carry out their orders? If that was the case, then she was surprised she was still in her position. The Elders didn't mess around when someone failed.

"Ma'am?"

She swallowed and cleared her throat. "You have your orders. Follow them."

"I just want to be clear that we'll be bringing the couple in alive."

"If you find them."

The agent's voice went hard as he said, "Oh, we'll find them."

Janice disconnected from the call and looked around her office. At one time, everything had gone her way. She hadn't aspired to run this division of the Saints, but she was glad she had taken the job. It had gotten her close to those in the Saints who could help her attain the positions she really wanted.

Never in her dreams did she think some IB and a spy would ruin her hopes. She had all kinds of resources at her disposal, and yet she couldn't bring either of them in. There had been only one threat to her, but it was that one threat that scared her most of all.

The sound of her phone ringing split the silence. Her head jerked to the mobile lying on the desk. Her heart was pounding as she reached for the phone and saw there was no caller ID. With shaking hands, she answered. "Hello?"

"I thought we discussed this."

The moment the male voice, raspy with age, reached her, she closed her eyes. "We did."

"Then why are Maks and the woman still not in custody?"

Janice swallowed hard. "They got lucky. They'll be brought in today."

"Hmm," came the reply. "And what is your explanation for not following my orders explicitly?"

"I-I don't know what you mean?"

"You know *exactly* what I mean. I said I wanted Maks brought in alive. Yet you told your team to take a shot if they had it."

It was on the tip of her tongue to lie, but she thought better of it. No one but the team she'd called upon to track Maks and Eden had known what her order was. So, either one of them had told on her... or...her office was bugged. Janice didn't even have to wonder. She realized that she was being spied on.

"Wise of you not to try and lie," he told her. "You've been good for us, Janice. You've always done what was expected and beyond. Look how far you've come. However," he said with a dramatic pause, "if you continue in this vein, then everything will be snuffed out like a candle. You're upset that Maks and the woman are eluding you. He's one of our very best. It was never going to be easy bringing him in."

She drew in a deep breath. "Sir, he could know sensitive secrets. Wouldn't it be better if he was eliminated?"

"Without a doubt."

"I don't understand," she said with a frown.

He sighed loudly, letting her know that he was irritated. "It isn't for you to know. It's for you to follow orders."

"Yes, sir."

"I hope you can, Janice. Your family has been a part of us for generations. I knew your father well. I was the one who placed your sister in our organization. Your family has an unblemished reputation. You wouldn't want to ruin that now, would you?"

It was a low blow for him to bring up her family since she was estranged from them. But Janice got the point. "No, sir, I wouldn't."

"That's good to hear. Now, bring in Maks and Eden so we can put an end to all of this. Today."

The line went dead. Janice didn't slam the phone down. If her office was bugged, they were no doubt watching her, as well. She knew for a fact that the Saints monitored others in the organization. Why did she think she was above that? Because her family was well known in the group?

She wanted to roll her eyes but managed to hold back just in time. Janice walked around her desk and went to sit down. She stilled, feeling the hairs on the back of her neck rise. Just as she was about to turn and see if there was a camera behind her, she stopped herself. Instead, she called back the unit of men she'd sent after Maks and Eden. The commander picked up on the second ring.

"Tell me everything that happened last night," she said. "Including exact locations."

27

He didn't want it to end. Maks wished he could stop time. The past thirty-three hours had been the best of his life. Not once had he or Eden put on clothes. They had slept in each other's arms, made love numerous times, and talked about everything.

Maks couldn't remember ever speaking so much at one time, but he had really enjoyed it. Eden's take on things made him pause and look at stuff from her point of view. He didn't always agree with her, but it was nice to get someone's fresh outlook. The fact that she was willing to see his side spoke to how openminded she was.

And her body. His cock twitched, growing hard just thinking about the many and various ways they'd pleasured each other. He knew for sure that he would never tire of her. He could wake up beside her every day for the rest of his life and be a happy man.

She lay sleeping in his arms after they'd had passionate sex. He'd been unable to sleep, though he had rested his eyes, body, and mind. Now, he envisioned what it would be like as they left the cave. There was a nearby village, which the Saints would no doubt be watching. It was where someone in their predicament would head. But not Maks.

His gaze slid to Eden. The trek was going to be difficult, but he knew she could make it. He'd make sure of it.

"You're staring," she murmured before her eyes fluttered open and she smiled at him.

His lips curved in response. "You're just so damn cute when you sleep. Do you know you snore?"

She was instantly affronted. "I do not."

"Light, baby snores," he said with a smile he couldn't contain.

She flattened her lips and gave him a playful slap on his abdomen. "Very funny."

The easy way they teased each other wasn't something Maks was used to, but he enjoyed it. He hadn't had this kind of effortless relationship in... well, ages. The fact that it was so easy gave him pause. But how could he turn away from something that made him feel so good?'

Eden rubbed her nose, then stretched after yawning. "It's time, isn't it?"

"Just about. I was letting you sleep as long as I could."

She sat up and pulled her knees to her chest as she looked at the entrance. "I have to admit, I'm loath to leave the warmth here and venture back out into the cold. How far do we have to go?"

"It's a bit."

Her head swiveled to him as she raised a brow. "A bit? Is that calculated in miles, perhaps?"

He chuckled and sat up. "It's longer than you'd like, but shorter than I would've gone on my own."

"Ah. That's as clear as mud."

"I thought you'd like that."

"I had no idea you were such a smartass," she replied with a grin.

The smile slowly slipped from his face. "We could stay another day."

"No," she said with a shake of her dark blond locks. "We've had a respite. It's time we get things back on track. We've had more time than I expected, and it was nice. The world might not know it needs saving, but that doesn't mean we sit here. We've got work to do."

Maks rose to his feet and held out his hand. He pulled Eden up beside him and looked into her hazel eyes. She flashed him a smile then turned and began to dress. Maks did the same. When he finished, he put out the fire so their eyes could become adjusted to the darkness.

"It isn't quite dawn yet," he told her. "We'll head out so the darkness can give us cover."

"Makes sense."

They sat in silence for several minutes. Maks finally reached next to him and took her hand in his. "I need you to remember everything I'm about to tell you."

"Okay. Why?"

"If something happens to me, you've got to keep going."

"What?" she said in outrage. "You're talking nonsense."

He shook his head. "I'm not, and you know it. They nearly took a shot at you the other night. They're looking to kill, which I expected."

"Oh," she whispered in a soft voice.

Maks swallowed and wished he could see her face. "We're going to leave here and head west."

"West," she repeated.

"There is a village at the base of the mountain, but we're not going there because the Saints will be waiting for us. We're going to continue heading west. If something happens to me, get to Oradea and the train station there. Look for locker D33."

"Oradea train station. Locker D33."

He smiled even though she couldn't see it. "That's right. The ticket to gain access is in my jacket pocket."

"Okay."

"There's a burner phone in there, programmed with the Loughmans' number. Call them, and they can get you to a safe location and then out of the country."

Eden blew out a breath. "I'll never remember all of that."

"Sure, you will."

"No. My brain doesn't work that way."

He tightened his fingers on her hand. "Keep saying it over and over to yourself. I need to know that you'll be able to get away."

Maks could just make out the outline of her body, and he saw her turn her head to the side. He could only imagine what was running through her mind at this moment. There was a lot between them and Oradea, namely the Saints, the weather, and the mountain. There were so many variables, so many things that could go wrong. He would have to keep them moving fast in order to stay out of sight of the Saints.

Eden was stronger than she knew, and she was intelligent. Her instinct to survive would kick in, and she'd be fine. That was if he could get her off the mountain. That was the only thing that made him pause.

"I can do it," she finally said.

He pulled her against him and wrapped his arms around her. She held him tightly, neither saying the words they wanted. Maks had never shied away from a mission, no matter how dangerous. He wasn't scared of the Saints or what they'd do to him if he were caught.

But he was terrified of what they'd do to Eden.

More than that, he didn't want what he had found with Eden in the cave to end. For the first time in eons, he'd been able to be himself. He hadn't lied or had to pretend to be anyone else. He wasn't pushing for information from her or watching his words so he didn't say something he shouldn't. It had been the most relaxing, amazing time.

And now, it was ending.

"We're going to come back here," she said.

He smiled and leaned back as she looked up at him. "Yes. When this is all over, you and I are coming right back here for as long as we want."

"Right after you take me to dinner."

"Exactly," he said with a chuckle.

She cleared her throat. "Well, now that we've got that figured out, we should head out."

"Yes." But he didn't release her.

They stood as they were for another few minutes, each taking in every second they could. Finally, he bent down and retrieved her coat and then helped her put it on. He slipped his own jacket on and fastened it against the cold.

As he walked to the entrance, he paused and turned to her, pulling her into his arms for one last, lingering kiss. He ended it as she pressed her cheek against his chest. When she stepped back, both of them retrieved their packs and settled them on their shoulders.

"Let me have a look first," he told her.

Maks moved the opening just enough to unlatch the cover and look outside. The darkness allowed him to hide a bit, but also anyone else. When he didn't see anything near, he slipped outside and pressed himself against the side of the mountain. His gaze swept the area, including the path to the cave. He spotted bear tracks that were a few hours old, going in the opposite direction they were headed.

Several minutes ticked by as he waited for any movement. Finally, he said Eden's name. She came out just as he did. Once he made sure the covering to the cave was secure once more, he moved in front of Eden, and they began walking. The snow was higher than before, but it was packed, allowing them to move somewhat easier than when they had come to the mountain. Maks was happy with the distance they were covering, but he checked over his shoulder often to see if anyone was coming up behind them.

The sky lightened from black to gray to pale blue. In the distance, he saw a storm headed their way. All he could hope for was that it moved slowly. Luck wasn't on their side, however. The storm reached them within the hour, bringing with it gusts of wind and thick snowfall. The middle of a blizzard was no time to be out on a mountain, but there was no turning back for them now. Their only choice was to keep going.

Maks took Eden's hand so they could stay together. The wind whipped around them, making it impossible for them to talk. He had to slow their pace some, but even then, they were still making headway.

What felt like an eternity later, the wind finally died down enough that they weren't walking against it. He halted to give them a rest, and Eden collapsed against a tree.

"It's official. I hate winter. I most especially detest blizzards," she said.

He chuckled as he handed her a water bottle. "You dreaming of a beach?"

"You know it. White sand, turquoise waters, and a fruity alcoholic beverage in my hand, complete with a tiny umbrella. I've asked the bartender for extra cherries, and he's gladly complied."

"Extra cherries, huh?" Maks learned something new about her constantly.

She nodded her head, her eyes closed. "Yep. They're particularly good in the hot sun against the clear blue sky."

"Anyone with you?"

Her eyes opened as she brought the water to her lips and drank. Then she said, "You."

"Hmm. I've not been to a beach in some time. Do you have a favorite?"

"Nope. I'm easy. Just somewhere I can wear a bathing suit and not freeze my tush off."

Maks smiled as he looked around. The freshly fallen snow was going to make it harder for them to walk, but there was no way around it. "You've talked me into it. I definitely need a vacation."

"Without a doubt. I'll make all the plans. All you need to do is show up."

"That I can do."

She pushed away from the tree and handed him what was left of the water. "I'm okay."

"I know."

He finished the water and stowed the empty bottle in his pack. There was only one left, along with two protein bars. It was going to have to last them until they reached their destination.

bit. Eden rolled her eyes as she recalled how long Maks had said the journey would be. She couldn't see the sun behind the clouds, but she was certain it was somewhere above them, which meant they'd been walking for hours.

At first, she'd been doing just fine. Then the blizzard hit. Eden had nearly been pulled off her feet from the wind a couple of times. Had Maks not had her hand, she was certain she would've been.

As difficult as that was, it was nothing compared to moving through thick, freshly fallen snow. Her jeans were damp, and her toes were numb. She really did hate anything to do with snow and winter now. It didn't matter how much she envisioned lying on a beach or sitting in a sauna, nothing was going to warm her until she got out of the weather and into dry clothes.

Maks made her repeat where she would go if anything happened to him at least every two minutes. Well, she might be exaggerating. It might be every three minutes, but she had to admit that she wasn't going to forget it now.

She watched him, wondering how he could keep going as if the cold wasn't affecting him. He was like a machine. Except she knew for a fact that he was all man. Hot, hard, and mouthwatering.

"You're staring," he threw her words from this morning back at her.

Eden laughed. "You're pretty hot, do you know that?"

"If you say so."

"Pffft. You know you are."

He glanced at her, grinning. "As long as you think it, that's all that matters."

"I bet women fall all over you, don't they?"

"I'll admit that I don't have a hard time getting women, if that's what you want to know."

She found herself getting a little jealous. It was her fault, though. She's the one who brought it up.

He tugged her closer. "I only want you, though."

That brought a smile to her face. "Thank you for saying that."

"It's the truth."

Suddenly it didn't matter that she was becoming a human popsicle. She was with Maks, who said he wanted her, and only her.

He halted and faced her. "You believe me?"

"Yes. Of course."

"I have a surprise for you."

She raised her brows. "You found us a beach?"

"Nearly as good. Look," he said and glanced to the side.

She followed his gaze and spotted the roofs of houses that made up a village. Her eyes teared up. "Really? We're here?"

"Ready to get warm?"

"Do you even have to ask that?"

He chuckled as they set off to the village. Maks took them around to the back of some businesses and brought them through narrow alleys. His gaze moved constantly, and she knew he was searching for Saints. The problem was, they could be anywhere.

"We'll only be here a little while," he told her.

"As long as I can get warm."

"And hopefully get a secure connection."

That brightened her day. "That would be fabulous."

True to his word, Maks found them a small house on the edge of the village that looked as if it hadn't had occupants in over a month. There was a fine coating of dust everywhere. While she set down her pack and removed her coat, Maks checked around inside the house.

"You want to make use of the shower while I check around outside?" he asked.

As if she would refuse that. Eden wanted to take a long shower, but she made it a quick one. It warmed her and allowed her to get into clean clothes. She hurried back downstairs to find Maks waiting for her.

"I feel like a new woman," she said with a smile.

He winked at her. "Everything is good here. I'm going to get us some food. I'll be back shortly. You need anything?"

"I can do some work with the files we have printed."

"Lock the door behind me. I'll knock three times, pause, and then knock once more."

He gave her a quick kiss, then was gone.

Eden locked the door and went to her pack, where she took out the files on the Saints. She took them to the sofa and spread them out on the floor before her. She was missing something, but she couldn't figure out what it was. She needed to see it a different way, but she wasn't sure how long they'd be here. She needed to be able to gather everything together quickly.

Still, she pulled out a piece of paper and began to list what she knew in order of when it happened. She was on the third sheet when the knock startled her. Eden jumped but counted the three knocks. There was a pause, then one single knock.

With her heart pounding, she got to her feet and went to the door to unlock it. She opened it an inch to look outside and saw bright blue eyes staring at her. With a sigh, she opened the door.

"Everything all right?" Maks asked as he walked in.

She closed and locked the door after him. "I was just immersed in work, and you startled me."

"Sorry about that."

That's when she smelled the food. She hurried to the kitchen after him. "What did you get?"

"As much as I could. Help yourself," he said as he took packages out of the bag.

Eden was famished and began eating the first thing she opened. She had no idea what it was, and she didn't care. All that mattered was that it was food and not another protein bar, though she was thankful for them when they would've starved.

"Did you see anything concerning?" she asked.

Maks shook his head. "Not at all, which means I need to be worried."

"The Saints are everywhere."

"That they are. I paid a young boy to get the food so I didn't have to go into the store."

She nodded, impressed. "Great idea."

"It's getting late, so we might be able to stay the night, but we should probably only stay a little while."

"Where are we headed, exactly?"

He shrugged as he finished his food and set the empty container aside. "I have no idea. I'm just trying to stay ahead of the Saints to give you time to work."

She took another bite, wondering how long they could keep it up.

"What is it?" he pressed.

Eden shrugged one shoulder. "Not only do I need a secure internet connection, but I need time to work, to spread this out and look at everything in multiple ways."

"Which you can't do with us moving constantly."

She twisted her lips as she wrinkled her nose. "No. Sorry."

"Internet means a city with reliable service. I had thought Oradea was a last resort, but it might be exactly what we need."

"How far is that?"

"Not far if we take a car."

And by take, he meant steal. Eden didn't like taking things that weren't hers, but desperate times called for desperate measures.

"The earlier, the better?" she asked.

He nodded and wiped his mouth with a paper napkin. "The good thing about these small villages is that they don't have CCTV cameras."

"That you know of."

"Sometimes people see more than cameras. Trust me, I know how to keep my head down. You finish up here. I spotted a few vehicles that could be what we need. I'll find us one and come back for you."

Eden followed him to the door, locking it once more as she returned to her meal. As she finished eating, she put on her boots, hating that they were still cold from their mountain trek. At least this time they would be in a car. Hopefully, one with a functional heater. Either way, she wasn't walking in the snow, and that made her night.

She finished packing away the food and making sure everything was in the same place it had been when they arrived when Maks knocked on the door with his code. She let him in, and they gathered their belongings before they climbed into the stolen car. In moments, they were out on the road.

"Do you think someone will notice the vehicle is gone?"

He shook his head as he drove. "It'll be a little while. We'll change cars before then."

"Oh."

And just like that, she found that living a life of crime wasn't as bad as she'd thought it would be. Of course, she wasn't really living such a life. She was just trying to survive by doing whatever she could.

29

Loughman Ranch
Texas

Callie rubbed her tired eyes and closed them for just a moment. They felt like sandpaper, but she'd already tried to sleep. Wyatt had been happy to be woken up for sex, but not even that could help her get some rest.

She lowered her face into her hands as her elbows rested on the desk. Stressed didn't begin to cover what she felt. When Wyatt asked what was causing such an emotion, she couldn't pinpoint it. It was just a feeling from the overwatch she'd been doing around the world.

The problem with that was there was *so much*. They had all believed that the Saints were everywhere, but to realize they truly *were* everywhere left her sick to her stomach. Everyone at the ranch was actively working on ways to expose and bring down the organization. The problem was that they didn't have anything concrete to go on. It was all circumstantial.

And since they couldn't put faces or names to those who ran the secretive group, they were shooting in the dark.

At least Maks was out there looking, as well. If only she'd heard from him again and knew he was all right. It was ridiculous, really. Maks was perfectly capable of taking care of himself as he had for years. But he was part of their family now. He'd risked his life to help them, and she wanted to make sure he didn't need help now.

"You can't keep doing this," Wyatt said as he came into the room.

Callie jerked her head up and found him holding two cups in his hands.

"Don't get too happy," he told her as he handed her a mug. "It's herbal tea. You've had enough caffeine."

She shot him an annoyed look, even as she knew he was right. "Thank you."

"You're going to make yourself sick if you keep this up."

"I can't help it. I know there's something big coming, but I don't know what."

His dark brows drew together as he lowered himself into the rolling chair next to her. "You haven't mentioned anything like that."

"I don't know." She shook her head and set aside the mug. "It's just a feeling. I shouldn't have put it in those words because I have no context. We haven't heard from Maks, we still have nothing concrete on anyone high up in the Saints, and I'm exhausted and probably seeing things that aren't there."

"You don't see things that aren't there. Maybe

it's because you're so tired that you can't see exactly what it is."

She hated to admit it, but he was probably right. Wyatt was always right. And she was definitely not going to tell her man that. "My eyes do hurt."

"Come on," he said as he took her hand and pulled her up as he stood. "If nothing else, come to bed and just lay in my arms to rest your eyes and your brain."

Her tea and the computers forgotten, Callie let Wyatt pull her to their bedroom in the bunker below the ground. The others had been asleep for hours. Living in such tight quarters with everyone made for an interesting dynamic. There were frayed nerves and tempers, but the one thing they all did was their best to get past something, forgive, and try to do better the next time.

Wyatt lay atop the covers in the darkened room and held out his arms for her. Callie crawled in beside him and rested her head on his chest—her favorite spot—as his arms came around her. She closed her eyes and let herself relax.

"It's going to be okay," Wyatt said in a low voice.

She swallowed. "I'm not sure it is."

"We defeated the Saints twice. With the chemical Ragnarök, and when they came to kill us."

"I know all of that, and believe me, I think about it every day. But, honey, they're a massive organization that has hundreds of thousands at their beck and call."

"And we have just shy of a dozen people."

She nodded, keeping her eyes closed. "Exactly.

They could've wiped us out that day. They could've brought more and more men in. Why didn't they?"

"Because it would have drawn too much attention and scrutiny to themselves."

"That's a load of bull, and you know it."

Wyatt released a long breath. "All I know is that we've succeeded where others failed. We have a good team with people we can trust."

"And we're pinned down here because if we go out, we'll probably be killed."

He put his hand on her head and kissed her forehead. "Callie, I love you more than life itself. I'd do anything for you. I also know you're a worrier, but I trust your instincts. If you think there's something, then there's something."

"I don't know anymore."

"Stop thinking, babe. Just rest."

Knowing she didn't have any other choice, Callie did just that. Her mind drifted, and she found herself falling asleep. She eagerly reached for it, grasping it like a lifeline. Because she had to be on top of her game for Wyatt and the rest of her family. All of them needed her because while she could direct them, she was the only one who knew how to hack into places. And that's where she knew the best information would be.

Her thoughts melted, one by one, as she fell deeper and deeper into sleep. Suddenly, a clip from a news broadcast playing in the background of her computer ran through her mind. She stiffened and jerked upright.

"Babe? What is it?" Wyatt asked, his deep voice filled with concern.

A foreboding chill ran down Callie's spine. "I hope nothing."

"What do you need?" He was already swinging his legs over the bed as he sat up.

Callie rushed from the bed, slipping on the floor in her socks as she raced to her computer. She prayed she was misremembering what she'd heard. The news from all over the world ran as background noise as she worked. It made it easy for her to switch over to certain countries if she needed something.

She reached her desk and didn't bother to sit in the chair as she began typing on the keyboard, her heart hammering in her chest.

"Callie, you're scaring the shit out of me," Wyatt stated.

She hit enter. The clip from earlier pulled up, her translation software on the computer translating the German to English. The floor felt as if it tipped sideways. This. This is what had been nagging at her for hours.

"Callie?"

Slowly, she turned to face Wyatt. "We were so stupid."

His gold eyes glanced at the computer monitor before focusing on her. "What are you talking about?"

"This," she said and stepped to the side so he could see the news clip.

Her gaze never left his face as he watched the entire thing. Twice. Only when he returned his eyes to her did she feel the first sting of tears. Wyatt said nothing as he pulled her into his arms. For several minutes, they stayed as they were.

"We thought we won," she whispered. "Turns out, the Saints are having the last laugh."

Wyatt pulled back to look at her. "The scientist told us we had the only sample. He's dead now, so he can't make any more. We know the Saints couldn't reproduce Ragnarök."

"This isn't Ragnarök. This virus is something else entirely. It first came on the news a few weeks ago. I didn't pay much attention because I figured it was just another type of flu that comes every few years. It's already killed several hundred people in two weeks. Something like this doesn't just happen. This is the Saints."

"Can you pull up how far this is spreading?"

"I'll get you everything you want to know."

He issued a nod. "Start. I'll wake the others."

Callie watched him walk away before she sat in her chair and rolled up to her desk. Then she began keying in all the information she was searching for. A map of the world filled one screen, and as she found outbreaks of this new virus, she added them to the map, showing the spread. She was just finishing by the time everyone walked in.

"I fucking hate the Saints," Cullen stated angrily.

Callie licked her lips. "They haven't named it yet, but as you can see, it has traveled fast in two weeks." She typed in another set of words and hit enter. "I've projected that in another two weeks, it'll have covered all of Europe and half of North America. A week after that, the rest of the world will be hit."

Owen blew out a breath. "Do we know where it originated?"

"Germany. It's spread through touch, sneezing, and coughing. The regular things."

Natalie glanced at Owen before she and Mia exchanged worried glances.

Kate, who was a medical doctor and had fallen in love with the patriarch of the family, Orrin, said, "I read about this. At first, it was only thought to be another strain of the flu. Obviously, someone got it wrong."

"Maybe on purpose," Wyatt said.

Orrin crossed his arms over his chest. "Callie's right. This is the Saints. I knew they would come at us again. We should've thought it would be with something biological. We need to hope for the best and prepare for the worst. That means we need to contact Lev and Reyna as well as seeing about getting ahold of Maks. He's in Europe. He needs to watch out for this."

"I'm calling Lev now," Cullen said as he pulled out his mobile.

Wyatt met her gaze. "Try Maks. Maybe we'll get lucky and get him."

Callie called Maks again and again, but there was no answer. The grim faces of her family made the knot in her stomach tighten. She started to dial Maks again when Wyatt put his hand over hers.

"Baby, you need to rest."

She shook her head. "I can't."

"You have to," Kate said. "We need you, and you need to stay healthy. We all do. Rest is the best thing right now."

Orrin nodded in agreement with his lover. "I'll stay up and continue trying to get Maks. I have a few other numbers we can try."

"We'll take turns," Mia said. "You've done enough. Get some sleep."

Knowing when everyone was against her, Callie rose and let Wyatt take her back to their room. She wasn't expecting to sleep with everything going on. But in the safety of Wyatt's arms, she found that she soon drifted away into the nothingness of slumber.

30

Maks grew more and more concerned the longer he drove. It wasn't odd for some parts of Romania to be desolate instead of the hubbub of bigger cities. But something was going on. Groups of people were outside of stores, fighting to get in while some houses looked to be boarded up.

This was new. He glanced at Eden to find her sleeping. They had changed cars twice now. Maks turned on the radio and found a station with a news brief. All that was being talked about was some kind of virus spreading fast throughout Europe. Apparently, it was something new that no known antibiotics or antivirals could handle. In fact, several hundred people had already died from it.

His thoughts immediately went to the Saints. This was exactly something they would do. They had wanted to unleash Ragnarök upon the world. He couldn't get many facts, like where the virus had started, if any medical officials knew where it had come from, or how quickly it was spreading.

He kept the radio volume down as he

continued listening. Every twenty minutes or so there was a new update, and each time the number of individuals who were showing symptoms of the disease increased. It wasn't until he heard that it began in Germany that he grew more concerned than before.

Maks took in mention of the symptoms. He did a scan of his body both mentally and physically to see if he had any of them. Then he looked at Eden. He couldn't see anything with his eyes, but he'd ask her once she woke.

If the chaos was happening in the small villages, he could only imagine how much worse it would be in the cities. Unfortunately, that's where they needed to go for the secure internet. But did he want to chance either of their lives? They'd been doing that from the moment they set out to destroy the Saints. It didn't matter if it was a bullet or a virus, the Saints were gunning for them.

"So be it," Maks murmured and continued driving.

They were forty minutes outside of Oradea when Eden woke. She stretched and covered her mouth when she yawned. Her hazel eyes sought him as she smiled. "I needed that, apparently."

"It's all that sex you wanted."

She laughed. "It had nothing to do with you keeping me up to have sex."

He smiled at the easy way they joked. "All right. You win. I'll take half the blame."

"Actually, I'm pretty sure it was all me." She reached over and touched his arm.

Little gestures like that always affected him deeply. He was coming to seek out Eden's touch.

And he knew that the more he did it, the more he would fall for her. Falling? He wasn't fooling anyone. He had already fallen head over heels for her, and it didn't matter when. It had happened without him even knowing it. Not that he could've stopped it had he wanted to.

And he didn't want to.

"You okay?" she asked, a tinge of worry in her voice.

Maks turned off the radio. "I noticed people acting weird."

"Weird how?"

"Fighting to get groceries and drawing curtains closed."

Eden's brows drew together. "Like they were hiding from something."

"Yeah. A flu-like virus, apparently. It began in Germany a few weeks ago. The death toll is what has gained everyone's interest, as well as how fast it's spreading."

"And how fast *is* it spreading?"

He glanced at her. "Fast. Only the remotest of regions in Europe are unaffected. It's gotten into Russia, Asia, and Africa. The first case in the States has also been reported."

"These super flu bugs happen about every other year." She shrugged. "That's all this is, right?"

"Remember when I told you about Ragnarök?"

She nodded slowly, her face going pale. "You think this is the Saints."

"With the rate this is moving through people and the death toll of those infected, it has all the earmarks of the Saints. And those other superbugs you spoke about? I know for a fact that the Saints were involved with one of them. My guess is that they had their hand in all of them. Testing them to see how quickly it could move."

"I think I'm going to be sick," she said and turned her head to look out the window.

Maks sent her a worried glance. "Do I need to pull over?"

"No. I just...why is this happening? Why does this have to happen?" She looked at him then. "Who the hell are these people that they think they can make decisions like this? They're not God. They can't decide when it's someone's time to die, and they certainly don't have the right to unleash some virus on the world and then sit back and watch as thousands perish."

Maks felt the pain in her words, her helplessness and anger. He understood it all because they were the same emotions he felt within himself. "Now more than ever, I'm positive the Saints need to be ended. We're going to find someplace to hide out. You'll get to work, and I'll make sure we have food and anything else we need."

"You can't go out there. You could get infected."

"We might already be infected."

She swallowed and took a deep breath. "What are the symptoms?"

He rattled them off as she said no to each one. "I'm fine, as well."

"Good."

The silence that filled the car was fraught with tension and agitation. When Maks reached the edges of the city, he noticed that there were few people on the streets. Those who were, had their arms laden with bags of food as they rushed home.

"Where are we going to stay?" Eden asked.

Maks had prepared for all kinds of eventualities, but not this one. How did one prepare for a pandemic? "I'll find us something."

They drove past stores where fights were breaking out over food, and authorities struggled to keep the peace. Restaurants were getting takeout orders faster than they could make the food. Visitors were desperately trying to get on trains, buses, and planes to get home.

"It has an apocalyptic feel to it," Eden said in a small voice.

Maks had to agree with her. He drove around the city three times, searching for a place. With the hysteria, he wanted to make sure he found the right spot. He'd circled the block a few times, noting that one of the finer houses looked unoccupied. He pulled the car to the side of the road and parked.

"Stay here. Keep the doors locked," he told her.

Eden nodded, her eyes wide as she watched him.

"I'll be right back."

"Hurry," she said.

Maks got out and closed the door. Immediately, there was a click as she locked it. He smiled inwardly as he went to the sidewalk and walked back the way he'd come. The guest house was yellow with a Spanish-style roof and a wrought iron fence. He glanced around him to see if anyone was watching as he approached the gate. It took little for him to pick the lock and open it.

Then he went up the path to the stairs. He

climbed them and stood in front of the wooden door. A look into the glass on the door showed that no one was home. Once more, he picked the lock and opened the door.

Maks said hello in Romanian, but no one answered. He quickly went from room to room and found it as deserted as he'd hoped. He hurried back outside and went to the car. In short order, he had his pack, and Eden stood beside him with hers. He put his hand on the small of her back and guided her to number 27.

She said nothing as he closed the gate behind him, locking it. Only when they were inside, did she let out a sigh. "This is a nice place."

"It's a guest house, and the owner rents out rooms. I think we got lucky that no one was here."

"How did you know about this place?"

"I keep my eye on a couple of houses in each country in case I need a place to hide out."

"Like a safe house?"

He shrugged. "Something like that."

"I'm guessing there's no food."

Maks walked to the kitchen and opened the fridge. A peek in the cabinets showed there was little to nothing. "I'm going to have to get us some."

"I don't want you to go out."

"I don't want to either, but we have to eat. Trust me. I'll be careful. Before I go anywhere, let's get you set up."

Eden chose one of the bedrooms where she could spread everything out. Once they had a secure connection, Maks waited until she set the gun beside her and gave him a nod. Then he leaned down and placed his lips on hers.

"Be safe," she said.

He shot her a wink. "Always."

"Maks," she called when he turned away.

He paused and looked back at her. "Yes?"

"I... You better come back to me."

"I will," he promised.

31

E den was more terrified now than ever before. You could look for men with guns, you could hide from them. Viruses? Germs? They were in places you never thought to look. And there was no getting away from them.

She opened the laptop, but instead of searching for the Saints, she looked for updates on the virus. Eden decided to check the main news stations in the States where she learned that the virus had already mutated once, and that over five hundred people in Europe had already died from it. It struck the old, the young, and the healthy.

Flipping from one news source to another, she gathered all the information she could. The fact that she and Maks were very near the epicenter of the outbreak frightened her. No one had been able to identify how the virus had begun, which immediately made Eden think of the Saints.

If they had been willing to go through with Ragnarök, and had made viruses similar to this current one before, then who was to say they weren't behind this one? It wasn't some random act of God or a freak of nature. This was something that had been given to the human race. And at the rate it was taking individuals and spreading, it was clear that this was a culling of the herd.

Ragnarök had been a way to control the population by determining who would be able to have children. If you were one of the select few the Saints chose, then you got the antidote. This virus wasn't much different. Eden could guess that every Saint would no doubt have the antibodies in place to prevent them from getting sick.

That would make the Saints easy to pick out in such chaos. Though that didn't help with the fear that threaded through her, choking her. She thought back to the people she'd been around, wondering if any of them had been sick. While she couldn't think of any that had shown symptoms, that didn't mean they weren't infected.

It didn't mean that she wasn't infected.

"Stop," she demanded when her mind began to race with *what-ifs*.

The only thing she could control was her work. Maks was counting on her to find something. The longer she sat there looking at news outlets as they spoke about this new virus, the further behind she'd be. It was getting them nowhere.

She closed all the news tabs and put on some music at a low volume. Then she went looking for some tape in the house. She found some, along with some string. She went back up to the room and took down the pictures so she had a blank wall to work with. Then she used the tape and hung up what she had found by date. Her brain worked better when she could see information in several different ways.

Once that was done, she stepped back and looked at it for a moment. Then she went to the computer and put in one of the pen drives. The files were compressed, so she had to expand them before she could look through any of it. All of it took time. At first glance, the files didn't seem to show much, but she knew there was more there.

Eden wished she had a printer, but she had a pen and some paper, and that was enough. She made notes, sorting through the numerous pages in the first of over a hundred files on the drive. A few things caught her eye, so she switched to the internet and did a few searches, though she came up empty. That didn't worry her, at least for the moment. She knew she would have to dig deeper, and that was just one of the many layers an information broker had to sort through to get what they were looking for.

She heard something below. Eden picked up the gun and quietly walked out of the room. She pressed herself against the wall and listened. Heavy footfalls came from the kitchen, stopping at the foot of the stairs.

"Eden?" Maks called.

She sighed and turned the corner to find him with one foot on the stair and a hand on the banister. "You scared me."

"Sorry I was gone so long. Things are rather crazy out there," he said.

She frowned. "I've not been keeping track of time. Did you find everything we'll need?"

"I hope so. Pickings are slim."

"I can only imagine."

He jerked his chin to her. "How are you faring?"

"Well, I have to admit, I spent some time investigating the virus."

"I don't blame you. Did you find out anything new?"

"Over five hundred deaths in Europe alone, and climbing."

Maks let out a whistle. "That's even more since I first heard of it."

"This scares me in a way that men with guns doesn't."

"Honestly, it does me, as well."

She sagged at his confession. "Thank you for saying that. Even if it isn't true."

"It's true," he said with a lopsided smile.

"I was thinking that the Saints would've vaccinated themselves against this."

His brows rose as he nodded. "That's definitely a possibility. I don't know if they'd vaccinate all the Saints, but certainly the ones who are high up in the chain of command."

"It'll be a good way to pick them out in a crowd, though. Won't it?"

"If they're not worried about getting sick, absolutely. I'm always on the lookout for Saints. I didn't see anyone that would draw my attention today, but then again, everyone seemed too intent on getting what they needed and getting home."

Eden shifted her feet. "I've only just gotten into the first drive. I wasn't expecting so much information. It's going to take me a while."

"I have a feeling we'll be here for some time."

"Too bad we couldn't have stayed at your cabin. We had just about everything we needed there."

"We certainly did," he said with a grin.

Eden glanced down the hall. "I guess I'll get back to work."

"All right."

She returned to the bedroom and her computer and turned off the music. She could hear Maks moving around in the kitchen, putting things away and looking through cabinets. It had been a while since they'd eaten lunch, but she wasn't hungry. Fear could do that to a person.

For the next few hours, Eden worked through each file, making notes and doing a basic search online for things she uncovered. It wasn't until she smelled something delicious that she looked up and found Maks standing in the doorway with a plate of food and a glass of wine.

"I could get used to this," she said with a smile as she set aside the computer.

Maks smiled. "I wasn't sure if you wanted to eat while you worked."

"A break sounds great. Let's go downstairs."

They made their way to the first floor and the small table in the kitchen. She looked at the food on her plate, then up at Maks.

"What?" he asked.

"If I'd been the one preparing this meal, I would've dumped the tuna out of the can onto a lump on the plates. I certainly wouldn't have made it all pretty with the different olives, slices of various cheeses, and crackers."

Maks shrugged. "I'd already cleaned all my guns, so I had to do something busy with my hands.

Since you needed to eat, it was the perfect opportunity."

"Do you always do this with your food?"

He snorted and pulled a face. "I would've eaten the tuna out of the can."

They shared a laugh, both reaching for their forks at the same time.

Eden was mildly surprised to find that the tuna had been seasoned. "This is good. What's in it?"

"Garlic, onions, and lemon juice."

"So simple, but really packs a punch. I might hire you as my cook."

His bright blue eyes crinkled at the corners as he popped a cracker and some cheese into his mouth. "There are some important documents on the drives. I'm sure you'll know them when you get to them."

"That's the problem. It's taking time to sort through what's junk and what's important. As I mentioned, there is a lot there. Where did you get the information?"

"A laptop. I'd spotted a man inside the FSB. He wasn't one of them, but he was obviously important by the way everyone treated him. No one said his name. When I asked about him, I was told I didn't need to know anything."

She swallowed her bite of olive. "And you just happened to be in this man's office and copied files."

Maks shrugged. "Something like that. I followed him for a few days. He changed offices each day, but he was always put in one of the best ones in the building. I knew he would eventually be put in my boss's office sooner or later. And I knew the space like the back of my hand, including how to sneak in."

"No one checked the office before he used it?"

"Nope. I waited in there while he worked and took phone calls."

"So, you know what he looks like."

"Damn right, I do."

She set down her fork. "He's Russian?"

"That's the tricky part. I heard him speaking Russian, English, Italian, and Turkish. I know dialects, but I couldn't tell where he's from. He's an older man. I'd put him in his mid to late fifties."

"Did anyone come to see him in the office?"

Maks shook his head. "Never. He went there to take calls and send emails. He left to visit others in the building. During one of those times, I got the information off the computer and copied it to the drive."

"It took up both?"

"Only one. The other contains things I've gathered from other computers in the FSB. I can help you sort through the files."

She lifted her glass of wine to him. "Much appreciated. I know some Russian, but not nearly enough. My translator is working overtime, and it's taking a lot of time."

"As soon as we're finished, we'll head up and start going through them."

Not for the first time, Eden realized how lucky she was to have Maks. He not only made her feel safe—especially now—but the man had a way of calming her in any situation. It took nerves of steel to do what he did. She was awed by him.

In more ways than one.

When the meal was finished, they went up to the room where she'd been working. She showed him where she was. In less than five minutes, he went through what had taken her hours to look at before because she didn't know the language.

"You are certainly handy to have around," she told him.

Maks pulled her close and pressed his lips to hers. "I'm glad you think so."

It would be so easy to forget the files and spend the night in his arms. That's all Eden wanted to do, but the world was falling apart. What she wanted would have to wait until later.

As one, they turned back to the work at hand.

The world might be falling into utter pandemonium, but being in the house with Eden, Maks found a sense of contentment he hadn't dared to dream could be his. For four days, they worked through the pages of intel he'd gathered. He went out twice more for supplies, and each time, things were more and more dangerous and chaotic out there.

They had the basic essentials at the house. And they had each other. When they took breaks from looking through the intel, they checked on how the virus was progressing around the world. The sheer number of fatalities struck terror in Maks. He wanted to check in with his family to see if they were all right, but he didn't dare.

The Saints would be monitoring them for just such a communication. Maks couldn't do that to them or to Eden. The only thing he could do was hold out hope and focus all his attention on what they had.

The nights, however, were the best. He got to hold Eden in his arms. Sometimes, they talked.

Other times, they just held each other. Whether it was before they fell asleep or first thing in the morning, they always turned to each other and made love. Each time bringing him closer and closer to her so that he could no longer deny that he loved her.

Eden was the love of his life, the one he'd never thought to find. He'd accepted his Fate, which was what made it all the sweeter that they were together now.

He also accepted that this might be the only time they had together. The knowledge was a bitter pill to swallow, but if it meant Eden, his family and friends, and the rest of the world could go on in safety, then it was worth it.

A new dawn was breaking. Their fifth day in the city. He would need to go out for food later. It was becoming scarcer with people hoarding as well as those too sick to deliver food to those who weren't. If something didn't stop the Saints and this virus soon, then...

He couldn't even complete the thought. Maks released a long breath and turned his head toward Eden's to inhale the coconut smell of her shampoo. It made him smile, thinking about how she wanted to go to a beach. He really wanted to take her. He prayed that he got to do that and so much more. She deserved it.

Her head shifted as she stretched and looked at him. She smiled sleepily. "You're frowning."

"Am I?" He immediately smoothed out his brow.

"Mm-hmm. That means you were thinking about everything again. I thought this was the one place we agreed not to think about the Saints or the virus."

He grinned and gave her a soft kiss. "You're right. Sorry."

Her lips twisted. "No apology necessary. I do it, as well. We can't help it."

"How are you feeling?"

"Just tired, but that's from working such long hours. You're the one getting out. How are you?"

He shrugged as he took stock of his body. "I'm fine."

Eden sat up and shoved her blond locks away from her face. "How much longer do you think we can stay here?"

"We aren't going anywhere until we get through everything. How much more do we have?"

"I don't think there's much. What's going to take time is putting it all together. With your help, I've been able to do a lot of research as we went through the files. Once we complete that, then it's just a matter of sorting through it all and putting it in order. There might also be more research involved, but it shouldn't be anywhere near what I've already done."

Maks ran his hand up and down her bare back. "Want some breakfast? I think there's still a little bit of sausage left."

"I can wait for lunch for that. I'll go with my usual."

He chuckled. "You mean coffee and toast."

"Yep," she replied with a smile and got out of bed.

She sauntered into the bathroom, glancing over her shoulder at him. He stayed in bed until she turned on the shower. Then he rose to dress and make his way downstairs to start the coffee. As he was leaving the room, he saw his jacket had fallen. Maks picked it up to put it back on the chair, and the burner phone he'd gotten fell out.

He powered it on, thinking of the Loughmans. That's when he saw the numerous calls that had tried to come through. He recognized the number and immediately called Callie.

"About damn time," she answered testily. "Now, tell me you're okay."

He sat on the edge of the bed. "I'm good. Eden's good. We're holed up in a house in Romania. How are all of you?"

"So far, so good." Callie sighed. "Maks, this virus was the Saints."

"Yeah, we figured that out for ourselves. I don't know how the States are, but I can tell you that things here are grim."

"Maks, its Wyatt," the eldest Loughman brother said as he joined the conversation. "Do you think you and Eden can get home?"

Maks glanced into the bathroom. "There's nothing we'd like more, but I don't think that's possible. The trains haven't run in days, and I hear getting on flights is damn near impossible. There is also talk that they're going to shut down the borders soon to try and contain whatever the hell this thing is."

"It's a strain of the flu," Callie said. "One that has a lot of other really horrible things in it. At least, that's what some of the private messages from the CDC to the Department of Justice are saying."

Maks ran his hand down his face. "Is there any hope for a vaccine?"

"Not yet," Wyatt answered.

Callie snorted. "Everyone is just trying to keep it contained. Have you seen the death totals?"

"Not as of this morning. We just woke up. I've been helping Eden translate the pages of intel I stole from the Saints in the hopes that there's something in there we can use to bring them down."

"Anything we can help with?" Callie offered.

Wyatt immediately said, "We've got extra hands here. Send over anything you think we can assist with."

"Thanks for the offer. We might. We've been limiting our time on the internet for fear that they're monitoring things."

Callie snorted louder this time. "Of course, they're monitoring it. But you're right, if you send over a huge batch of data, that will raise some flags."

"Let me talk to Eden. There might be something we can send over. She wants to get through all the files first. She's making a wall with documents and what she's found."

"Is she looking for something in particular?" Wyatt asked.

Maks got to his feet and walked from the room and down the stairs. "I've not prodded her. She has a way of finding information that I would've overlooked."

"Might be wise to let her do her thing," Callie said. "Once she finishes this wall, you might be able to both see something."

"That's what I'm counting on. If things go well,

it might be today. The problem is that I had no idea how much intel I'd gathered. I didn't think there was much in any of it, but it turns out, I was wrong. Eden has uncovered a lot of things I wasn't even aware of."

There was a smile in Callie's voice when she said, "I can't wait to meet her. I bet there is so much I could learn from her."

"I'm pretty sure the feeling is mutual," Maks said.

Wyatt blew out a breath. "We've been on enough missions together that I know you're thinking ahead. What's going through your mind?"

Maks was silent for a moment as he listened to the sound of the water from the shower. "Before the virus, it was just making sure that I kept us ahead of the Saints. I know how to deal with men with guns. This, however, is something else entirely. Food is still available, but it isn't as easily accessible as before. We aren't starving, but that's low on my list of concerns when there are so many coming down with this illness. My worry is that I'll pick it up. If I'm sick, then I can't keep us away from the Saints. Eden is smart, and she's learning quickly, but it isn't enough."

"She's not trained," Callie said.

Maks blew out a breath. "Then there's the problem of if Eden gets sick."

"Do you have any plans in place for either scenario?" Wyatt asked.

"There's nowhere to go, nothing to do. It's why I haven't moved us since we got here."

"That's probably the smart thing."

Maks leaned back against the counter. "How are all of you holding up?"

"We're secluded here on the ranch, which makes it easier. Callie is monitoring everything with the help of Natalie and Mia. We take turns scouting the property. The good thing is that with the ranch and the garden Natalie started a few months ago, we're doing pretty good. We go into town once a week for the things we can't get anywhere else. Things here aren't as bad as where you are, but we're ahead of things at the ranch. We're keeping our distance from others and already self-isolating."

Maks wasn't surprised by the news. "That's good. From what I hear, it's making its way through the US at a good rate, but not nearly what's happened here."

"We had time to see what was happening and prepare. At least, some of us," Callie said sarcastically. "Some people in the government are just dumbasses of the first order."

That made Maks chuckle. "I'll keep you all posted of things on this end."

"We'll do the same," Wyatt said. "If things get too hairy over there—"

"I won't call," Maks interrupted him.

Wyatt sighed loudly. "You've done a lot for us. You were even there for Lev. You're good at what you do, Maks, but you should take help when you can."

"I'm not putting all of you in danger. I'll figure things out with Eden. One way or another, this thing with the Saints is coming to an end. They've done enough."

Callie said, "I'm in total agreement. However, I think it's prudent if we share what we have. That means we need to send you what we have, which, I hate to admit, isn't much. It'll be everything on Ragnarök and all that debacle. In order to do that, I'm going to create an encrypted server where we can share things. I don't know why I didn't think of it sooner, but this will actually help us. Eden can send over everything she has, and we'll be able to help. Besides, there might be a kernel of info in our intel somewhere that could be just what we need."

"That would be nice." The water shut off overhead. "I'm going to keep the phone on. Send me a text when you get the server set up and you're sure it can't be hacked."

Callie made an annoyed sound. "Anything can be hacked. This will be difficult to find, though, and even harder to get in. Plus, I'll set up firewalls to alert me if someone tries to gain access without permission. Just like I have on everything here. That way, I can destroy everything in the servers and drives to wipe it clean before anyone can find anything."

"And before you freak out—" Wyatt began.

Callie quickly interjected, "Like he did."

"—she's made backups of everything we have."

"Three backups," Callie amended. "One for each brother."

Maks nodded, always impressed by Callie. "Sounds good. Thank you."

"Stay safe."

"You, too." Maks then disconnected the call.

He was making the coffee when Eden came down the stairs in fresh clothes and wet hair.

She raised her brows when she noticed the cell phone on the counter. "Everything okay?"

"Wyatt and Callie had been calling. I forgot about getting in touch with them as we've been working. I called them back."

"They're not infected with this virus, are they?"

"Thankfully, no. They're also being very safe."

Eden got out the loaf of bread and took out two slices for the toaster. "You're worried about them."

It wasn't a question. "I am. They're also worried about us. Wyatt even offered to find some way to come and get us."

"You sound surprised," she stated while returning the bread to the pantry.

"It would be suicide for them to try something like that."

She propped a hand on the counter and shot him a flat look. "Would you do it for them?"

"If I was able, yes."

"So why is it any different if someone does it for you?"

Maks parted his lips to answer, but he realized there wasn't anything he could say.

Eden rolled her eyes as she laughed. "That's what I thought. They consider you a friend, maybe even family, which means they want to help you. You risked your life for them."

"Maybe," he replied with a shrug.

"Which means, you did. And you didn't think twice about it, did you?"

He held her hazel eyes and shook his head.

"Exactly. Maks, you're an amazing guy with some truly special—and a little terrifying—skills.

You're going to help others, and sometimes, others are going to help you."

He reached out and pulled her against him. "You mean, like you?"

"Me?" she asked, surprised filling her face. "What do you mean?"

"You've helped me."

Eden snorted as she slid her arms around his neck. "Now you're just teasing."

"I'm not. You've brought calm into my life. An ease I had forgotten."

She wrinkled her nose. "I'm not sure that's a good thing in your line of work."

"Trust me, it's not dulling anything. Holding you at night, it's let me be...me."

"Really?" she asked with a bright smile. "I'm doing that?"

She was doing that and so very much more. "Oh, yes."

Eden rose up on her toes as she leaned her head toward his. "I do like this side of you. Did I ever tell you that flattery will get you everywhere?"

"You haven't, but it's good to know."

He couldn't stop smiling. Even when they shared a kiss, he couldn't believe that they had found something wonderful amid such a dark time. It didn't seem possible, and yet it was. His heart was nearly bursting with emotion.

Maks pulled back. "There's a couple of things I need to tell you."

"Okay," she said with half-closed eyes. "But only if you give me another kiss when you're finished."

He chuckled. "Callie is setting up an encrypted

server to upload all of their data. She's going to share the location with us so we can put everything we have in there, as well. That's in case something happens to us. They'll be able to get the information."

"Sounds like a good idea. What do you think?"

"I trust Callie, if that's what you're asking. She knows what she's doing, and I'm confident that it'll be a good place to store everything."

Eden nodded solemnly. "In case we both get sick or are killed by the Saints."

"There's that as well, yes. Callie also said they'd help you with whatever you need. She's eager to meet you."

"I can't wait to meet her, as well. All of them, actually. It'll be nice to put faces with names."

Maks noticed that they were both talking as if the virus or the Saints weren't going to impede them. Perhaps it was a good way to look at things. Especially now.

The toast popped up, breaking their gaze. Eden grabbed her breakfast as he took down two mugs and poured their coffee. They said nothing as they climbed the stairs and started their work for the day.

It wasn't until a few hours later that Eden sat back and blew out a breath. "That's it."

Maks stilled as he swiveled his head to her. "What's it?"

"That was the last page in the last file of the second drive. We've looked through it all. I've done initial research on all of it. Now is when I need to go through and give greater attention to anything that I flagged before."

He couldn't believe they had finally reached the end. At that moment, the cell phone dinged with a text. He recognized Callie's number and looked at the message. It was a link to what he assumed was the server she'd set up. Before he could call to see if it was from her, the phone rang.

"It's from me," Callie said when he answered. "I knew you'd be wary. Wanted you to know that I sent it, and it's all fine."

Maks chuckled. "Thanks. We'll start getting everything sent over shortly."

He disconnected the line and gave the phone to Eden so she could see the link. In short order, she began sending the files from the drives to the encrypted server. Meanwhile, he looked around the room at the papers scattered everywhere.

"Where is that paper on...?" Eden trailed off.

He would help her if he knew what she was looking for, but he'd learned quickly that it was easier to let her do her own thing. Curious, he watched as she tiptoed in the spaces between the papers, bent to shuffle some around, moved to another spot, picked up two papers, then returned to the bed.

She was in her own world as she jotted something down on the computer then turned to the side where some paper and pen sat. She wrote something there, as well. Then she handed him what she'd picked up from the floor and pointed to the left side of the wall.

"Can you hang that between the fourth and fifth papers?" she asked.

Maks did as she asked. When he turned back, she had another page. And another. Then another.

33

"Holy hell," Maks muttered.

Eden blinked, unable to believe that it had finally all come together. She stared at the wall, noting what was linked to what. To top it off, there were even a few names that she had gotten from the pen drives and her research. Names that obviously meant something to Maks given his shocked expression.

"Am I seeing that correctly?" he asked.

She nodded and came to stand beside him. "Yeah. Because I'm seeing it, as well."

Maks took several steps back and sank heavily onto the bed and then ran a hand down his face before his gaze returned to the wall. "That's...fuck. It was right before me the entire time."

"What?"

"Not what, *who*."

She stared at the wall and the names there. "They did everything in their power to keep their identities from being known. You can't blame yourself."

"*Fuck*," he said again.

Eden walked to him and put a hand on his shoulder. "What do we do now?"

"Tell the entire damn world," he bit out.

"The problem is going to be finding out who to deliver this to, who isn't a Saint."

Maks surged to his feet and went to the wall to stare at the pages and rope that linked events to different people. He put his hand on his hips and slowly shook his head. "You don't recognize these names, do you?"

"No," she answered.

He pointed to the one on the far right. "He was my captain in the Army."

"Are you sure? People can have the same names."

Maks walked to where the name was located next to a person who had been killed. "I know because of the date. We were on a mission in Chile then. Just thirty klicks from where this man was killed."

That wasn't a coincidence, that was for sure. Eden couldn't imagine how upset Maks must be at discovering this information. But he wasn't finished.

"This man," Maks said as he walked to the name nearest him, "recruited me into the FSB. And this one..." He continued to the next name and swallowed. Maks stared at the name for a moment. "This bastard is from old money. He has his hands in a little bit of everything, and if you ask him what he does for a living, he'll laugh and tell you some cockamamie story that's nothing but lies."

Eden frowned at the last statement. "You aren't

just acquainted with..."—she paused to read the name—"Jeffery Sumners. You know him."

"Yeah, I know him. He's a family friend. My grandfather and he were pretty tight. At least that's what I was told. Jeff remained in contact with my father throughout the years and even helped my dad get ahead in his work. Jeff was like that favorite uncle you always see in the movies. The kind who stays away for a while then shows up out of the blue with presents for everyone."

There were two other names on the wall, and Eden was afraid that Maks was going to know who they were, as well. Her gaze locked on him, taking in his rigid form, the tense way he held his shoulders.

His head swiveled to hers, their gazes colliding. "I know all five of these names."

"Do you think they can get us to the top of the Saints? Is there any way we could get them to tell us who is running the organization?"

"What do you see when you look at this wall?" he asked instead.

She blinked, unsure of where he was going with this. "I see deeds done in an effort to get the Saints what they want. Be it killing people who were causing issues, getting the people they wanted into office, starting—and even ending—wars between countries to boost economies, not to mention this virus and probably many, many others."

"Why did you put all of this up on the wall?"

Eden shrugged, trying to find the words. "When there is this much information to go through, I like to see it in different ways. Getting it online is nice, but it all starts to blur together after a while. I like to see it in a different setting. Usually, there's a pattern somewhere."

"Is there a pattern here?"

Her gaze slid to the wall as she looked over every piece of paper, followed every line of thread that had been marked with different colors to differentiate the people. Eden took a step back. Then another, and another. She took it all in again, her heart beating faster each time. There was a pattern. And no one would have known any of it had Maks not stolen the intel that he had.

She turned her head to him. "There's a pattern."

"What is it?" he asked softly.

Eden licked her lips. "You've found the leaders of the Saints."

"Not me. You."

"I'm not the one who risked my life to get the documents."

Maks' lips twisted briefly. "I've sat on most of that for months. If it hadn't been for you, I wouldn't even know any of this. You did it. You found the answers."

"We both did it." She walked to him and reached for his hand. "Since you've told me about the Saints, I've envisioned a table full of stuffy old men running this secret organization."

He shrugged and looked at the wall. "They are in their sixties and seventies. Well, hell, Jeff may be in his eighties."

Eden jerked her chin to the last name on the list. "But not all the names are men."

"No, they aren't."

"You know all five names up there. I'm guessing they were part of your life somehow."

"Captain Jonathan Miller, Evgeni Turgenev, Jeffery Sumners, Timothy Smith, and Evangeline Popov. Each one of them has come into my life in some way that put me on the course I'm on now. I met Stacy through Evangeline. She owned a little coffee shop in near the base. She noticed me staring at Stacy and urged me to ask her out. I didn't. The next time I went in, Stacy came to me. She told me that Evangeline mentioned that I was interested."

She gave him a nod to continue. It was obvious whatever he was about to tell her was difficult, but she didn't rush him.

Finally, Maks said, "All these years I've believed that Stacy died that day she and the team attacked my squad. I recently discovered that isn't the case."

"I suppose she got lucky. How did you find out? Did she contact you or something?"

"I saw her at SynTech."

Eden's stomach pitched her to feet as she took in what he said. "Who?"

"Your boss. She changed her name and continued working for the Saints."

"Janice?" Eden replied in a strangled voice. She couldn't comprehend what was happening, but somehow it all made sense.

Maks dropped his gaze to the floor as he went quiet.

Eden wasn't sure what to say about any of that, so she didn't reply. Maks never let go of her hand while he was delving into his memories. She hated that these people had left such a mark on him.

Some he considered friends, and to realize that they had manipulated him must be difficult to accept.

"It's time we bring them down," she said.

Maks' bright blue eyes slid to her. "How?"

"In this day and age, we don't need to get to a news source for word to get out. We get it out ourselves. Not to mention, we know a hacker."

A smile finally softened his lips. "Callie."

"That's right. But we'll have to be careful about how we put this out. Not only do we need proof of who these people are and how they're involved, we need to tell the world they're involved with this pandemic that's hit us."

Maks blew out a breath. "That's not going to be easy."

"I can do it. I just need some time to get everything together. And I'm going to be online. They might take notice of what I'm going to do. I was being careful before. This time, I won't be."

"Do what you need to do. I'll prepare for any...visitors."

She gaped at him. "You can't honestly think to hold them off on your own? As good as you are, you don't have nearly enough weapons."

"I know where to get some," he answered with a smile.

Eden wasn't sure if she should be happy at that news or worried. They weren't in his house in Hungary that had insulated walls to protect against bullets. It was only a matter of time before the Saints gained access to this house with all its windows.

"Wait," she said when he started out of the room. "What if we went to a better location?"

He raised his brows in question. "The city is on lockdown. Where could we go that the Saints won't be? Staying here will give us a little time until they pin down our location."

"I may be way off base here since I don't do this for a living, and while you're right, it will take them a little while to find us, the fact is, they *will* find us. And no matter how many guns you have, they'll hunt us down before I can finish what I need to do."

That caught Maks' attention. "Can you send it to Callie to do?"

"No. I can't tell her what I'm looking for. I'll know when I start my search. It has to be me."

"Which means you need more time than you'd have here."

"Exactly."

His chest expanded as he drew in a breath. "I have an idea. It's going to be tricky, but it just might work."

"You've not led us wrong so far."

"You might not be so quick to say that after you see what I have planned."

"Is it going to keep us safe?"

He lifted one shoulder. "Safer than remaining here and fighting it out."

"Then I'm good with it."

"Gather what you need. We'll be leaving as soon as we can."

He turned on his heel and left the room. Eden reached for the mobile phone he'd left behind and took pictures of the wall. Not only was she going to need this, but she also wanted to send it to Callie.

After that, Eden began dismantling the wall from left to right, keeping everything in order so she could put it back together if she needed to later. Not that she would forget any of it. How could she? In all her imaginings, she'd never once thought she would be involved in something as big and horrible as this. History was being made, and she was a part of it. All she could hope for was that she and Maks succeeded. It was a long shot, but they had no choice but to take it.

To sit idly by would not only mean the continuation of the Saints but also more and more deaths. Not that putting information out there about the Saints would stop the epidemic, but it certainly couldn't hurt. People had a right to know that the freedom they believed in was nothing but a figment of their imagination.

She wasn't going to let that happen. Every person out there had a right to know the truth. They might riot, they might freak out, or they might continue on as they had been. She didn't care. The truth was all that mattered right at this moment.

It made her physically ill to know that people were dying because the Saints had decided to play God. Was the world overpopulated? Yes. Were humans destroying the Earth? Yes. Should something be done? Yes.

But the right way. Not by killing innocents.

The more Eden thought about it, the more riled up she became. She had packed everything into her backpack and was walking to the door when Maks appeared. Even now, in a scary situation with the ultimate villain chasing them, she found herself smiling at him.

"You sure about this?" he asked. "Once we start, there's no turning back."

Eden adjusted the pack on her shoulder. "What other choice do we have? There is no bunker we can go to."

"Actually, there is."

She blinked before narrowing her eyes on him. "Really?"

"It's not easy to get to, and I expect we'll find Saints there."

Eden pushed past him to go downstairs to get her coat. "Sounds like we need to get moving."

34

W hat they were doing was insane, and yet Maks knew they didn't really have a choice. Eden was right. They couldn't have stayed in that house for very long before the Saints arrived and killed them. At least with this plan, they stood a chance. It wasn't much of one, but it was better than the other options.

That was his thought before they left the safety of the guest house. Once they were outside, he wasn't so sure he'd made the right decision. But the look on Eden's face said she wasn't going back— only forward.

The night helped to shield them from prying eyes. Yet, there were more people out than he liked. And he knew most of were probably Saints. While he and Eden zigzagged their way through the streets and houses, he saw several policemen in uniforms. His trained eyes spotted even more in plain clothes. However, there were still others like Eden and him, who were just trying to make it through another day.

Maks took her hand and led her toward the river that split the city. There was a direct route, but he took his time picking out which direction they would go to avoid running into anyone. It wasn't just because he didn't want the Saints to catch him, he was also doing his best to keep them away from anyone who might be infected. The likelihood that the virus was airborne was high, so it wouldn't matter about keeping their distance, but he was still being cautious.

They kept low, running from one spot to another and avoiding the lights from the lamps above. The shadows were many, and he used them to their advantage.

Maks glanced to make sure no one was coming. He squeezed Eden's hand to let her know they were about to make a run for it to the next shadow cluster. Just as he was taking the first step out, he heard a voice near him. His arms quickly reached out and grabbed Eden, yanking her against his chest as he held her still and melded them both into the shadows.

Two men, one in a policeman's uniform, strolled past, sharing a cigarette. Neither he nor Eden moved until the men were long gone. Maks lowered his arms and retook her hand. Then they were off. The rest of their trek to the river happened without incident.

"Now what?" Eden asked when they arrived.

They were hunkered down behind some cars, looking at the river. Maks rose up enough to peer over the hood of the car to see the boats tied up. Some were houseboats where he saw lights within and people moving about. Others were smaller vessels that looked empty, bobbing softly in the water.

"Stay here," he told her. "I'm going to find us a boat."

She nodded, determination in her gaze.

He leaned in and gave her a quick kiss before he made his way down to the water. There was little movement on the docks. That didn't mean there weren't people in the buildings nearby looking down at him, though. He went to the first small boat that looked like it had seen its fair share of years. Despite the age, it had been well maintained.

Maks slipped aboard and took a quick look around. He didn't find any keys, but then he hadn't expected to. Maks then motioned with his hands for Eden to join him. She followed his path exactly, keeping low and remaining in the shadows. Once she was on board, he untied the boat and pushed away from the dock to drift out into the river. He went to the helm, turning the wheel to point the bow in the direction he was headed, which just happened to be downriver.

"Stay low," he told her.

Eden sat on the floor of the boat. Her eyes blinked up at him. She was scared, but she was strong. He knew finding her had been a godsend. Without her skills, he wouldn't have the information on the Saints and who was running it. They were a long way from taking the organization down, but they were headed in the right direction.

Maks let the vessel drift farther from the city. No one shouted anything about seeing a boat, so he hoped that meant that no one had noticed them. It was why he hadn't started the engine. He didn't want the noise. Luckily, the direction he was headed was downriver. The current was taking them there. All he needed to do was steer the boat to keep it from going ashore. Everything was going fine until he hit some rough currents that wanted to yank the vessel straight into shore. They were getting to the outskirts of Oradea, but weren't far enough away yet for him to start the engine.

He fought the current as long as he could before he had no choice but to hotwire the engine to keep them from crashing. The moment the motor roared to life, he throttled the boat on low and maneuvered them safely into the center of the river.

A few minutes later, he passed a boat going toward the city. He saw a family of five—three young children huddled with their mother as the father steered—clearly fearful and nervously looking his way. Maks gave them a nod and kept going. That was just the first of many vehicles on the water.

He glanced at Eden. "Lots more people out here than I thought."

"They're trying to get away. The river seems like a good idea."

Maks shrugged. "I'm not sure there is anywhere they can go that's safe. But the river at least allows you to see people coming. As long as you're moving. It's when you stop that you have to worry."

"And they'll need to stop for provisions eventually."

"Yep. We would've been better off up on that mountain in the cave."

"Don't tease me," she said with a laugh. "You know I'm fond of that place."

He chuckled and looked at her. "It's just getting there and getting back that's the problem."

"Cold weather and I don't mix."

"You've lived in Vienna for how long?"

"Three years."

He shook his head. "And you never got used to the cold?"

"No, you can't use Vienna like that. The weather gets chilly, yes, but I was able to get warm quickly. That's vastly different from being up on a mountain in ten feet of snow."

"It wasn't ten feet," he said, unable to hold back his smile.

She nodded. "You're right. It was twenty."

At this, he laughed, holding in the sound so it didn't carry on the water. "It was more like three feet."

"Perception is reality, and my reality was that it was twenty feet," she said, a smile on her face. Then she sobered. "Where are we going?"

He drew in a breath and looked forward. "There's an old Nazi bunker about five miles downriver."

"A what?" she asked in shock.

"Someone unearthed it a few years back. They're being found all over Europe. Most don't even make headlines now. This one didn't."

"Then how did you find out about it?"

He paused for a moment. "I overheard some people talking about it."

"You mean those in the FSB? Or the Saints?"

"I believe they were Saints."

"Do you know if the Saints will be there for sure?"

Maks shrugged as he glanced at her. "I assume they will be. They were there the last time I visited the bunker."

"You've been there before?" she asked as she shifted to get more comfortable.

"Several times. I was curious about it. They've not excavated all of it. I found another way in and explored different parts of it."

"How long ago was that?"

"Two months. I doubt they got the section I was in. I stashed supplies in the bunker as well as outside of it. I also took the opportunity and made some upgrades."

She made a sound in the back of her throat. "Are you telling me you actually knew you'd be coming here?"

"I always prepare. I've got stashes like this all over the world. Especially in places I know I can get to easily. The bunker sounded like a great place for me to lay low if I ever needed it."

"Then why didn't we come here first?"

"Because I suspected there would be Saints there. I wanted us to slip into Oradea quietly and unnoticed. We couldn't have done that in the bunker."

Eden shoved her hair out of her face. "I'm not sure I see how going there now is any different than going there when we first arrived. If any Saints are there, then we'll have to fight them. Right?"

"If we had chosen that as our base when we got here, then I would've had to clear out everyone so they didn't discover us when you were on the internet."

"Good point. Except I'm going to be on the internet again."

He steered farther away from an oncoming vessel. "We don't need a whole lot of time now. It's just getting it out to the world."

"Which may take some time. Not as long as it took to gather all the intel, though."

"The bunker will allow me to hold the Saints off for several hours. Maybe even a day if we get to the right spot."

Eden looked up at the night sky. "That will work. I don't see me needing anything longer than a handful of hours."

"You need to accept there will be opposition. The Saints will do everything they can to stop you."

"I've been thinking of that. Callie can help."

"And she'll be more than happy to do it. What are you thinking?"

Eden smiled as she turned her head to him. "I'm thinking that she hacks into all the news outlets around the world that she can, and we distribute what we have."

Maks jerked his head to her. "That's a bold move. If it can be done, it'll accomplish exactly what we want."

"A lot of it will be on Callie's shoulders. Even if we can only get to a couple of countries, once it's out there, it's out there."

"The Saints will move quickly to have it removed."

Eden laughed softly. "Do you have any idea how many conspiracy theorists are out there?"

"Obviously more than I realize."

"They look for shit like this. If they get a hold of it, and we'll make sure they do, then they'll help us spread it."

Maks nodded as he began to smile. "Get it out to as many as possible globally. The Saints will try to take it down, and they'll succeed. But then the conspiracy theorists will keep it alive because it'll look suspicious. That's rather brilliant."

"I have my moments," she said with a little shrug.

"I wouldn't have thought of that. I definitely tip my hat to you."

"We make a good team," she said and reached over to touch his leg.

He lowered his hand and let his fingers brush her hair. "We're getting close."

They went silent then. He throttled down the motor until it was barely running. When they got as close as he dared, he turned the boat toward shore. Maks motioned for Eden to take the wheel while he went to the front of the boat and grabbed the line. When they got close enough, he readied himself and jumped onto land, pulling the boat with the rope as he did.

Eden turned off the engine as Maks tied the vessel to a tall tree to keep it there just in case they needed a getaway vehicle. He held out his hands as Eden tossed him first his pack, then hers. Maks set them on the ground beside him and reached for her. Eden leapt from the boat, landing against him so he could steady her.

"We'll hike the rest of the way," he said in a

whisper as they put on their packs. "It's about two klicks. Ready?"

"As I'll ever be," she said with a wink.

His smile died as he faced away from her. He had no idea what awaited them at the bunker. All he could do was hope that he hadn't led them into a worse situation.

35

Washington, DC

"Good evening, Mr. Sumners," the beautiful flight attendant said as he climbed upon his private Learjet.

He gave her a nod and made his way to his seat. Jeff sat down and looked out the window. He'd known a trip to Europe would be coming, but he hadn't expected to be making it now. Especially with the virus working as well as it was. Flying to Europe was going to bring scrutiny upon him. Then again, he'd always been able to shrug off such things. He would again.

The gorgeous brunette smiled at him as she brought his whisky. "We're about ready to depart. Don't forget to buckle your seat belt."

"Of course, not," he replied as he took the drink and set it on the table in front of him.

He'd already slept with her twice. Some men had a thing for blondes. For him, it was brunettes. The smarter they were, the more he wanted them.

He couldn't stand anyone who was dumb. And he rewarded his employees very well.

He checked his watch to see the time before he pulled his phone from his pocket and dialed. It was answered on the second ring. The tremor of fear he heard in Janice's voice made him smile. "You failed."

"I need more time," she hurried to say.

"You've had plenty. I'm handling things on my own from here on out in regards to Maks."

There was a beat of silence. "And what does that mean for me?"

In the background he heard the door of Janice's home being busted down. He listened patiently as the phone dropped and there was a brief struggle. Then a moment later a deep voice said, "It's done, sir."

"You've never let me down. Good work. Take a few days off."

The line went dead. Jeff set the phone on the table before him and looked out the window. The plane lurched forward as it began taxiing down the runway. His gaze landed on the woman. He really should try to remember her name, but names meant nothing to him. She got him hard and gave him release. To add a cherry on top, she was so pretty that he couldn't stop looking at her.

Unfortunately, there was a chance that she would contract the virus the Saints had unleashed upon the world. It was too bad, really. He liked her. However, there were a hundred women just like her waiting to take her place.

And they were always eager to work for him— and spread their legs. They never hesitated to do whatever he requested because they got paid handsomely. That was everything in the world. It all came down to money. Who had it, who knew how to make it, and who knew how to use it to their advantage. There was so much money in his accounts now that he couldn't spend it all if he tried.

He mocked the stupid ones who gave away their fortunes to help the needy. Didn't anyone understand that the poor and needy would always be like that unless they learned how to pull themselves out of the muck like he had? In his opinion, if they didn't have the will or drive to make something of themselves, then they needed to remain just as they were.

Jeff settled back with his drink as the plane soared through the air, headed toward Romania of all places. He'd never cared for the country, but then again, he wasn't going there on holiday. He was headed there because that's where Maks was.

He swirled the amber liquid in his glass, thinking back to the years he'd known Maks and the Petrov family. From an early age, he'd seen something in Maks that alerted him to the potential waiting to be found. And had he found it.

Maks didn't know it, but he had been the one to push Maks to join the military. It was all done behind the scenes, so no one knew. The way Maks had blossomed in the Army had been more than what Jeff had expected. Much more.

After that, it had taken nothing to get Maks to go down the roads he wanted. Jeff just had to open certain doors for him and wait, and Maks unknowingly complied. Things had gone exactly to plan. Right up until Maks met that stupid woman.

Just when Jeff thought he'd have to kill her, he'd found another use for the bitch. She had fallen into the fold rather easily. It had been almost too simple to convince her that Maks needed the Saints as much as the Saints needed him. All would've worked out perfectly. It should've worked out like the rest of Jeff's plans. But things had gone sideways.

When Maks left Stacy, the woman was severely wounded, half his team was dead, and he was a changed man. Enough that Jeff became concerned that he wasn't going to be able to recruit Maks. The rest of the Elders began to doubt his vision of Maks taking his place one day. Jeff was able to convince them to give Maks another try.

They spent weeks surveilling him, waiting to see if Maks would go to someone and begin looking into the Saints since they didn't know everything Stacy had told him before Maks shot her. Jeff agreed with two other Elders that the woman might have told Maks everything in a last-ditch bid to get him to their side. Thankfully, Jeff worried for nothing.

Once they were assured that Maks was walking down the path they wanted again, Jeff made sure that Maks was offered a position with the CIA. It was right up Maks' alley. Sure enough, he took it. After proving himself there, Jeff made sure that Maks was moved to Russia to infiltrate the FSB.

Maks kept performing just as expected. He had no idea he was taking out targets sent by the Elders. Jeff made sure that Maks had so many orders and missions coming from both the CIA and the FSB that he had no time to consider anything else. And Maks hadn't.

Until a week ago.

Jeff drained the last of the whisky. He was getting old. Too old to be doing this shit. Maks should be with him, being groomed to take his place the moment Jeff died. Instead, Maks had fooled them all.

He still couldn't believe that Maks had betrayed them. Jeff had kept such a close eye on him. How could this have happened? Unless...

"No," Jeff whispered to himself.

There was no way that Maks had been planning this since he believed his lover died. There's no way someone could've walked away from their life, their family, to hunt down an organization the size and scope of the Saints. It would be suicide. And Maks was smarter than that. Yet there was a part of Jeff that knew Maks was smart enough and patient enough to do just that.

Jeff briefly closed his eyes and sighed. "This wasn't how this was supposed to go."

He didn't want to kill Maks, but the man was giving Jeff no other option. Since no one seemed to be able to bring Maks in, it was now up to Jeff to stop all of this nonsense. The future of the Saints, the future of the *world* depended on it.

36

Creepy didn't begin to describe the area. Eden felt as if a thousand eyes of the dead watched her. A shiver of apprehension ran down her spine. She knew the bunker would be a great place for them to hole up and fight against the Saints. At the same time, she couldn't shake the feeling that this was the last place they should be.

She gently tugged on Maks' hand to get his attention. He stopped immediately and looked at her over his shoulder. The moon was bright enough that she could make out him raising his brows in question.

"Is there somewhere else we can go?" she whispered.

His brows drew together as he turned to her. "It's the best place."

"I know. It's just..." She trailed off and shrugged. She couldn't put into words her feeling of foreboding.

Maks tightened his fingers with hers. "It's going to be dangerous anywhere we go. We've got to stay away from people because of the virus, but also get somewhere we can defend ourselves. This is the best place I know of around here. We can't leave Romania, and traveling is—"

She cut him off with a nod and her finger over his lips. "I know. I'm sorry. I just have a bad feeling."

"So do I," he admitted.

He gently pressed his lips to hers and gave her a smile. Eden forced herself to return it. This was a no-win situation. There weren't any better options, no matter how much she wished there were.

They walked over the snow-covered ground, meandering through bushes and trees weighed down with snow until she spotted the top of a bunker rising from the ground. It wasn't at the top of a hill as some were. This one was hidden in plain sight. However, if she hadn't been looking for it or known of its existence, Eden was certain she would've walked right past it.

There was no movement around the bunker. Then again, all she could see was a small part of it. She followed Maks as he walked them around the back. The moon went behind the clouds, cutting off what little light there was. She was fumbling in the dark, but Maks knew exactly what he was doing.

Within moments of moving aside some brush, he was ushering her inside. Eden glanced at the concrete door that was at least a foot thick. Shouldn't the hinges have been rusty and creaked when opened? Probably, but Maks had said that he had scoped this place out before. Which meant that he had likely taken care of any squeaking.

He closed and barred the door behind them. Then he flicked on the light of his phone and took her hand as he walked past her. Eden coughed at the damp, dank smell but kept pace with him. They passed several doorways and halls that jutted off in different directions. She hoped that she didn't have to navigate the bunker by herself because there was no way she'd remember how to get out.

The sound of voices halted them in their tracks. Maks lowered his phone to hide the majority of the light. Eden stood right behind him, her breathing loud to her ears. They stood like that for several minutes before the voices moved off, and they began walking again.

To her shock, Maks took them to a stairway that led down. He zigzagged them through different corridors first one way and then the other, turning her around completely. Until finally, he stopped beside what looked like a solid wall.

"Hold this," he said in a whisper.

Eden took his phone and held up the light to shine against him and the wall. She frowned at the old picture of Hitler staring back at her. The glass was intact, but the photo hadn't withstood the elements. It was faded and yellow. And no matter how much she tried, there was no getting away from those beady, black eyes watching her.

Maks, however, didn't seem to care. He pushed the bottom corner of the picture upward so that the entire thing swiveled on the nail holding it. Eden's lips parted in astonishment as she saw a number pad there. Maks quickly keyed in a code and the wall moved. Clearly this bunker wasn't always out of commission. Someone had retrofitted at least parts of it since World War II. This must have been what Maks said he had upgraded.

"Come on," he told her as he put his hands on the slab and pushed.

It swung open, and lights clicked on as he walked in. Eden leaned to the side and took in the room. It appeared to be a conference room of sorts. There was a long table, several chairs, lights swinging from the low ceiling and along the wall, as well as a table in the back that held radio equipment.

Maks set his pack on the table and walked to the electronics. He flipped some switches and leaned down to look at something. Eden was slower to walk in. She was entering a place that had been used in WWII against the allies. Evil people had used this room. She wanted to turn and run, but she realized that this was now their place to use *against* evil people.

Eden slowly walked inside. Maks turned and briefly looked her way. She let her gaze roam over the area, taking what must have been high tech equipment for the forties. Looking at it now, she wasn't even sure how to work any of it.

"You all right?" Maks asked as he walked to her.

Eden snapped her head to him. "Yeah. It's just...weird...to be in here. I've seen some of these on the television, but never in person. Maybe it's just me, but the air feels heavy."

"It's not you. A lot of people died around this bunker, on both sides of the war. You're feeling the residual energy."

"I don't like it."

He grinned. "I'd be worried if you did."

She cleared her throat. "Now what do we do?"

"We're going to lock ourselves in this room."

Eden watched dumbfounded as Maks walked to the door. "You can't be serious."

"There's a way out, I promise. I've used this a few times," he told her as he touched a button near the door and it closed on its own.

The moment it slid shut, Eden felt a chill run down her spine. "How do you know the Saints don't know about this place?"

"They haven't gotten to this part of the bunker. They're on the other side."

"We heard them on the way here."

Maks faced her. "They were on the other side of the wall. They might be concrete, but voices still carry. This side of the bunker is blocked off. It will prevent them from gaining access. I know about the blockage because I found it. I also found out how to clear it. I then made sure they couldn't break through it easily, and added the extra security to the door in case they somehow did. And before you ask, they haven't found the way in that we used. I know this because of the way I stacked the brush around the door. I'd have known if it had been moved."

There was no reason for Eden not to believe him. It was just the place that was getting under her nerves. "I trust you."

"You'll get past this place soon enough. Now, the equipment here is old, but the Saints have been running new lines for wireless internet," he said with a smile.

Eden chuckled. "You want to use their internet to get the word out about them?"

"Damn straight, I do. Rather ironic, isn't it?"

"I think it's perfect."

He flashed her a smile. "Shall we get to work, then?"

"We need to let Callie and the others know what we're doing."

Maks reached into his pocket and pulled out the cell phone. "It's secure. The only number in there is Callie's. Call her and let them know what's going on. Then start your research."

"And where will you be?" she asked, suddenly afraid that he was going to leave her alone.

He walked around the table and took her hands in his. "No one but me knows how to get through that door. No one other than the two of us even knows that door is there. You're going to be safe."

"The minute I start my search, they're going to be alerted."

"Which is why I need to get the guns and ammo I have stashed. They aren't far. I'll be back by the time you get off the phone with Callie."

Eden wanted to hold him there, tell him that they didn't need the guns, but she knew it for the lie it was. "You're coming back to me."

"I'm coming back to you. There's nothing that will keep me from you. Not even death."

"I'm not strong enough to do this on my own. I need you here."

His hands ran up her arms to cup her face. His bright blue eyes held hers as he gazed at her. "That's where you're wrong. You don't need anyone. You're the strongest person I know. And that's what's going to win us the day."

Eden wanted to believe him, but she could feel her heart thundering in her chest, ice running in her veins. There was so much she wanted to say to him. She wanted to thank him for rescuing her and showing her the truth. She wanted to tell him how much joy he'd brought into her life despite the danger they were in. And she wanted to tell him that she loved him. But it all stuck in her throat when he pressed his lips to hers.

The kiss was scorching, igniting the desire with in her. It was so intense that for a moment, it blanketed the fear. All too soon, the kiss was over.

"I'll be back before you know it," Maks whispered.

Then he was opening the heavy door. Just before he walked through it, he paused and looked at her. "I love you."

She blinked, her heart skipping a beat as the words registered. Eden rushed to the door, even as it was closing. "I love you, too," she said as it slid shut. She slammed her hands against the concrete and then rested her head upon it.

Had he heard her? She couldn't be sure, but it didn't matter. She was going to tell him when he returned. For now, she had work to do. Eden took a deep breath and straightened. Then she turned and walked to the table to retrieve the phone. She dialed the number and put the phone on speaker as she grabbed her pack and began to unpack everything that was in it.

"Maks?" asked a female voice when the line connected.

"Um...it's Eden."

"About time I got to talk to you. I'm Callie."

Eden smiled at the phone. "I've heard a lot about you, Callie."

"We're going to need to get a drink when all this is over."

"More than one," Callie said with a laugh.

"Is everything all right with y'all?"

Eden heard the Texas twang and grinned. "So far. We're in an old Nazi bunker Maks found. Unfortunately, the Saints are in part of it, as well."

"It'll be a great defense though," came a deep voice. "I'm Wyatt Loughman, Eden."

Callie chimed in and said, "I'm his better half."

The two shared a laugh before Wyatt said, "Where's Maks?"

"He went to retrieve some guns that he'd stored nearby. At least that's what he told me. I'm not happy he left."

"It's never easy being left behind," Callie said.

Wyatt asked, "Did Maks say he was coming back?"

"Yep. Just as soon as he got the guns."

"Then he'll be back," Wyatt told her. "We got the files you uploaded. That's quite a lot of information."

Eden opened the laptop as she pulled out an old chair and wiped the dust from it. "It certainly is. What neither of you knows yet is that Maks identified the Elders. You'll find five names in the documents. I took a photo of my wall, and they're there, as well. Maks knows all five of the people. They've been a part of his life in one way or another."

"Shit," Wyatt mumbled.

"I can't imagine he took that well," Callie said.

Eden swallowed, thinking about how

devastated—and angry—Maks had been. "No. He didn't take it well at all."

"What's the plan now?" Wyatt asked.

Eden glanced at the closed door, hoping that Maks would return any second. "We decided to come here so I could do a last bit of research. Then we want to send out everything, well...everywhere."

"I can help with that," Callie chimed in.

"I was hoping you'd say that. Now, we know the Saints are going to shut us down as soon as it goes out. However, if we can get it to all the news stations around the world, it'll at least be seen."

Wyatt asked, "If they're going to take it down, what's the point? There has to be a better way."

"Not really," Callie said. "If we're lucky, people will start asking questions."

Eden smiled. "And that's the next part. We know the Saints will pull the information down and say that some hackers got in and wanted to cause a stir. Which we are. But the real thing is getting this intel out to the right people. And the right people now are the conspiracy theorists."

"Oh, that's brilliant," Callie said with a laugh.

Wyatt chuckled. "Damn. That's smart. If the conspiracy theorists get a hold of this, they won't let it go."

"That's what we're hoping for. Now, it probably won't end the Saints immediately, but if enough people start to question and dig, they can't kill thousands at once." The minute the words were out of Eden's mouth, she thought of the virus. "Except that's what they're doing. I didn't think about that. I just feel like everyone else should know what we do."

"You can't make people believe what they don't want to believe," Wyatt told her.

Callie snorted. "Maybe not, but if the information keeps getting out there, then people will start taking notice."

Eden frowned at the words. "What do you mean?"

"Well," Callie said, drawing out the word. "You and Maks came up with a great plan. I'd like to add to it."

"I'm all ears," Eden said.

"We keep hacking into the news outlets. We go big first, all over the world. When that gets pulled, we then target major cities on different continents, rotating but continuing to toss out the information."

"All the while, we'll also give it to the conspiracy theorists, who will also run with it," Eden said with a smile. "I like the way you think."

Wyatt made a sound. "Two peas in a pod. God help us when you two get together."

"Oh, it's happening, hot stuff. Prepare yourself," Callie warned him.

Eden smiled, liking the two of them immensely. "Thank you for your help."

"Anytime," Callie replied.

"Eden, has Maks said how the two of you are going to get out of Romania?" Wyatt asked.

She knew he wasn't asking because of the virus, but in regard to the Saints. "I've not asked him."

"Maks always has a plan," Callie said.

Wyatt was silent for a beat. "He always does. Listen, Eden, we're going to do whatever we can to help the two of you. It's not going to be easy since we have an ocean between us. All I ask is that you keep us informed. Send texts when you can to update us. This won't be our first time getting friends out of Europe and back home. If we did it once, we can do it again."

"I'm grateful. Truly. Have there been any updates on the virus? Any vaccine news?"

"None," Callie said angrily. "I know the Saints have it."

Eden perked up at that news, thinking of the Saints in the bunker. "Do you think they all do?"

37

The two bags of guns, ammunition, and grenades were weighty, but that didn't slow Maks down. He picked his way carefully along the river's edge. Close enough to hear the water, but far enough away that no one would see him if they were on a boat.

He was nearly to the bunker when he heard a motor. It wasn't going slowly as others did. Instead, it seemed to be moving fast. Maks paused and squatted down in the brush to look out over the water. It didn't take long for the vessel to appear. It was big and sleek and expensive. And it parked right in front of the bunker.

No doubt someone high up in the Saints had arrived. Had they come to gloat at how well the virus was spreading throughout the world? Or had the Saints found something in the bunker? The latter option surely wouldn't bring someone in the middle of the night.

Maks couldn't make out who was getting off the boat. He counted six armed men with the newcomer, not including the driver. They quickly disappeared inside the bunker. Maks didn't care what they were doing right now. The fact that a senior member of the Saints was there only made him eager to unleash the intel on the world so he could start taking out the organization.

He straightened and hurried to the bunker. Once he reached his entrance, he squatted once more and listened to see if anyone was near. Then he opened the door wide enough for him to get in and shut the door behind him. Maks wanted to run to Eden, but the sound of the guns and ammo jangling might be heard. He had to settle for walking quickly.

Finally, he reached the hidden entrance. He set down one of the bags and was straightening when the sound of a lighter filled the silence, followed a second later by the flare of fire as someone lit a cigarette. Maks jerked his head in the direction, his free hand having already palmed the gun at his waist.

"There were great things in store for you, Maks. If only you would've stayed on the path I chose."

He frowned, recognizing the voice. But he couldn't place it. Maks stared into the darkness where the end of the cigarette glowed red. The man drew in a deep breath, burning through the tobacco and causing red light to fill his face. Maks found himself staring into the dark eyes of none other than Jeffery Sumners.

Jeffery blew smoke out of his mouth. "You know, don't you?"

"I know it all."

"Not all of it, dear boy. There are a great many things you don't know. You would have, though. I chose you a long time ago to take my position with the other Elders after I died."

Maks jerked his head back, utterly revolted. "Why would you ever think I'd want any part of the Saints?"

"You have a killer instinct. You're able to do what must be done for the greater good."

Fury ripped through Maks. "You think this virus you unleashed is for the greater good?"

"Absolutely," Jeff said and held the cigarette away from his face. "Do you know why the Spartans were so dominant? They didn't allow the weak, diseased, or lame to live. Look at animals in the wild. Only the strong survive. That's how it's supposed to be. Instead, it's the sick and lame who dictate our lives. Government spending keeps those unwilling to work fed. They pay medical bills for people who shouldn't be alive. Billions of dollars are spent every year for drugs and surgeries because people don't want to do the right thing and lose weight themselves. They want a quick, easy fix to everything. We, as a species, are lazy. We've become weak. It's time for the strong to take control."

Maks couldn't believe the filth pouring from Jeff's mouth. "You honestly believe you're doing good."

"I know I am. The world is overpopulated. Countries are polluting our air, the rivers and oceans. We're raping the Earth without a thought to the future. All in the name of sustaining our numbers. The Earth simply can't handle that. There are too many people. Since your friends stopped Ragnarök, this was our other option.

Though, to be fair, we'd planned to release both of them almost simultaneously anyway." He took another puff from the cigarette and exhaled. "The Earth has been screaming at us for decades that we're hurting her. Why should everyone have to die simply because others don't listen? That's why the Saints were formed a thousand years ago. It's why we stepped up and did what no one else could."

"Thousands have died. Innocents!" Maks yelled.

———

The sound of Maks' voice through the door alerted Eden. She paused in her typing, trying to listen. He would never have yelled if everything was going right. He was talking now. And there was someone else there. No matter how hard she tried, though, she couldn't make out what was being said. Since Maks hadn't come into the room, then whoever was out there with him wasn't friendly.

Eden sent a quick text to Callie, letting them know what was going on. Then she went back to her research. Things were coming in quickly. She couldn't believe the Saints had found them already. She'd only been online for ten minutes, but in that little bit of time, she had uncovered quite a bit.

She was linked to the server Callie had set up, so Callie could see exactly what she was uncovering. All the while, Callie was hacking into the news outlets around the globe. As soon as Eden hit send, everything she and Maks had found would go viral.

"And more will die," Jeff said calmly.

Maks tightened his hand on the gun. He wanted to lift it and fire, ending Jeff's life. But if he was here, then the rest of the Saints knew Maks' location. They didn't, however, know where Eden was. He was going to do whatever was necessary to ensure it remained that way.

"If my grandfather had really known who you were, he never would've befriended you."

Jeff chuckled and dropped the cigarette to the ground where he stepped on it, grinding it out. "Your grandfather knew. He was in the Saints, as well. Not nearly as high up as I am, but he did his part."

"I don't believe you."

"I don't care if you do or don't. The truth is that your grandfather thought the Saints were exactly what the world needed." A flick of a switch made light suddenly flood the corridor.

Maks didn't look away from Jeff's face. In all his years, he'd never hated anyone as much as he did Jeff right in this instant. He wanted to hurt the man, to cause him so much pain that he screamed for death.

Jeff shrugged and leaned a shoulder against the wall. "You look just like your grandfather. You have the same mentality. He should've climbed higher in the Saints than he did. He would've done nicely as an Elder."

"Shut the fuck up."

"Your father didn't have it in him, though," Jeff continued as if he didn't hear Maks. "We all knew that. He was too...weak. He wouldn't have joined us, and then we would've had to kill him. I made the choice to not tell him about the Saints. But I remained friendly with the family in the hopes that one of his children would join us. Then you came along."

Maks raised the gun and pointed it at Jeff's face. "You have no right to make decisions for the rest of humanity."

"Look around, son. There is nothing but lies out there. People are so sick of hearing them that they don't even pay attention to anything anymore. They vote someone into office simply because they can talk to a crowd. That kind of gift is great, but it doesn't always make for a good leader. The proof of that has shown up many times in the past. When it's apparent that people can't vote properly, we do it for them. When they can't get a good candidate to run for office, we produce one for them."

"You have an answer for everything."

"The truth hurts."

"Is that all you have to say with a gun pointed at your face?"

Jeff smiled, unfazed. "Kill me. It won't stop what's out there now."

Maks twisted his lips. "You said the truth hurts. You couldn't be more right. You and every Elder of the Saints is about to be outed to the world. Your organization will come under fire. Everything you've built will be destroyed."

"You aren't the first to threaten such things. It hasn't happened before. It won't now. There isn't anything you have that could do that."

For the first time since seeing Jeff, Maks smiled.

"Actually, I do. All the time you thought I was working for you, I've been undercover stealing intel and gathering information. I didn't realize how much I had until I sorted through it. I have proof that ties you and the other four Elders to several murders."

Jeff's dark eyes held approval as he nodded. "See? I told you that you had what it took to be an Elder."

Eden finished the last of her search and put it in a document. Then she hit send. All she could hope for now was that people actually paid attention and didn't dismiss it. There was a lot of information, but with Callie's help, the two of them had put it together in such a way that it made sense.

"It's going," Callie said through the speaker.

Eden couldn't believe Callie had actually hacked all the news sources. Even now, Eden held her breath. Maks was still on the other side of the door, speaking with someone. Was he buying her time to get everything out?

"Holy shit," Callie said in a soft voice. "It's out there, Eden. All of it. On all the news channels in the US. Oh, now Europe. And Asia."

Eden dropped her head into her hands, tears welling in her eyes. They had done it. They had given the world the information on the Saints. She prayed it was enough to bring down the organization. So many people had lost their lives because of the Saints. It was time that stopped.

She wiped at her eyes and lifted her head.

"What about the conspiracy theorists? Can you tell if they're picking it up?"

"They certainly are," Callie said with a laugh.

"Eden?" Wyatt asked. "Is Maks still talking with someone?"

Eden glanced at the door, unease rippling through her. "Yes."

"Stay there. Don't go out. Maks has a plan. Trust him," Wyatt told her.

As if Eden had any other choice.

"It's time for the people of this world to make their own choices, be they right or wrong. It's time their votes counted. And if that means the end of Earth, then that's what will happen. But there are hundreds of people out there working to right what's been done to the planet. They could pull it off."

Jeff lifted one shoulder, his long, camel-colored coat moving with him. "Maybe they will. Neither I nor any of the other Saints want to chance that, though. We're going to ensure that the Earth continues. Do you honestly think this is the first time we've done population control? Where do you think the Black Plague came from? The Spanish Flu, and all the others? They don't just happen, my boy. They're created and unleashed. Same with wars. Some we let get out of hand, some we contain."

"You make me sick. You're playing God, and no one should have that right."

"I have that right because I made sure of it!" Jeff

bellowed as he pushed away from the wall. He was no longer calm. Anger contorted his features as his lined faced reddened. "You think because you're born that you have rights? You have nothing. Nothing! The only reason you have what you have is because I've allowed it."

Maks' finger moved to the trigger. All he had to do was squeeze. A silence fell between them, and Maks let it grow. He was utterly disgusted with the individual who called himself a person before him.

Suddenly, a faint buzzing came from Jeff's coat pocket.

Maks realized it was the man's phone. He smiled then. "The Saints are done. Over. Everything I had is now out in the world. You can take it down, but it'll go back up again."

"Because your friends the Loughmans are helping you? Don't count on them for too long. The entire ranch will be obliterated in a few days."

"You can kill us all. But the truth is out there now. Others have seen it. I gather that's why your phone is ringing. They want to alert you to what's happening. The bottom line is that you're fucked, old man."

Jeff's smile was cold, his eyes filled with hatred. "You could've had it all. You chose wrong, Maks. Now you're going to die. Same with the woman helping you. And I'm going to make you watch what I do to her."

Maks lowered his gun. "You'll never get to her. You'll never even find her."

"The hell I won't," Jeff shouted, spittle flying from his mouth.

He took a step toward Maks and then froze. He

blinked, his face locked in a macabre look of fear and anger. Jeff then pitched forward, his arms by his sides. He landed on his face before he rolled over, his body twitching slightly as he stared up at Maks, his eyes begging for help.

Maks squatted beside him, unsure if it had been a stroke or heart attack that got the bastard, not that it mattered. "Karma's a bitch, old man. May you rot in Hell."

He didn't wait for Jeff to breathe his last. Maks got to his feet, his gun raised as he waited for men to come pouring out, guns blazing. But as the seconds passed, there was no one. Maks didn't take his eyes from the space where Jeff had been. He spotted a light in the darkness. A doorway that Jeff must have come through.

Maks wasn't sure why Jeff had come alone. Maybe because the bastard knew Maks would have a lot to say, and Jeff didn't want anyone else hearing anything. It didn't matter anymore. The man was dead.

"One Elder down," he murmured.

Maks turned and went to the picture of Hitler and opened the door to the room beyond. Eden was right there, a gun pointed at his head. The minute she saw him, she lowered it and ran into his arms.

"I love you," she said. "I love you so much."

Maks held her tight, marveling at the fact that he was still alive with the woman who had stolen his heart in his arms. "Jeff found me."

Eden leaned back to look at him. Together, the two of them walked from the room to see Jeff Sumners on the ground, dead. Maks frowned when

Eden dropped to her knees and began to rummage through Jeff's coat pockets.

"What are you doing?"

She glanced at him. "He's an Elder. Don't you think he'd have a vaccine for the virus with him?"

Without a second's hesitation, Maks was beside her, searching.

EPILOGUE

California

T he sounds of the cello woke Eden. She smiled as she sat up and rose from the bed to pad barefoot down the hall to where Maks sat on the porch with the morning sun shining. She stood in the doorway, listening to him for several minutes until he finished the song.

He looked at her then and smiled. "Morning."

"Morning," she said with a grin as she walked to him and gave him a kiss. "That's the second-best way of being woken in the morning."

"I couldn't resist. It was just a perfect day."

Eden had to agree with him. Not only were the temperatures mild with only a slight chill in the air, they were also back on American soil. Over the last few days, she found it difficult to believe that the week before had actually happened.

A few days ago she had found a news article about an American woman who had died in Vienna of a home invasion. There was Janice's picture in the article, which speculated the invasion had occurred because of the virus epidemic. But Eden and Maks both knew that the Saints had killed her. Eden couldn't even bring herself to feel sorry for Janice.

Maks stood and put the cello away before they walked into the house together. Neither turned on the news or the radio. They didn't need to know what was going on in the world, because they had been a part of it. They had indeed found a vaccine in Jeff's coat and had immediately taken it to the local authorities so it could be replicated.

Once that happened, it didn't take long for the Romanians to give it to other countries, and everyone began vaccinating against the vile strain of flu. Unfortunately, before that happened, many hundreds of thousands died—all because of the Saints.

As for the organization, they had done what they could to stop the spread of information about them. But once it was leaked that they were the ones who had designed and spread the virus, the cry for their arrests couldn't be drowned out by anyone—not even the Saints. The remaining four Elders were arrested. In a plea deal, they had all given up a plethora of names of those associated with them.

It was a witch hunt, but then again, she and Maks had always known it would be. The main thing was that the world was safe again. Somewhat. There would always be danger out there. There'd always be someone who thought they were doing the right thing, when in fact, they were the villains. Thankfully, there were also men like Maks, willing to risk their lives for others.

Maks stopped by the kitchen island and shook his head. "You look damn good in my shirt."

"Do I?" she asked seductively. "Do you like it better on me. Or off?"

"Is that really even a question?"

They laughed and walked into each other's arms. "I love you," she said.

"I love you." He gave her a soft kiss.

Eden then pulled back and looked into his bright blue eyes. "Are you ready for today?"

"Yes. No." He shook his head. "Let's put it off another day."

"If you want, but it's always going to be difficult. The Saints are finished. Jeffery is no more. There's no longer a reason for your family to think you're dead."

He gave her a lopsided grin. "You're just too damn smart. I'm really glad you're coming with me."

"I'll always be by your side."

An hour later, they got out of the rental car in front of a San Francisco home. Eden stood on the curb and waited for Maks to walk to her. They had only gotten halfway down the walk when the front door of the house opened. An older woman with light brown hair and bright blue eyes came out on the porch.

Her gaze was locked on Maks, her hand over her heart. "Alex? Is that you?"

"Hi, Mom. It's me."

Eden watched with tears pouring out of her eyes as Maks' mom rushed down the steps and into Maks' arms. It wasn't long before his father joined them. It warmed Eden's heart to see Maks rejoin his family. His mother was the first to call his siblings so everyone could come over. There would be a ton of questions for Maks, and Eden knew that he wouldn't be able to answer them all. But it didn't matter. He was home, back where he belonged.

And they were together.

He took her hand and pulled her with him as the four of them walked through the doorway. His mother and father embraced her as the laughter and happiness filled the house. And she knew it was just the beginning of their lives together.

THANK YOU!

Thank you for reading **THE GUARDIAN**. I hope you enjoyed it! If you liked this book — or any of my other releases — please consider rating the book at the online retailer of your choice. Your ratings and reviews help other readers find new favorites, and of course there is no better or more appreciated support for an author than word of mouth recommendations from happy readers. Thanks again for your interest in my books!

Donna Grant
www.DonnaGrant.com
www.MotherofDragonsBooks.com

In case you missed it, check out book one in the *Sons of Texas* series, THE HERO!

THE HERO

THE HERO'S HOMECOMING

Owen Loughman is a highly-decorated Navy SEAL who has a thirst for action. But there's one thing he hasn't been able to forget: his high school sweetheart, Natalie. After more than a decade away, Owen has returned home to the ranch in Texas for a dangerous new mission that puts him face-to-face with Natalie and an outside menace that threatens everything he holds dear. He'll risk it all to keep Natalie safe—and win her heart.

Natalie Dixon has had a lifetime of heartache since Owen was deployed. Fourteen years and one bad marriage later, she finds herself mixed up with the Loughmans again. With her life on the line against an enemy she can't fight alone, it's Owen's strong shoulders, smoldering eyes, and sensuous smile that she turns to. When danger closes in, how much will she risk to stay with the only man she's ever loved?

Order *The Hero* now!

Read on for an excerpt from THE HERO, the first book in the Sons of Texas series that began it all...

1

September

The blades of the chopper cut through the air with a whomp, whomp noise that Owen Loughman had come to find soothing. He sat back with his eyes closed in the seat of the Blackhawk helicopter, trying to figure out why he'd been pulled from his mission with his SEAL team in Afghanistan.

Not surprisingly, he'd been told exactly nothing.

He cracked open an eye and glanced at the cockpit. The two men piloting wore solid black. No military designation. No adornment of any kind. Obviously CIA.

Owen had witnessed—and experienced—his fair share of craziness since becoming a SEAL. CIA agents thought they kept themselves under the radar. It was the biggest load of shit. Everyone recognized them immediately.

It wasn't the fact that he hadn't gotten details of why he and his team had their mission halted after a week in the desert. It wasn't that he'd been shoved onto a plane in the Middle East without explanation. It wasn't even that no one had so much as looked at him since he'd landed in the States and was promptly put on the Blackhawk.

He was a Navy SEAL. He was prepared for anything—any and all surprises. No, the unease had everything to do with the CIA. He didn't trust the government bastards.

The disquiet feeling that saved his life countless times began to stir. He blew out a breath and opened his eyes as he turned his head to look out the open door of the chopper.

Texas.

He would recognize his beloved state anywhere. He hadn't been back in . . . he had to stop and count . . . ten years. He couldn't believe it had been that long. Where had the time gone?

The last time he'd seen Texas was the day he'd graduated from the University of Texas and joined the Navy. From the time he was in junior high, he'd known he would make his life in the military. It was who the Loughmans were, dating all the way back to the Revolutionary War.

He'd been the only one to follow in his father's footsteps and choose the Navy, though. Wyatt, his older brother, chose the Marines, along with Cullen, his younger brother.

He couldn't recall the last time he'd spoken to his brothers. Their family wasn't close. He blamed it on their father, because it was easy. Though in truth, the fault lay with each of them.

The chopper began its descent. His gaze took in the rolling hills and the cattle scattering to get away from the noise. Then he spotted the two-story, white house with black trim that brought back a flood of memories.

Home.

He rested his hands on his thighs covered in desert-colored cammies, wishing his gun hadn't been taken from him in Afghanistan. Just what the hell was he doing back home?

The Blackhawk landed a hundred yards from the house. The pilot turned in his seat and looked at Owen through the tinted screen of his helmet. "We've reached your destination, Lieutenant Commander."

He unbuckled his seatbelt and grabbed his pack before jumping out of the open doors, his gaze perusing the area as memories flooded back. No sooner had his feet hit the ground than the Blackhawk was airborne again.

He glanced up, watching the chopper disappear. Then his gaze slid to the house. It looked . . . empty, desolate. Which couldn't be right since his aunt and uncle lived there.

Owen took a deep breath of the fresh Texas air. And stilled. He smelled death.

He hurried to the side of the house and squatted, flattening his back against the porch railing. Quietly, he lowered his pack to the ground before he cautiously looked around the corner.

Aunt Charlotte's numerous hanging plants that she lovingly cultivated still dotted the wrap-around porch, swinging in the breeze. An empty rocker teetered.

It was quiet. Too quiet.

He silently crept to the front steps. If anybody

was there, they were inside the house. He glanced behind him. The open landscape allowed him to see anyone coming. The scattered trees were large enough to hide a foe, but even they were too far away for someone to surprise him.

Except for the oak out back. He would have to tread carefully there.

He hurried up the five steps to the porch and flattened himself against the house beside the front entryway. Slowly, he opened the screen door. Just in time, he recalled the squeak if opened all the way.

Keeping away from the glass inset into the wood, he rested the frame of the screen on his forearm as he put his hand on the knob. Then, with a deep breath, he twisted and gave a slight push.

The heavy door opened noiselessly. When no gunfire erupted, he peeked inside the house. When he saw nothing, he quickly entered, his hand catching the screen to close it without a sound behind him. He moved to the side of the foyer and listened for any noise.

The house remained as soundless and still as before. On silent feet, he walked to his left. He glanced up the stairs but chose to look around the ground floor first. The front room, the one his mother had used as a music room, had been turned into a formal living area by his aunt.

His gaze searched the space. As if pulled to them, he spotted two holes in the wall. Bullet holes. A sinking feeling filled him.

For long seconds, he stared at the marred drywall, hoping it was his mind playing tricks on him.

But there was no denying the truth that was before him. Had his father's work once more followed him home? It infuriated him that Orrin hadn't taken precautions to keep his family safe as he'd promised.

Moving to the wall, he touched the holes. The bullets had been removed, but by the size of the openings, he surmised they were 7.62mm. Military grade.

His eyes slid to the next room. He knew what he would find. His mind screamed for him to turn and walk away. The house had seen so much death, and as always, he was the one to find it.

He hadn't run away when he was a boy. He wouldn't do it now. Though his years with the SEALs had shown him unbelievable ways a person could kill—and be killed—nothing could compare to knowing it had struck your family.

Again.

Owen swallowed and walked through the doorway to the large living area with the eight-foot-wide stone fireplace. The first thing he saw was the blood. It coated the recliner, which was also riddled with bullet holes.

He clenched his jaw, anger kindling in his gut. His fears were confirmed. Uncle Virgil and Aunt Charlotte were dead. As he stood in the living room where he and his brothers had watched TV, opened Christmas gifts, fought, and played, the primal side of him—the beast the Navy had shaped and trained —demanded justice.

Justice his mother hadn't gotten.

He slowly turned the haze of rage and anguish into cold fury that could be directed with reprisal so horrible the screams of the men who had killed his family would reverberate in Hell.

Pulling his eyes away from the recliner, he slowly moved around the living area. Debris from the gun battle littered the floor, making it so he had to carefully choose where to set his feet so as not to make noise.

He reached the arched double entry into the kitchen and felt his chest squeeze in fury. The shooters had found Aunt Charlotte there. By the dough still on the counter, she'd been making her famous bread. The blood pool on the floor was large, as was the pattern of splatter on the walls.

A floorboard creaked behind him. He whirled around, his arm jerking up and back to hit the intruder. At the last minute, he recognized the dark gold eyes and stopped his assault.

"Wyatt."

His elder brother gave a firm nod in greeting. "Owen."

He frowned as he looked at Wyatt's face covered with a thick beard. His dark hair was unkempt and long. Wyatt stood still as stone, his gaze moving from one place to the next.

Having gone undercover enough times himself, Owen recognized the reason for Wyatt's appearance. His brother had always been quiet. A loner. Only the Loughmans knew the cause.

And no one spoke of it.

Now, Wyatt appeared even more serious, if that were possible. He was leaner than Owen remembered, more lethal and vicious. Wyatt wore black camo with no insignia. So that's where his brother had disappeared to. Delta Force.

Despite Wyatt's icy demeanor, not even he could hide the anger that sizzled in his eyes or the way his hands clenched at his sides.

Men like he and Wyatt knew only one way to seek vengeance—blood. Whoever had done this to their family was about to see just what the Loughman brothers were capable of.

Wyatt stepped around him into the kitchen and stopped next to the pool of blood. His gaze remained on it for a moment before he met Owen's gaze. "There's nothing upstairs."

He opened his mouth to speak when the sound of another chopper filled the air. Both brothers hurried to the front of the house. Sliding against the wall, they peeked out the windows to see another man in green fatigues appear in the doorway of the Blackhawk.

"I'll be damned," he murmured when Cullen jumped from the helicopter before it landed.

Cullen's cap was pulled low over his face as he stood staring at the house. He didn't move even as the chopper took off, the sound fading quickly.

Owen looked at Wyatt to find a frown on his brother's face. Nothing ever changed. He pushed away from the wall and walked out the front of the house. The sight of his younger brother brought a smile. Too bad the reunion was tarnished with death. But that seemed to be the curse of the Loughmans.

Cullen dropped his pack from his shoulder and smiled when he caught sight of him. Owen jumped off the porch and met Cullen halfway, enfolding him in a hug.

They pounded each other on the back in

greeting. His then held his younger brother at arm's length and looked into hazel eyes so like their mother's as Cullen removed his hat. If he thought Wyatt had changed, it was nothing compared to Cullen.

Cullen's gaze held a cynical edge, showing suspicion that only someone who had been neck-deep in war would understand. His hair was kept in the typical style of the Marines—high and tight—with the sides shaved close to his head and only a quarter inch spiked on top.

"Damn, it's been a while," Cullen said with a bright smile.

He playfully slapped Cullen on the cheek, but he couldn't hold his smile. Not when he knew what had brought them together. "You've grown up, little brother."

Cullen's laughter died as his gaze moved over Owen's shoulder. The grin was gone, the hardness back in place. "Wyatt."

Owen turned around to find Wyatt on the porch, watching them. Life as a Loughman hadn't been easy for any of them, but particularly Wyatt. Owen still remembered being a young boy, how people used to be envious of their ranch. For a few years, the siblings had lived a life of wonder and joy.

But it all shattered one stormy day.

None of the boys had been the same since. Owen looked between his two brothers, hating that the tension was already back.

"What's going on?" Cullen asked as his sharp gaze looked around. "Where are Uncle Virgil and Aunt Charlotte?"

Wyatt leaned against the post. "Dead."

Cullen's eyes become intense. "How?"

"I'd say at least five men," Owen said.

Wyatt added, "Six." He walked down the steps and pointed to the ground. "Two came in the front. Another two from the back, and I spotted two more sets of footprints around the barns."

Owen scrubbed a hand down his face. This was a hit. Pure and simple. But against his aunt and uncle, who were some of the best human beings he'd ever known? This wasn't about Charlotte and Virgil. This was about something else. He immediately thought of his father. But it could be because of one of them, as well. He and his brothers had enemies of their own.

That soured his stomach. Hadn't he sworn he wouldn't allow such things to touch his family again?

He walked back into the house and to the living area, followed by Cullen and Wyatt. He looked at the recliner where their uncle had been killed to the fireplace where one of the shotguns hung.

"It's untouched," Cullen stated.

Owen glanced around the room. "Virgil never got to it."

"He didn't stand a chance against such firepower," Wyatt stated.

Cullen strode to the kitchen and stood quietly for several minutes. When he spoke, his voice was low and filled with raw fury. "I'll not stop until I find out who did this."

"We feel the same," Owen said, fully understanding how Cullen felt.

Cullen released a breath and faced his brothers.

"I was in the middle of a mission when my team was pulled. No way was I picked up and immediately brought here just because they were murdered."

"You weren't the only one, kid," Wyatt said. "I was on a mission, too."

Owen crossed his arms over his chest. "Make that all three of us. I can't think of any of my enemies who would know to track me here."

"Me either," Cullen replied.

Wyatt gave a single shake of his head.

Owen's anger burned brightly. "This involves Dad. It has to."

A muscle ticked in Wyatt's jaw. Owen ignored the telltale sign that Wyatt was furious and frowned when he heard the sound of an automobile approaching. The three instantly fanned out. Cullen took the back door while Owen positioned himself at the front. Wyatt squatted behind the sofa in the formal living room.

The motor shut off, and a moment later, a vehicle door closed. Owen glanced out the window and caught sight of the front of a dark gray BMW 6 Series.

Seconds ticked by without the sound of anyone approaching. Wyatt turned his head toward the back of the house when the front door was thrown open, and someone stepped inside. Owen stilled a second before he grabbed the slim form.

He had the intruder flipped onto their back immediately. In the next moment, Owen found himself on the floor, staring at the ceiling. He jumped to his feet and tried to look beneath the baseball cap of the person, but he couldn't make out anything.

Owen didn't waste any time getting the advantage and slamming the person against the wall. There was a gasp that sounded distinctly feminine as the air in the intruder's lungs was forced out.

That caught his attention. With a shove, he knocked the hat off. A wealth of light brown hair tumbled free.

All the breath left him as he stared into green eyes he feared he'd never see again.

"Natalie?"

"Hi, boys," she said off-handedly.

He frowned, suddenly furious to find her there. "What the hell are you doing here?"

"She's looking for me," came a voice behind them.

"Callie?" Wyatt asked in a strangled voice full of surprise and annoyance as he stood.

Callie Reed glared at each of them as she walked around Owen and nodded to Natalie. He released Natalie, and she moved to stand beside Callie. He exchanged a look with his brothers, though Wyatt couldn't stop staring at Callie.

"Someone please tell us what's going on?" Owen demanded.

Callie shrugged. "I work here."

Green eyes met his. "I came to help."

ABOUT THE AUTHOR

New York Times and *USA Today* bestselling author Donna Grant has been praised for her "totally addictive" and "unique and sensual" stories. She's written more than one hundred novels spanning multiple genres of romance including the *New York Times* bestselling *Dark Kings* series featuring immortal Highlander shape shifting dragons who are daring, untamed, and seductive. She lives with her dog in Texas.

Connect with Donna online:
www.donnagrant.com
www.MotherofDragonsBooks.com

facebook.com/AuthorDonnaGrant

instagram.com/dgauthor

bookbub.com/authors/donna-grant

goodreads.com/donna_grant

pinterest.com/donnagrant1